A LITTLE NONSENSE

CHRISTMAS KEY BOOK FIVE

STEPHANIE TAYLOR

For my dad and our summer walks along the River Coln. I wish there were still 10,000 messengers to deliver all the messages.
Yours—always, Eina

"A little nonsense every now and then,
is relished by the wisest men."
—*Willy Wonka*, Roald Dahl

DON'T MISS OUT ON NEW RELEASES...

Want to find out what happens next in the Christmas Key series? Love romance novels? Sign up for new release alerts from Stephanie Taylor so you don't miss a thing!

Sign me up!

1

HOLLY BAXTER STANDS IN THE WIND LIKE A PILLAR, TALL AND STRAIGHT, the breeze lifting her long, light brown hair from her shoulders. She inhales deeply, arms folded as she watches the activity on Christmas Key with a smile. The sky is so clear and blue that it looks like it's been lovingly hand-painted by an artist who's framed it with waving palm trees and turquoise water.

The dock has been busy for weeks with boats full of construction materials and workers arriving every day. The men glisten under the tropical October sun, their muscles bulging as they shoulder huge beams and pieces of wood, carrying them to the spot where the new dock is being built. Holly waves at the project manager from Island Paradise Excursions, who is staying on the island for the first couple of days as they begin construction on the dock that will allow bigger boats to come ashore and deliver tourists and visitors to her little island for day trips and short stays.

"Mayor!" A voice carries to her on the wind, and Holly turns her attention from the dock to Main Street. Vance Guy is standing outside his new shop next door to Mistletoe Morning Brew. He raises a hand to her in greeting and a wide smile breaks across his face. Vance has recently opened the island's first bookstore, A Sleigh Full of Books, and the pace of the island seems to be settling over him quite nicely.

Holly steps from the sandy shoreline onto the paved road of Main Street, beaming at Vance as he lifts a box of books from the most recent delivery and carries them through the open door of his shop. "Hey, Vance! How's business?"

The inside of A Sleigh Full of Books is starting to come together, and Holly hardly remembers the empty, dusty space that had sat empty for years before Vance moved in. She steps inside and looks around at the shelves that Vance has installed along the walls of the narrow shop. A wind chime rings by the open back door. The whole space smells like freshly cut and sanded wood and salty ocean breeze. Holly inhales deeply.

"Where do you think I should shelve this?" Vance holds up a book with a narrow spine. He frowns at it. "I don't even remember ordering it."

Holly steps over an open box of books and holds out a hand. Vance passes the book to her and she turns it over, skimming the back. "I don't think you'll have to shelve it," she says, smiling at the obscure-looking book. "I'm pretty sure Calista snuck this into your order. Want me to drop it off with her at the salon?"

Vance peers over Holly's shoulder. "You think she ordered a book called *The Evil Mother-in-law*?" He frowns. "Wait—good point. Yeah, drop it off with her." With a chuckle of amusement and a shake of his head, Vance bends over and pulls the flaps of a box open to reveal stacks of new releases and best-sellers. Vance and Calista Guy's move from Toronto to the island with their young twin sons had been followed closely by the arrival of his mother, Idora. The transition to having her mother-in-law living in their house has been a rocky one for Calista, to say the least.

Holly tucks the book under her arm and surveys the shop. Vance has installed a small counter in the corner so that he has a view of the front door and of Main Street, and through the open back door, the frame of a wooden deck is visible. He's cleared the brush from behind the store and started constructing a reading deck that will soon be covered in outdoor furniture and will hopefully invite patrons to come over from next door with coffee in hand to browse and read.

It's all coming together, just like the new dock, and Holly gives it a final look of approval.

"It looks great so far, Vance," she says, stepping through the open door again and standing on the sidewalk. "Let me know if you need anything, okay?"

"Will do," Vance says distractedly, lifting another stack of hardcover books from the box and setting them on a shelf. Holly watches for another second as he scans the shop and tries to picture where everything will go. "Oh, hey—would you mind telling Calista that I'm going to stay here and work late today?"

"You got it," Holly says, patting the doorframe before she steps off the curb and onto the only paved street on the island.

The sun hits her scalp and warms her skin as she looks both ways. From the west, Dr. Fiona Potts is approaching in her golf cart. Holly lifts a hand to her as she crosses the street. Fiona slows and comes to a stop next to her best friend, tossing her thick, wavy strawberry-blonde braid over one shoulder as she ducks to see Holly's face from under the roof of her cart.

"Where you headed, stranger?" Fiona smiles at her. She lifts her sunglasses with one hand, the other hand still resting on the steering wheel. "It can't be quitting time yet!"

"It's not," Holly assures her. "I'm inventing errands to run so that I can take a break from wedding plans." She nods at the wide window of the Christmas Key B&B across the street and they both glance in that direction to see Bonnie Lane, Holly's assistant, chatting animatedly on the phone at their shared desk space.

"So when do we all get to hear about this mysterious Bridezilla?" Fiona asks, turning back to look at Holly. "This drama has been building for months."

"I know." Holly rolls her eyes. She and Bonnie have been working closely with a bride since springtime, trying desperately to meet her every demand and to ensure that her vision for the perfect, private island wedding is brought to fruition on Christmas Key. At first her demands had been amusing and bewildering, but once Holly and Bonnie learned the identity of their October bride, her request for secrecy had made more sense.

"I'll be able to tell you all about it soon. She actually made me and Bonnie sign non-disclosure agreements that threaten to take away everything we own if we reveal the identity of the bride and groom before the wedding."

"Is that even legal?" Fiona scoffs. She holds out her left arm and motions for Wyatt Bender to drive around her as she idles in the street, chatting with Holly.

"She had her lawyers draw it up, so I would assume so..." A blur of motion on the other side of Main Street catches Holly's attention and she looks over in time to see Marco, the island's resident parrot, swoop down into the open bar of Jack Frosty's next door to the B&B. "Hey, how come Marco is out and about? I haven't seen him anywhere but perched on Cap's shoulder for the past few months."

Fiona turns and catches sight of the bird. He's resting on the wooden counter that faces Main Street, flapping his wings as Leo Buckhunter—the bar's proprietor, Holly's uncle, and Fiona's recently-minted fiancé—tries to shoo him away. A cloud passes over Buckhunter's laid-back face as he swats a dishtowel near the bird, hoping it will send him swooping back across the street to North Star Cigars and onto the shoulder of his cantankerous master.

Holly laughs as Buckhunter mutters curse words at the parrot, finally giving up and tossing the dishtowel back over his shoulder as he goes back to bussing tables after lunch.

"Speaking of weddings," Holly says, catching Fiona's eye and giving her an eyebrow wiggle.

Fiona holds up a hand. She slides her sunglasses back on. "We're not talking about it yet. And by 'we,' I mean your uncle. He refuses to talk about it."

"But you guys have been engaged for months," Holly presses, cutting her gaze back to Buckhunter on the other side of the street. Fiona had bravely done the proposing over dinner at Buckhunter's house one evening in the spring, and everyone on the island has been anticipating a quick, casual wedding ever since. But Buckhunter's reticence to talk about it and make definite plans are throwing a wrench in the whole thing. Holly has half a mind to talk to him about it herself, but Fiona's warning look tells her to leave it alone.

"I have a patient in half an hour." Fiona changes the subject as she looks at her watch. "I was just running up to see how Hal was doing. Katelynn called this morning and wanted me to check on him." Hal Pillory, one of the island's long-time residents, has recently had some memory issues that required his granddaughter, Katelynn, to move down to Christmas Key with her own teenage son to care for him.

Holly nods and pats the roof of Fiona's cart. "Then don't let me keep you, Doc. Will I see you tonight at the Ho Ho?"

"I've treated four cases of hemorrhoids this week and given two enemas," Fiona says wryly. "Do *you* think I need a drink?"

"See you there around seven." Holly steps onto the sidewalk and waves as her best friend pulls back into the street and drives towards Hal Pillory's bungalow.

At the corner of Main Street, just before the turn onto the aptly named Holly Lane, the island's mayor stops in front of Poinsettia Plaza and takes one more look at the book she's agreed to drop off at the Scissors & Ribbons salon. Millie Bradford, one of Holly's favorite neighbors, is back at work and adjusting to her life as a widow after unexpectedly losing her husband, Ray, to a heart attack while Holly had been off the island in May. She looks through the giant picture window now and spots Millie as she makes careful notes in a ledger on the front counter inside the salon.

"Hey, Millie," Holly says cheerfully, pushing open the door to the quiet salon. "How are things?"

"Oh, hi, honey." Millie slides her reading glasses off her face and sets them on top of the open ledger. She drops the pencil in her hand and comes around the counter to offer Holly a hug. "Things are good. How about you? Are you and Bonnie getting things ready for this big, mysterious wedding?" As Millie hugs her and then steps back, the light from outside catches on the gold hoops that always dangle from her ears.

"I think we're just about ready," Holly says with a smile. "Is Calista in today?"

"Oh, sure, she's here." Millie waves a hand towards the back of the salon. "She's got Cap in there now, giving him a massage." As the island's resident masseuse, Calista's time is always in high demand, which serves two purposes, really: it keeps the salon busy, and it keeps Calista out of the house and away from her mother-in-law.

"Vance asked me to drop this off with her," Holly says, handing over the book. "And he also wanted to let her know that he was staying late at the bookstore and working on getting it all put together."

Millie takes the book from Holly and inspects the title with an amused smile. "How are things coming together over there?"

"Looking good so far," Holly assures her. "He's got lots of new releases, and the back deck is under construction."

"And how about the dock?"

"Construction is in full-swing." Of course Millie knows this—everyone knows this. On an island the size of Christmas Key, there isn't much that everyone *doesn't* already know, but talking about things like construction and what's going on with their neighbors is always a way to banter and chit-chat to pass the time. "Will you be at the Ho Ho tonight? Fiona and I are headed over. And I'm sure Bonnie will join us."

"Oh, you girls," Millie says. She sets the book on the front counter and rests a fist on her hip. "I might join you. Sometimes it's fun to be around everyone and listen to music and have a drink, but sometimes it still makes me miss Ray too much," she admits.

Holly reaches out and puts a hand on Millie's arm. "I know," she says, remembering the way Ray and Millie had danced together to every song, wearing a groove in the rough floorboards of Joe Sacamano's open-air bar on the beach as they swayed to Sinatra. "But being around all of us might be good for you. We love you, Mil."

Millie smiles at her sadly. "I know. I love you all, too. I don't know how I would've gotten through the past few months without you."

The women share a quiet moment together before Holly squeezes Millie's arm. "I better head back over to the B&B and make sure Bonnie isn't drowning in wedding details. See you tonight, if you decide to join us."

Millie holds up a hand in farewell and waves at Holly through the front window as she jogs back across Main Street towards the B&B.

"Why is this damn bird harassing me?" Buckhunter calls out as Holly walks past Jack Frosty's. "I thought he was surgically attached to Cap's shoulder!"

Holly pauses and stands in front of Marco. The bird tilts his head to one side inquisitively, looking at Holly with one bored eye. "What's up, little buddy?" she coos to the parrot.

"Maybe you want him to join you at the B&B so he stops picking french fries off the plates of my customers?"

"Cap is getting a massage right now." Holly tips her head toward Scissors & Ribbons. "I'm sure he'll be back to pick up his faithful companion as soon as he's done there."

Buckhunter rolls his eyes. He's got a plate in each hand, and he's wearing a baseball cap that's turned around backwards. "Why don't you bring Pucci over here and drop him off, then I can just turn this place into a bar-slash-animal shelter."

Holly gives her uncle a winning smile. "No thanks. Pucci would rather hang with me and Bonnie at the B&B than with his grumpy Uncle Buckhunter over here."

"Cute." Buckhunter turns his back and walks over to the bar to deliver the dirty dishes. "I saw you and Fiona talking a few minutes ago. Are you coming—"

"To the Ho Ho tonight?" Holly finishes for him. "Yeah, I'll be there. You?"

"Of course. I always close things down early on Friday nights so I can join you guys." Buckhunter hustles around behind the bar as he talks to Holly, acknowledging the hand of his lone customer signaling for more water. It's Gwen, one of the triplets who own the island's only gift shop/grocery store, and she's quietly picking at her grouper salad with a fork while she turns the pages of a magazine on the table.

"Okay, I'll see you there," Holly says, holding out a finger for Marco to nudge with his feathered head. After he's finished interacting with her, Holly walks the few steps to the B&B's front door and rushes up the stairs and into the lobby of her small hotel. Aside from the construction crew, there are no guests staying on the island at the moment, so she passes by the unmanned front desk, grabbing a mint from a silver bowl next to the telephone.

"Bon?" Holly calls out as she strides down the hallway. Her legs are bare and tanned, her cut-off shorts frayed. Her t-shirt is well-worn. She frequently jokes that she's the only mayor in the country who goes to work in shorts and wears a bikini instead of undergarments, but she never takes for granted the life she gets to lead on her beautiful island. "What did I miss?"

"Hey, sugar," Bonnie Lane says, looking up from the white wicker desk in the B&B's bright, open office. Their window looks out onto Main Street, and Pucci, Holly's golden retriever, keeps watch from his spot on the dog bed in the corner of the office nearly every day.

"How many times did Bridezilla call?" Holly kicks off her Birkenstocks and pulls her feet up under her thighs on her desk chair. They'd taken to calling Kitta Banks "Bridezilla" months before as a way to stop themselves from accidentally calling her by her real name in front of the other islanders. But the fact that Bridezilla was actually a fitting name made them giggle, so they'd stuck with it.

"Only seven or eight," Bonnie says, giving Holly a wink from across the desk. Their computers are turned back-to-back, and they sit that way all day long, sharing gossip over hot or iced coffees from Mistletoe Morning Brew and watching the world pass by on Main Street.

"Should we go over the details again?" Holly asks, pulling up a folder on her desktop. Kitta Banks is one of the most recognizable movie stars in Hollywood, and her decision to get married on Christmas Key both thrills and terrifies its mayor. She's spent several near-sleepless nights recently, tossing and turning as she imagines the glitterati that are about to descend on her little island.

All the eyes of the world will focus on Christmas Key for that moment, and the pictures and stories that are released following Kitta's nuptials with Deacon Avaloy will give people another glimpse of the island that was made briefly famous on the reality show *Wild Tropics*. The thought of it makes Holly's stomach flip like it's filled with tiny acrobats.

Bonnie glances around the office as if spies might be hiding in its every nook and cranny. "What do you think of Deacon Avaloy?" she whispers.

Holly arches an eyebrow as she scrolls through her computerized list of wedding details. "I think he's really good-looking."

"Well, I think he's a snake in the grass," Bonnie retorts loudly before clamping a hand over her own red lips. "Oops," she says in a quieter voice. "You know how these political types are, and I don't trust them."

"Fair enough." Holly pecks at her keyboard and makes a face like she half agrees with Bonnie. Deacon Avaloy has already been tapped as a potential Democratic candidate for the next presidential election, and with his thick head of dark hair, cheekbones that could cut glass, and muscular figure, he's a perfect physical match for his willowy blonde bride-to-be. In fact, she and Bonnie have both right-fully compared the couple to the late JFK Jr. and his wife, Carolyn Bessette Kennedy.

"Anyhow," Bonnie goes on. "They'll bring all of their famous friends here and I'm sure whatever photographers they use will make the island look like a million bucks, so there's always that."

"Of course," Holly says absentmindedly, picking up a pen and tapping it against her teeth as she thinks.

"What's eatin' you today, sugar?" Bonnie frowns at her from across the desk.

"Nothing." Holly sets the pen down. "It's just that we're helping to plan this big wedding for complete strangers, and I'm really starting to wonder why Fiona and Buckhunter won't let us help them plan theirs. Or why they won't even *talk* about it."

"Mmm, mmm, mmm," Bonnie says, wagging her fingers as she shakes her head back-and-forth. "Do not go there, doll. I've interfered with a friend's romantic life before, and it does not end well."

"I'm not trying to interfere, Bon, I'm just curious...I want to help."

"Nope." Bonnie sets her lips in a firm line. "If they won't talk about it, then there's a reason. If we get into it, Buckhunter will act like he's got a burr in his saddle, and we need to stay far away from that mess, you hear?"

Holly shrugs her shoulders reluctantly. "Yeah, I guess."

"Holly Jean Baxter, you do as I say on this one, alright?"

"Okay, okay, okay," Holly says, pulling her face into a small pout. "I won't interfere. I promise."

"Now," Bonnie says, sliding her pink and yellow reading glasses onto her face. "Let's run through the timeline again and the list of things we need to do. We're at T-minus nine days and counting until this shindig, and we still need to get the chapel in shape and solidify our plans for who's staying in what room once the guests all arrive."

For the time being, Holly is distracted by the work that needs to be done. But there's something tickling at the back of her brain— something about the way Fiona slid her sunglasses back on instead of meeting her best friend's eye when she asked about the wedding. Whatever it is, it'll come out eventually. Holly picks up her pen and grabs a notepad and starts jotting down the list of things to do as Bonnie rattles them off.

2

"HOLLY BAXTER," MARIA AGNELLI CROWS, CORNERING HOLLY AT THE Ho Ho Hideaway that night. "I might die in my sleep tonight, and if I do, I don't want to go without knowing who's getting married on this tiny rock in the middle of the sea."

Holly leans down to hear Mrs. Agnelli over the music that's playing loudly in the bar. She smiles as she realizes that the older woman is trying to pry the information out of her about Kitta Banks and Deacon Avaloy, and there's a tiny part of her that wants to just whisper the truth in Mrs. Agnelli's ear. She's a cantankerous old woman, to be sure, but Holly adores her and would like nothing more than to give her the scoop on their famous visitors.

"No can do, Mrs. Agnelli," Holly says with regret. "They made us promise to keep it under wraps until their arrival date."

Mrs. Agnelli makes a sour face and holds the straw of her daiquiri to her lips with a small, knotted hand. "I'll buy your next drink," she says, trying to tempt Holly. Eighty-six-year old Maria Agnelli has very little patience for nonsense like secret weddings, and she clearly plans on dogging Holly until she gets the information she's looking for.

Holly laughs and leans in close to Mrs. Agnelli's ear. "If I could tell anyone, you'd be the first to know."

Somehow this seems to appease Mrs. Agnelli (although it could have been the effects of daiquiri number two), because she reaches up and pats Holly's smooth cheek. "I know you would, girl. I know you would." She looks at Holly for a long moment before tottering away on her cranky hip and starting up a conversation with Bonnie at the bar.

"What are you drinking, Mayor?" Holly actually isn't drinking anything yet, but she turns at the sound of the familiar voice. It's Jake, the island's only police officer, looking at her intently with a beer in his hand. "Get you something?"

Holly pulls her hair up with both hands and takes the hair tie from around her wrist to secure it in a low ponytail. "I could go for a blended margarita, if Joe's making any."

"He could probably be convinced." Jake smiles at her, and a million unspoken thoughts pass between them. Jake and Holly have been an on-and-off item for the past few years, and most recently, they've been on good terms.

"Then yes," Holly says, scanning the small crowd for Fiona. "I'd love one."

Jake's back is strong and muscular under his white t-shirt and Holly admires the way he cuts through the crowd, making polite chit-chat with the other islanders. She'd gone to Europe in the spring with River O'Leary, the former pro baseball player who'd come to Christmas Key the summer before and swept her off her feet, but the adventure had had the opposite affect on Holly than River had intended: rather than giving her a taste of the world that tempted her to take a bigger bite, it had sent her fleeing back to the comfort of her little island...and to Jake.

"Hey," Fiona says breathlessly. Her hair is unbraided and loose now, spilling over her freckled shoulders. "What did I miss?"

"Not a thing," Holly promises her. "Jake is at the bar getting me a margarita."

"Ohhhh." Fiona nudges Holly with her elbow and wiggles her

eyebrows suggestively. "He trying to get you tipsy so you'll need a ride home?"

Holly laughs. "Maybe, except..." Her eyes trail across the bar and land on Katelynn Pillory.

"Oh," Fiona says flatly. "Right."

"It's fine, Fee. Jake and I are just fine."

"You just said 'fine' twice in the same sentence. That means you are *not* fine. One fine means you might be fine. Two fines means they cancel each other out and leave you *un*-fine."

"If you say so, Fee. But anyway, we aren't together. We're just friends with a long history."

"Uh huh." Fiona looks unconvinced.

"We are. And that's all." Holly puts a hand on her friend's arm to end the conversation as Jake makes his way over to them with her margarita in hand. "Thanks, Officer Zavaroni," she says, smiling at him evenly. "I was ready for this." Holly holds up the drink in a small toast before taking the first sip.

"No problem." Jake turns to Fiona. "Hey, Doc. What's up?"

"Not too much. Just talking to Holly and admiring the view." She turns to the open front of the bar and sweeps a hand across the horizon to indicate the vast expanse of ocean and sandy beach.

"It is a pretty good view," Jake agrees, not taking his eyes off of Holly. A warm flush passes over her and she holds the straw of her margarita between her teeth to avoid having to say anything.

"So," Fiona says, her eyes glittering with mischief. "You here with Katelynn?" Katelynn Pillory is talking to all three of the triplets on the other side of the bar now, their sunny blondness surrounding her like a ring of bright light. A synchronized laugh rises into the air as the three identical women appreciate something Katelynn is saying.

"No." Jake shrugs. "She just called and asked for a ride. Logan agreed to stay in with Hal tonight and hold down the fort for an hour so that she could get out."

"She called and asked for a ride?" Fiona's chin dips low and she looks at him through her strawberry blonde eyebrows and lashes. "And you gave her one?"

"Yeah," Jake says.

"My friend," Fiona pats his strong forearm like she's delivering bad news to a patient in her office, "you two are here together."

Holly wants to step in and defend Jake, to remind Fiona that Katelynn puts in long days caring for her elderly grandfather and dealing with his confusion and memory loss and that she deserves a night out just like everyone else, but instead, she takes another drink and watches Jake squirm.

"Well, that isn't how I see it," Jake counters. He puts his beer to his lips and tips it back, taking a long pull.

It's partially amusing, this dance they've been doing for months, but there are moments—like this one—where Holly tires of the uncertainty of it all. She takes a step back from Jake and Fiona, feeling the smile fade from her face. "I'm going to go and take a stroll by the water," she says. "I'll be back in a few."

Inhaling the ocean air and listening to the roll and crash of the waves always clears Holly's head. She kicks off her Birkenstocks and leaves them at the foot of the stairs in front of the Ho Ho, walking barefoot through the sand that's cooling as the sun starts to descend over the water. She's got her drink in hand as she makes her way to the place where the water will lap over her feet.

It isn't that Jake might be interested in Katelynn, and it isn't that she and Katelynn have known each other since they were teenagers (back when Katelynn's high-school boyfriend decided that he might prefer Holly), it's that she's in such a precarious place in her own love life. She turned down a marriage proposal from Jake about a year and a half ago, and ever since, they've played a game of emotional tug-of-war trying to figure out how to live together on the island without breaking each other's hearts.

Her own feelings for River O'Leary had turned serious and thrown a wrench into her relationship with Jake, followed by the arrival on the island of the cast and crew of the reality show that had brought lusty, blonde Bridget Lindt into their lives. Jake and Bridget had fallen into a fast, on-camera dalliance that had led to a behind-the-scenes pregnancy, but the accident that caused Bridget to miscarry had derailed them and left Jake bereft. Since then, he and Holly have struggled with their unresolved feelings. There have been a string of conversations about whether they should stay away from each other or try things again, and ultimately, Holly is always the one to insist that they keep a little space between them for the time being.

"You looking to be alone, young lady, or can I join you?" Cap Duncan lumbers down the steps of the bar and towards Holly as she walks on the sand.

"Hey, Cap," Holly calls out, holding up her margarita. "I'm just enjoying the sunset, but you're welcome to join me."

Cap falls into step beside Holly. His hands are resting in the pockets of his shorts. He hasn't been drinking for a while now and has no desire to lose his grip on sobriety and become a thorn in everyone's side again. At one point, he'd decided to run against Holly for her seat as mayor, driving a wedge between them that had only receded when he stopped drinking and started dating Heddie Lang-Mueller.

"So we're gearing up for this big event, are we?" Cap asks, shuffling his feet through the sand and looking at the way the sun skitters across the waves.

"We are," Holly confirms. "And before you ask, I'm still not allowed to tell you who's getting married here."

"Oh, I wasn't going to ask." Cap shoots her a sidelong glance, a smirk on his face. "Most of us already know that it's Kitta Banks and Deacon Avaloy."

Holly stops walking. Her margarita nearly drops from her hands as she turns to Cap. "Are you kidding me?" she splutters. "Did Bonnie spill the beans? Because it wasn't me."

"No, no, no," Cap assures her. "Bonnie Lane's lips were sealed tighter than a drum." He tries to wipe the smile off his face. "For once."

"Then who?" Holly demands. She holds her glass with one hand splayed across the rim, letting it dangle at her side. "Who spread that around? Cap, you have to tell me. I could get in *big* trouble here. I signed an agreement to keep that under wraps!" Visions of lawsuits and an angry actress screaming at her down the phone line flash through Holly's mind.

"Oh, it's fine," Cap says calmly. "Maggie was cleaning up one evening and she came across the paperwork. I heard it all at Mistletoe Morning Brew the next day when I showed up to order a coffee and one of those lemon poppyseed muffins that Ellen and Carrie-Anne make. Have you tried one of thos—"

"Cap," Holly says seriously, leveling her gaze at him. "Maggie snooped through our paperwork and then told you all something that we all know is supposed to be a secret?"

Cap inhales through his nose, wiggling it around as he does. He thinks for a moment. "Well," he finally says. "I think her rationale was that it isn't *her* secret to keep. She's not bound to anyone on this one."

Holly shifts her weight from one bare foot to the other on the sand. Her cold margarita glass bumps against her thigh as it dangles next to her. "I would say she's bound to *me* on this one," Holly argues. "She's my employee, and as such—"

"Listen." It's Cap's turn to interrupt. "She's a harmless old bird. She came into the coffee shop and spilled the beans to me and Heddie, and I think one of the triplets might have been there. Maybe Wyatt." Cap stops and thinks. "Possibly Vance. And then Ellen and Carrie-Anne heard it, too." Holly lets her head roll back on her neck and her eyes gaze up at the clear evening sky. "Come to think of it, Millie might have been there picking up coffee for her and Calista," Cap adds, chewing on his lower lip.

Holly lowers her chin and stares at him. "This just keeps getting better and better."

"And that's pretty much it," he confirms. "Unless you count young Logan, who was there to see if I'd take him fishing. He seemed pretty excited about having a starlet on the island..."

Holly has already turned and started marching back to the bar. She needs to find Maggie and read her the riot act, and she's got to figure out how to mitigate this disaster before things get out of hand.

At the foot of the stairs that lead up to the Ho Ho Hideaway, Holly pauses to dump her now melted margarita into the sand. She lets the rest of the drink drip from the glass as she scans the crowd. No Maggie. She knows that the B&B is unmanned since the handful of construction workers who are staying there to build the dock have taken a quick trip back to the mainland to spend a Saturday at home, so of course Maggie won't be there either.

"Bon," Holly says, striding across the wooden floors on bare feet. "We need to go back to the office."

Bonnie sets her drink on the counter and dabs at the corner of her lips with a square cocktail napkin. "But sugar, it's Friday night!"

"I know. I wouldn't ask if it wasn't an emergency."

Bonnie looks into Holly's eyes for a minute before putting her hand on Holly's arm. Her red nails shine under the string of lights that Joe Sacamano has pinned up over the bar. "Okay, honey. If it's an emergency, then off we go."

Wyatt Bender has been sitting next to Bonnie on a stool at the bar, and he stands politely, wiping both hands down the front of his crisp Wrangler jeans. He's removed his cowboy hat and left it in his golf cart, and Holly can see a small trickle of sweat on his temple as he watches regretfully, clearly not wanting Bonnie to leave.

"Do you ladies need an escort?" Wyatt offers, pulling out his wallet to settle his tab with Joe.

"No, we're fine, Wyatt. I hardly had any of my drink so I'm good to drive. But thank you." Holly grabs Bonnie by the elbow and leads her out the side of the building and into the sandy parking lot. "Hop in," she says tersely, sliding into her hot pink golf cart and switching on the electric ignition. Her headlamps cut through the dusk.

"Sugar," Bonnie frowns as she climbs into the passenger seat. "Where are your shoes?"

But Holly is already backing up and maneuvering the cart onto December Drive. "I left them in the sand," she says, punching the gas. "I'll get them tomorrow."

"When Holly Baxter loses her shoes and doesn't finish her drink, I know we've got a live one on our hands." Bonnie grabs onto the frame of the cart and hangs on for safety. "But sugar? Would you mind slowing down just a hair? Ain't no emergency worth showing up dead for."

Holly expertly dodges a pothole in the sandy lane, swerving as they plunge into the dark foliage on Cinnamon Lane. She doesn't slow down.

3

"MAGGIE SUTTER!" HOLLY SHOUTS AS SHE HITS THE BRAKES. HER GOLF cart skids to a stop in the sandy road and Bonnie lurches forward in the passenger seat. "Don't you take another step--I see you!"

Holly is out of the cart before Bonnie even recovers her balance. Maggie pauses on her own front lawn about halfway between the street and the front door to her little yellow bungalow.

"What can I do for you, Mayor? Shouldn't you ladies be over at the Ho Ho with everyone else this evening?" Maggie consults the thin-banded watch on her left wrist. "You know I'm not much for the big crowds, but the two of you should probably be a couple of margaritas deep into the evening by now."

Holly ignores her and takes long steps across the front lawn as she closes the gap between them. "You had no right to go through that paperwork in my office and tell everyone who's getting married on Christmas Key," she says, her eyes stormy. "Do you know what kind of a situation that puts me in?"

Maggie's eyebrows knit together as she contemplates this. "Now, Holly," she says, holding up one hand. "I didn't go through your papers. I happened to see the file right there on your desk as I searched for a notepad to take back to the front desk. I wasn't snooping, I swear."

"There's a drawer full of notepads behind the front counter. Why didn't you just use one of those?" Holly folds her arms across her chest as she squares off with Maggie.

"Because those are just scratch pads, and that couple who was staying in the Seashell Suite wanted to know if they could take one home with the B&B's logo on it." Maggie's face is open; she doesn't appear to be lying.

"Oh."

Bonnie is out of the cart and walking up to the women, one hand on her lower back as she feigns injury from Holly's wild driving. "Sugar," she says, putting her other hand on Holly's arm. "I know you're upset, but we might want to take a step back here before things get ugly."

"Holly, I've never done you wrong," Maggie says. She shakes her head sadly. "Now I know spreading the information around the coffee shop was a mistake, and I'm sorry for that, but these people will never know that we all know. We're just a bunch of old biddies and geezers on an island in the middle of nowhere!"

Holly would agree with this, but she knows how quickly word spreads about anything on Christmas Key. "It still wasn't your news to share," Holly says, standing her ground. "If we're going to work together as a team, then we need to respect each other's boundaries."

"Now, honey," Bonnie says, reaching for both Holly's and Maggie's hands to hold in her own. "None of us mean to hurt one another around here. We're the nicest bunch of people you'd ever want to meet." She squeezes both of their hands. "But we get a little stir crazy sometimes and we can all admit that we're kind of isolated on this island. That need to gossip and make human connections can sometimes lead us astray."

Holly nods, conceding this fact. Maggie's eyes shift so that she's looking at the trunk of the palm tree in her front yard. It's wound with Christmas lights year round, and they haven't been switched on yet for the evening.

"Remember that time when you accidentally gossiped about the triplets' surprise birthday party and they found out about it?" Bonnie asks Holly, tugging at her hand to remind her.

"And remember when I told Mrs. Agnelli about you and Jake breaking up and he was furious that you would share the details with anyone else?"

Holly nods again. "You're right."

"So can we agree to disagree on this and try to figure out a way to minimize the damage?" Bonnie squeezes the women's hands again, looking each of them in the eye. "Are you two ready to hug this one out?"

Maggie steps forward and puts her arms out for Holly. There is the slightest hesitation from Holly as her stubbornness nearly wins out, but ultimately she'll forgive Maggie—she loves everyone on the island far too much to hold a grudge over something like this.

"Okay," Bonnie says, watching Holly hug the shorter, older woman tightly. "Now can we get back to the Ho Ho and finish our Friday evening?"

Holly is about to agree to a quick trip back to the beachside bar when her phone buzzes in her back pocket. It's a text message. She recognizes the area code and closes her eyes tightly, trying to imagine what it might be.

Holly. Why is People magazine contacting me about my upcoming wedding on Christmas Key? It's Kitta Banks. And even without hearing her voice, Holly senses the impatience and the demanding tone in her words.

"I think the Ho Ho might be out for tonight, Bon," she says, holding up the phone so that Bonnie can see the screen. She leans forward and squints, trying to make out the message without the aid of her reading glasses.

"Well that's a doozy, ain't it?" Bonnie stands up straight again, her face a mask of anticipation. "What do you think we should do about that?"

"I think we should head back to the office and make a few phone calls."

"Alright, boss. Let's go and try to mop up a gallon of spilled milk with a single Kleenex." Bonnie is already heading back to the golf cart. "We've got work to do."

THERE ARE FIVE VOICE MAILS WAITING FOR HOLLY AT THE OFFICE— three from Kitta and two from her manager threatening a call from their lawyer—and six emails. Holly is still barefoot, but she's completely forgotten that fact. The soles of her feet are dusty with sand as she pulls her knees up and rests her heels on the edge of her desk chair.

"Are you still mad at Maggie?" Bonnie asks, slipping on her pink and yellow reading glasses as she turns on her computer. The sky outside the office windows is dark and clear.

Holly sighs. "No. I'm not mad. I wish she hadn't done it, obviously. But our biggest issue now is making Kitta happy and trying to stop this from turning into a disaster." Instead of responding to the text, Holly dials the number she has for Kitta on her desk phone. It rings in her ear as she consults her silver watch: it's three hours earlier on the West coast.

"Explain." Kitta's voice comes through the phone without a greeting.

"Hi, Kitta," Holly says, looking at Bonnie across the tops of their computers. "It's Holly."

"I know. What happened?"

"Well, I have an elderly employee who came across some of my paperwork—"

"You don't have the paperwork on lockdown?" Kitta interrupts. "And your employees aren't aware of our non-disclosure agreement?"

"We're a pretty small operation here, Kitta," Holly says, exhaling. "It's basically just me and Bonnie in the office, and we've kept all the details of the wedding between the two of us. But this other employee happened to find a file I was keeping, and she mentioned it to another islander at the coffee shop the next morning."

Kitta is quiet on the other end of the phone, and Holly can imagine the face she knows so well from the movie screen, pouting prettily as she contemplates an unwelcome spread in *People* magazine about her upcoming top-secret nuptials.

"So this old lady mentioned it to *one* friend in a coffee shop, and suddenly I'm getting calls from reporters?"

Holly is at a loss here. "I don't know how that happened, Kitta—is it possible that the leak came from somewhere else? There's no way anyone on this island has a connection to a reporter at *People*, and it's even less likely that they'd think to take information like that and feed it to the gossip mill. I can guarantee that."

"Of course it wouldn't have come from my people." Kitta's tone is haughty and offended. "I surround myself with professionals, and none of my friends would dare do something like this."

"You have my apologies, Kitta. If there's any way this happened because of something or someone on Christmas Key, you know it was unintentional and not done with malice. Bonnie and I have both worked really hard to help you make this the wedding of your dreams, and we've been very discreet."

"Listen. I know I've been demanding," Kitta says. "But you have to understand what it's like to be me. People go through my *trash* looking for information that they can print and make money off of. It's ridiculous. And my relationship with Deacon is something that's precious to me. I have no desire to share our wedding with the world —yet."

"I understand."

"Good. Then we're on the same page." Kitta pauses. "This will be the last slip-up we have. Deacon and I arrive in one week, and the wedding is two days later. Do you think we can keep it under wraps until we've said our vows?"

"Absolutely," Holly says with certainty. "We've got it under control." Across the desk, Bonnie is chewing on the side of her thumb and looking nervous.

"Okay, I'll talk to you tomorrow." Without another word, Kitta ends the call.

"She'll talk to us tomorrow," Holly repeats to Bonnie, setting the phone back on its cradle.

"Of course she will. Several times, I'm sure." Bonnie exhales loudly and puts her fingers to her temples. "Let's think long and hard before we do this again."

Holly laughs. "You mean before we agree to host the wedding of an Oscar winning actress and a famous politician again?"

"Before we agree to host a wedding—period." Bonnie sets her reading glasses on the desk and picks up a pencil and notepad. "Now, what's next?"

Holly bites on her lower lip as she thinks. "Emergency village council meeting. Tomorrow is Saturday, but we're burning daylight here, so let's see if we can get everyone together here tomorrow afternoon at some point."

"You got it, Mayor."

Outside on Main Street, Jake drives by in his official police golf cart, slowing as he passes the well-lit B&B office window. He watches as Holly folds her arms over her chest and frowns. Her lips are moving and Bonnie is writing something on a notepad. Jake hits the gas again and drives on.

4

"I ALREADY KNOW WHO'S COMING, HOLLY." MARIA AGNELLI TAKES HER seat at the front of the B&B's dining room the next afternoon as the islanders all trickle in for the village council meeting. "I heard all about it after you left the Ho Ho last night."

Holly is standing next to the podium she uses as she heads up their monthly meetings, one hand on her hip as she counts heads. They've only got about half of the locals so far.

"That's exactly why we're here, Mrs. Agnelli." Holly avoids her gaze as she continues to count off every person who walks through the double doors. "We're at sixty-three right now," she says, leaning over to let Heddie Lang-Mueller know the head count. "At seventy-five, I say we start."

Heddie nods and continues organizing her legal pad and pens on the table next to Holly's podium. It's been her job to take meeting minutes for as long as anyone can remember, and Heddie takes her duties seriously. "Just tell me when you're ready," she says in her crisp German accent. As usual, Heddie is sitting ramrod straight in her chair, her fine gray-blonde hair swept up off her neck and pinned in a neat bun.

"I saw that gal in her last movie," Mrs. Agnelli continues, talking to no one in particular. "Didn't care for her." She turns and pats the chair next to hers so that Millie Bradford will join her up front. Since Ray's passing, the islanders have entered into an unspoken agreement to take turns watching Millie and making sure she's always got someone to sit next to or walk with, and she seems to appreciate it. She slides onto the chair next to Mrs. Agnelli's and sets her purse on the floor by her feet.

"And that's seventy-seven," Holly says, counting off the triplets and their husbands as they enter. "Let's call the meeting to order."

She picks up her pink marble gavel and bangs it against the matching block. "I'd like to call this emergency village council meeting to order," Holly says loudly, stepping behind the podium. "If you could take your seats, we'll get through this as quickly as possible and we can all get back to our regularly scheduled Saturday plans."

As mayor of a tropical paradise, Holly's daily dress code is exceedingly casual. But when she leads the village council meetings, she always attempts to step it up just a notch, trading in cutoffs for a sundress (though never giving up the bikini under her clothes, which is always there just in case she gets the chance to take an impromptu dip in the ocean).

Today she's wearing a bright yellow skirt covered in tiny blue flowers, and with it, a clean white tank top and a pair of nude colored sandals that tie around her ankles. She's captured her long, loose hair in a low ponytail, and even gone so far as to put on silver hoop earrings and mascara for the occasion.

"My Saturday afternoon plans include a nap and a cold beer," Maria Agnelli says loudly. "And if I'm lucky, maybe I'll catch Jake washing his golf cart without a shirt on." She turns and scans the crowd until her eyes land on Officer Zavaroni. He blushes underneath his deep tan.

"I called this meeting to talk about the upcoming wedding that we've all been buzzing about," Holly says, ignoring Mrs. Agnelli. "It's my understanding that, although Bonnie and I worked hard to keep the arrangements quiet per the bride's wishes, there's a leak in our boat and we're taking on water."

"And that leak's name is Maggie Sutter," Mrs. Agnelli offers, her voice carrying. Millie puts a hand on her arm, leaning in to shush her gently.

"It doesn't matter at this point how the word got around," Holly cautions. "What matters is that we move forward with a united front so that this wedding can happen the way the bride and groom want it to."

Fiona's hand goes up in the middle of the room. Holly pauses; it isn't like Fiona to put in her two cents while Holly is speaking at a village council meeting, so she nods at her. "Go ahead, Fee."

Fiona stands. "Now that we all know it's—wait, do we all know who's coming?"

"Kitta Banks and Deacon Avaloy," Holly confirms. A ripple of chatter moves through the crowd.

"Right. Now that we all know who it is, I guess what I'm wondering is whether we're all on deck for this event, or if we can be excused from the preparations. Do you need our help to pull this off?"

Holly is caught off guard by the flat way Fiona presents the question. She can usually count on her best friend to help with anything, and she's never known her to shy away from pitching in at a big event.

"Oh. Well," she says, scanning Fiona's blank face for clues. "No, of course you don't *have* to help. If anyone is opposed to being a part of the wedding crew, then I totally respect that. As always, your help is welcome and appreciated, but I understand that I'm not paying you for your time, so..."

"Great." Fiona sits down abruptly. Next to her, Buckhunter glances at his fiancee with a worried look. His eyes cut to Holly and they exchange a look as if to say *what gives?*

"Anyway," Holly goes on, trying to recalibrate her thoughts. "As I was saying, we need to make sure we meet Kitta and Deacon's expectations. We've obviously postponed construction of the dock for several days as the wedding team arrives and carries out the event, and all of the B&B's rooms are saved for the wedding party. We have a 'zero visitors' policy for the next week and a half, and with that in place, we can assure the bride and groom that this will be a totally private location for their ceremony."

Katelynn Pillory's hand climbs slowly into the air. Holly nods at her.

"Holly," Katelynn says, standing tentatively. Holly takes note of the fact that she's sitting next to Jake. "I am so, so sorry, but I had no idea we had a zero visitors policy for these weeks." She presses her palms together in front of her chest; this makes her look like she's about to drop to her knees and pray. "Logan's been working really hard all summer to save money," Katelynn scans the crowd, "and as a sidebar, thank you to all of you who've hired him for odd jobs and whatnot—but he's been saving up to help his friend Owen buy a ticket down here."

Holly taps her thumb against the podium gently as she listens. Next to her, Heddie is furiously taking notes.

"Anyway, Owen's parents agreed to let him come down for a couple of weeks, and he gets here tomorrow. I had *no* idea we had to get visitors approved, otherwise I would have. I'm so sorry," she says again.

Holly's mind races. "Okay. Owen's coming. That shouldn't be a problem," she says, thinking on her feet. "In fact, maybe he and Logan can help out with some of the preparations that might require the strength of two young men."

Katelynn is clearly relieved that Holly's amenable to her son's friend being on Christmas Key for the duration of the wedding. "Oh, of course they'll help! No problem."

"Then I think it's fine. As long as they adhere to the no photos policy that the rest of us are under." She looks around at the crowd as Katelynn sits down again. "And just as a reminder, we've all got to be firm about that. No matter how tempting it is when you have stars in your midst, you absolutely cannot approach them for autographs, photos, or to gush like fans. We have to treat them just as we would any other guests and give them their privacy as they enjoy the island. Do we have any issues with that?"

Everyone nods or looks at the person next to them with eyebrows raised. There seems to be a general consensus that this will be an easy rule to follow.

"Great. Then the only other thing we need to discuss is keeping further leaks from happening." Holly consults a list of ideas she's jotted down on a piece of paper. "First of all, we need to agree not to share anything about the wedding on social media." Only a small portion of the islanders even use Facebook, but she knows it's still a possibility. "Secondly, we can't share anything about it—even a teaser —with family or friends we might talk to on the phone." A few people grumble to their neighbors as they take this in. For many of them, sharing with loved ones on the mainland is their lifeline to home and family. "And to be absolutely sure that we honor our guests' wishes, we have to commit to *not* talking to anyone who might call or show up here in the interim looking for information. Got it?"

Slow nods bob around the B&B's dining room. They can't even imagine reporters washing onto their shores or hiding in the bushes to secretly obtain information, but Holly can.

"Okay, good. Then that's it. Let's just do our best to be helpful between now and the wedding, stay cool in the face of celebrity, and hopefully give Miss Banks and Mr. Avaloy the wedding of their dreams." With that, Holly taps the gavel again to indicate the close of the meeting.

The room instantly explodes into chatter and discussion, and people stand and mill around in groups.

"Hey, Fee," Holly says, making a beeline for her best friend. Fiona and Buckhunter have already left their seats and are moving towards the double-doors to exit the dining room. "Wait up."

Fiona stops and turns, all evidence of her curt question wiped from her face. "Hey, Hol."

Holly loops her arm through Fiona's and keeps walking. "Mind if I borrow your lady for a bit?" she asks Buckhunter, turning to glance at her uncle over her shoulder as they leave him behind.

"Not at all. I've got to get back to the bar anyway." Buckhunter runs a hand through his short hair and winks at Fiona. "I'll catch you later, huh?"

Fiona nods and gives him a half-smile as he walks around them and heads back out onto Main Street to go next door to Jack Frosty's. With this many islanders out and about for the village council meeting, he'll surely get some early dinner foot traffic or maybe a handful of people who want afternoon appetizers and drinks.

"Want to go for a swim?" Holly asks, leading Fiona through the lobby and out onto the front steps. Their arms are still looped together.

"At the beach?" Fiona squints in the afternoon sun. Main Street is heavy with people mingling and talking after the meeting, and the curb is lined bumper-to-bumper with golf carts. "You want to swim now?"

"Yeah." Holly points at the sky. "It's gorgeous today. It's Saturday. I've got a bikini on under this." She plucks at the thin strap of a lime green bikini that peeks out from under her white tank-top.

"Of course you do." Fiona laughs at her best friend, shaking her head. "I'd expect nothing less."

"I'll drive." Holly grabs Fiona's hand and pulls her to the sandy lot adjacent to the B&B before she can change her mind.

"What's the hurry? The ocean's not going anywhere."

"I'm just dying to get into the water." Holly slides behind the steering wheel. "Do we need to swing by your place for a swimsuit?"

Fiona sits gingerly on the passenger seat, rearranging her long sundress. "No, I've got a bikini on under this."

"Niiiiccceee," Holly says appreciatively.

"Hey, I learned from the best."

The women drive up Pine Cone Boulevard and end up at Candy Cane Beach in under three minutes. "Does this work for you?" Holly puts the cart in park and shuts it off.

"No complaints." Fiona digs through her bag and pulls out a pair of sunglasses. "Do we have towels?"

"Nah," Holly says, waving a hand. "I figured we could dry off in the sun afterward and then drive back in our suits. Towels are for amateurs."

In one swift movement, Holly pulls her tank top overhead and unzips her skirt, letting it fall in the sand at her feet. Fiona pulls her dress off and follows Holly to the water's edge.

"Shall we?" Holly rushes in without waiting for an answer. The water laps at her thighs and bare stomach, covering the bright pink bikini bottoms that don't match her lime green top. "Oh! It's perfect!" she calls back to Fiona, motioning for her to follow.

The women swim out a little and then float on their backs, watching the autumn sky as their hair drifts around them in the water. After a few minutes, Holly flips over and paddles closer to shore. Fiona does the same.

"So what's up?" Holly asks, standing up and walking a few steps as they get to shallower water.

"What's up with what?" Fiona tips her head and shakes it a little to get the water out of her left ear.

"That whole thing at the meeting? It's not like you to refuse to help out with something."

A shadow passes over Fiona's face and she tugs at her wet bikini bottoms, hiking them up over her curvy hips. "I just don't feel like being around wedding stuff. It's not a big deal."

"Uh, it kind of is," Holly argues, sitting at the very edge of the water so that the waves wash over her stretched out legs. "You're planning a wedding of your own, so it seems like it should be right up your alley."

Fiona sits next to her and pulls her knees up to her chin. Her long, wavy strawberry blonde hair hangs in wet tendrils down her back. She makes a noise that sounds like a cross between "Hmmm" and "Uhhhh."

"What's that for?"

With a deep breath, Fiona turns and looks at Holly. "He shoots down every idea I have. Everything I come up with is 'too much' or just not right for us," she says. "What's with that?"

"Buckhunter doesn't like any of your ideas?"

"Not just that, he seems totally uninterested in even talking about the wedding."

Holly contemplates this. Buckhunter is her uncle, but that doesn't offer her any particular insight into the man—at least not more than what Fiona already has as his fiancée. She's only known that they were related for just over a year, so other than sharing some DNA, she can't even guess at why he might be feeling a little reticent to throw himself into wedding planning.

"Have you asked him why he doesn't want to talk about it?" Holly asks carefully.

"Kind of. I mean, I asked him if we should just call it off."

Holly sputters. "You *what*? Why would you do that?"

"I don't know...I guess because it seemed like he was regretting saying yes to me." It's a reminder for them both that Fiona had gone the untraditional route and done the proposing herself, and a heated flush crawls up her neck and her cheeks as she remembers his pleased surprise when she'd popped the question over dinner at his place.

"You're letting the redhead in you show through," Holly says, scooping up a handful of water and tossing it at Fiona's arm. It splashes her, running in rivulets down her skin. "Stop being so fiery."

Fiona's shoulders relax as she sits and thinks. "I'm being a drama queen, aren't I?"

"Okay, 'drama queen' is a little extreme, but I think you're probably reading way too much into things. This is Buckhunter we're talking about, you know. He's a fifty-year-old bachelor who thinks that putting on a t-shirt instead of a tank top equals 'dressing up' for an event."

A smile creeps across Fiona's face. "Yeah, you're right. Maybe all the talk of dresses and flowers and rings is just out of his comfort zone."

"You're talking diamonds with Buckhunter? And wedding gowns?" Holly's eyebrows shoot up and she turns her head toward her friend in disbelief. "Those things are *not* in his area of expertise. Not only that, but imagine how he feels having some big wedding blow into town in a week. He's probably terrified that it'll give you big, crazy ideas."

"He should know me better than that. I'd be happy with some-thing simple. I tried showing him my Pinterest board—"

"You showed him your Pinterest board?" Holly shakes her head and puts an arm around Fiona's shoulders. Her skin is warm from the sun, her hair wet and cool against the inside of Holly's arm. "Honey, honey, honey. Mistake number one, right there. You never show a man your Pinterest wedding board. All that color-coordination. The cakes that look like they were made by elves and fairies. The cute signs that people hold up, and the perfectly-executed group photos. Those things are there to fuel *your* secret wedding fantasies—not his."

"Oh my god, Hol...you're right." Fiona's head drops and Holly leans in closer, putting her cheek against her best friend's damp scalp. She gives her a tight squeeze.

"Listen. You're not asking, but here's my advice: don't let him catch you on Pinterest. Stop all wedding talk until we get through this Kitta Banks carnival. Come help out and see what money can buy when you're a millionaire bride, but don't get hung up on having a picture perfect event of your own. You and Buckhunter will do exactly what's right for you. Sound fair?"

Fiona lifts her head and looks at Holly. "Sounds fair. I've been such a girl about this."

"Eh," Holly shakes Fiona gently with the arm that's still around her shoulder like she's trying to rattle some sense into her. "Since you are technically a girl, I'm going to let it slide this time."

"Should we take one more swim?" Fiona stands up and steps over the small waves as she heads back out into the water.

Holly grins at her friend's back, pleased that she's gotten to the bottom of the wedding issue. "Do coconuts grow on palm trees?"

5

JAKE PAUSES OUTSIDE THE DOOR OF MISTLETOE MORNING BREW THE
next morning with a folded newspaper under one arm. As the
island's only police officer he's essentially always on duty, but much
of his traditional work days end up being time spent socializing and
hanging out on Main Street, so he never minds the feeling that all
waking hours are work hours.

"Officer Zavaroni," Cap Duncan says with a nod, holding open
the door to the coffee shop. "After you."

Jake gives Cap a nod and walks into the air-conditioned shop.
Inside, a respectable group of Sunday morning coffee drinkers is
gathered at the tall bistro tables, sipping various brews and flaking off
bites of pastry with their forks.

"Hi, Jake!" Gwen calls out. She's seated at a table with her identical sisters, Glen and Gen. Their husbands aren't with them, and
they're happily gossiping and sharing a plate of croissants and
danish.

Jake waves at the ladies as he approaches the front counter.
"Morning, Ellen," he says to Ellen Jankowitz as she waits to take his
order.

"What can I get for you this fine morning?" Ellen leans a hip against the counter. Her wife, Carrie-Anne, is weaving through the café with a tray full of dirty cups and plates held aloft. They're both wearing purple t-shirts with words printed in white across their chests. Ellen's says: *"The suspense is terrible...I hope it'll last."*

"Let's see..." Jake consults the hand-written sign above the counter. "I'll have a Snozzberry Smoothie, please."

"One Snozzberry, coming right up." Ellen winks at him and takes his money.

Jake finds a table by the window and looks around the coffee shop. This month's literary theme for the interior decor is *Willy Wonka and the Chocolate Factory*, and every table's centerpiece is a glass jar filled with a different kind of candy. One table has rainbow-hued gum balls on it, another boasts striped peppermint sticks standing upright like straws in a jar. Cap's chosen a table with a container of Hershey's Kisses wrapped in silver foil and he turns it around and around, watching the light bounce off the candies as he waits for his coffee.

Outside on Main Street, Holly walks with purpose, her hair loose on her back as she makes her way to the dock. Jake nods and smiles absently at Carrie-Anne when she sets his drink in front of him, but his attention is on Holly as she puts her hands on both sides of her mouth and calls out to a group of men wearing deep tans and sweaty t-shirts. They stop what they're doing on the dock and turn to her.

Jake watches for a minute before picking up his smoothie and newspaper and walking out the door of the coffee shop.

"I wanted to know what the plan is for the next week," Holly is saying to a man whose hands are planted firmly on his hips. He's got a sun-bleached goatee and a bright orange baseball cap on his head.

"The plan is to keep working up until Thursday, then head back to Key West," the man says, looking over at Jake and giving him a perfunctory nod as he approaches. "You wanted us out of here for a long weekend, and we're trying to clean things up and get to a good breaking point by then."

"That's perfect," Holly says. "If you guys head out on Thursday morning, we can turn over all the rooms at the B&B and have them ready for the wedding party that's arriving Friday." She does the mental calculations on timing as she talks. "And incidentally, thanks again for taking those days off. We really appreciate your flexibility."

"Hey, not a problem. Our boss tells us we need to head home for a few days, we head home for a few days. My guys will be happy to spend a few nights in their own beds. Getting to spend yesterday with our families was a treat—although our wives might get tired of us napping on the couch and drinking six-packs all weekend." The other men laugh agreeably.

"You guys need help with anything today?" Jake offers. He's standing next to Holly and she looks up at him in surprise.

The foreman of the group glances around at the piles of wood and metal near the dock, hands still on his hips. "Well, Officer, we're just moving stuff today from the dock to the building site, and it's nothing but heavy lifting and transport, really. But we could use the extra hands and a golf cart—if you're up for it."

"I'm up for it," Jake says amiably. As much as he loves doing the small things that the other islanders ask of him—lifting boxes, helping to re-string Christmas lights from the eaves of bungalows—there's a part of him that longs to spend a day doing some real labor. "Let me run home and change, and I'll meet you back here."

"Deal." The man turns back to Holly. "We've got a boat arriving in, what, an hour?" He consults his paint-splattered wrist watch.

Holly points at the horizon. "Sooner." The delivery boat is approaching from not far off, and on it should be both a week's worth of groceries to stock the shelves of Tinsel & Tidings Gift Shop, and a sixteen-year-old boy from Ohio named Owen.

"Then we need to get moving." The men spring into action as Jake climbs behind the wheel of his golf cart in front of Mistletoe Morning Brew. Holly pulls her phone out of the back pocket of her white shorts and types a quick text to Katelynn Pillory: *Logan's friend is approaching. Boat should be at the dock in less than twenty.* She hits send.

❄

"OWEN!" LOGAN PILLORY IS WAVING BOTH ARMS TO GET HIS FRIEND'S attention as the boat's captain steers it gently towards the dock. "Dude, you're here!" The excitement on his face makes Holly smile. How could she be mad at Katelynn for inviting a friend of Logan's to visit the island and entertain him for a bit? After all, Logan's worked hard to amuse himself as the only teenager on Christmas Key, and he's dived headfirst into the local economy by making himself the master of odd jobs for the island's residents.

"Holly," Logan says, turning to her with a big smile as she stands next to him. "Hi." His innocent crush on Holly is widely known, though she does her best to ignore it, even in the face of his blushing and stammering.

"So your buddy is here, huh?" Holly squints at the boat as the captain cuts the engine and drifts towards the dock. "What are you two going to do first?"

Logan shrugs. "Probably talk about everyone we know from home and then head to the beach."

"Sounds about right." Holly's arms are folded across her chest and she leans over to Logan, bumping him with her right shoulder. "I hope you guys have fun."

"We will." Logan turns his attention back to the boat as Owen hangs over the side, watching the hull bump softly into the dock. The captain jumps off the boat and grabs the rope to tie it off.

"And I'm serious about calling on you both to help out a bit—you know I've got your number," Holly says, taking a step back and pointing at Logan with her index finger. It's true that she has Logan's number; they'd been kayaking together when he first arrived, and Holly had helped him with his business fliers and advertising when he decided to offer up his services.

"Yeah, for sure." Logan's hair flops over his forehead as he nods. "Text me." As he says this, Owen is crossing the sand with a huge duffel bag over one shoulder. He hears his friend telling Holly to text him and shoots Logan an impressed look.

Rather than clarifying the exchange, Holly turns to Owen, smiling up at the boy. He's about six-foot-five and all hands and feet and kneecaps. "Hi, I'm Holly Baxter," she says, sticking out one hand to shake Owen's. "I'm the mayor of Christmas Key and a friend of Logan's mom's."

The mention of Katelynn and Holly's friendship deflates Logan's ego somewhat, and the mood shifts just slightly.

"Hey," Owen says, shaking Holly's hand with a big, hearty motion. "I'm Owen. I'm here to kick this guy's butt and get him in shape."

"Get *me* in shape?" Logan reaches over and shoves Owen playfully. "Dude, all I've done since I've been here is mow lawns and run on the beach. I'm in the best shape of my life." As if to prove it, Logan flexes one bicep, showing off the tan that's emerged from the burns he'd initially suffered through when he arrived.

"You do look pretty good. Too bad Cara isn't here to see it." Owen smirks at his friend. "She's single, by the way."

"Cara?" Logan's eyebrows shoot up. "Who cares." He glances at Holly to make sure she knows that, in fact, *he* doesn't care about Cara.

"Whatever, dude." Owen claps him on the back. "Show me your place."

The boys amble off with a wave to Holly, and she watches as they wander up Main Street. Logan points out businesses and people as he talks, and Owen is still holding his army green duffel bag casually over one shoulder by its handles.

The triplets emerge from the coffee shop then and grab the three hand trucks they've left by the front door of Mistletoe Morning Brew. The women maneuver the carts over to the boat to be loaded up with the items that they'll use to stock the shelves of their gift shop.

"Holly!" Glen calls out. "How are the wedding plans coming?"

"Everything is good," Holly assures her. "We've got the bride and groom arriving on Friday, so there's still a lot to do to prepare for that."

"We're happy to help, you know that." Gen bends over to lift a box full of cereals and packaged pasta onto her cart. "You know we love big events."

"I appreciate that," Holly says, handing Gen another box, this one laden with perishables like milk and butter and cheese. Gen sets the box on top of her pile and backs up her cart to make the first run over to Tinsel & Tidings.

"Was that Katelynn's boy greeting his friend?" Gwen asks, counting bottles of wine as she loads them onto her cart.

"Yep. That was Owen," Holly says. "They promised to help out with wedding stuff if we need them to, but I'm sure they'll spend most of Owen's visit in the water and on the beach."

"Or following you around," Gwen teases, nestling a bottle of Merlot in between a Cabernet Sauvignon and a Riesling.

"Oh, I'm sure they can find better things to do with their time..." Holly's attention is diverted by Bonnie waving at her from the front porch of the B&B, both arms flagging her down the same way Logan had done to Owen just minutes before. In one hand is the office phone, and on her face, a mix of terror and regret. "Hey, I've got to run," Holly says, touching Gwen lightly on the arm. "I'll see you ladies later."

Holly jogs up the sidewalk and stops in front of Bonnie. "What's up?"

Bonnie clutches the phone to her ample bosom and grits her teeth. "It's your mother," she says.

Holly takes two steps back and looks at the phone in Bonnie's hand like it's made of molten lava. "No," she says, making an X with her arms like she's trying to ward off a beast. "Uh uh."

"I was in the office working on some things for next weekend," Bonnie hisses. "And when the phone rang, I assumed it was Kitta calling. But it's Coco." She makes an apologetic face.

For a moment, Holly debates just walking away and pretending she never walked over to Bonnie in the first place, but instead, she holds out a hand. Bonnie passes her the phone.

"Hello?" Holly says in a cheerful voice. "This is Holly."

"You already know it's me," Coco says impatiently. Holly can imagine her tapping her acrylic French manicure on the marble countertop of her kitchen island. "I'm sure Bonnie gave you a warning as she flagged you down through the window of the office."

"Actually, it was from the front porch," Holly says drily. "What's up, Coco?"

There is a pause as Coco debates whether to take issue with her own daughter calling her 'Coco' instead of 'Mom.' She obviously decides to leave it alone and plunges ahead. "I hear there's a big wedding in the works."

"Yes, Buckhunter and Fiona are getting married," Holly says, skirting the real reason her mother is calling. There is no doubt in her mind that Coco not only knows who's getting married on Christmas Key the following weekend, but also what the bride is wearing, where they're going on their honeymoon, and whether they'll be immediately trying for children.

"Cute, Holly." Coco clears her throat. "I'll be on the boat that arrives Wednesday afternoon," she says. "I assume there'll be a room for me at the B&B for the week."

"No," Holly says, shaking her head and making wide eyes at Bonnie. Bonnie puts both hands over her mouth, her own eyes bulging as she anticipates the bad news. "Actually the B&B is full—we've booked the whole thing out for the wedding."

"Then set me up at your place." Coco is matter-of-fact about this, as if staying at Holly's house is a real option.

"Uhhh, well, I—"

"You what, Holly? And don't tell me you're remodeling the guest room again, because you already used that excuse."

Holly takes a deep breath and goes for it. "I don't think it's a good time for you to come down."

Coco says nothing. Holly can feel the frost in her mother's silence all the way from New Jersey.

"I am coming down on Wednesday." Coco pauses. "I have my ticket and I've made the arrangements. When two celebrities throw a wedding on our island, you can be damn sure that—as a co-owner of that particular piece of property—I'll be down there to make sure everything goes smoothly."

Holly's eyes roll so far back in her head that for a second, all Bonnie can see is the whites of her eyes. "Fine, Mother." Holly's tone is crisp. She knows Coco well enough to know that she won't be talking her out of this trip, and that having her mother there will add another layer of potential drama and disaster to an already stressful event.

"So I'll be staying with you, then?"

"Sure. You'll stay at my house." Holly clenches her jaw as she stares at Bonnie's cartoonish expression of dismay. There's no way she'll be staying at her own house during Coco's visit, so she'll have to relinquish the whole house and find somewhere else to go.

"Fabulous. I'm so thrilled to receive such a warm, inviting welcome from my only child," Coco says sarcastically. "I'll see you on Wednesday."

Holly ends the call by hitting the button on the cordless phone. Her eyes never leave Bonnie's face.

"Sugar," Bonnie says. She reaches out and puts both of her hands on Holly's bare arms. "You'll stay with me while she's here. And you can bring Pucci. I'll set the guest room up for you—it'll be nice. I promise."

This cheers Holly up—it really does—but she can't bring herself to smile. Any time Coco comes to town, Holly's spirits plummet. Her strained relationship with her mother has been her life-long cross to bear, but the icy, demanding way that Coco handles everyone and everything that crosses her path gets harder and harder for Holly to handle with each passing year.

"Thanks, Bon. But I'll check and see if Pucci can stay with Jake. He's already got a dog door there, and it'll be one less thing for me to worry about while we're dealing with Kitta and the wedding." She forces her lips to turn up at the corners, but the smile doesn't reach her eyes. "I, however, will take you up on the offer to crash in your guest room. There's no way I'm staying at my place with Coco."

"Understood." Bonnie takes the cordless phone from Holly's hand and sets it on the railing of the B&B's front porch. "Now, it's Sunday afternoon. Why don't we just head over to Jack Frosty's for something cold to drink and we can kick around a few more wedding ideas."

Bonnie wisely steers Holly away from the office, pushing her gently up the steps and into Buckhunter's bar.

Holly sighs. "You're right," she says, nodding at Bonnie as they pass the jukebox and pick a table in the center of the room. "And I might as well give Buckhunter the good news while we're here." She pulls out her chair and is about to sink into it when her uncle materializes at her side with two glasses of ice water for them.

"Give Buckhunter what good news?" He sets the waters on the table and wipes his hands on the front of his cutoff Levi's. His thin, over-washed Hawaiian shirt hangs limply over his strong chest, and the overhead fans make the fabric ripple against his tanned skin.

Holly gives Bonnie one last knowing look and turns her gaze up to Buckhunter's face. "Coco's coming," she says. "That's the good news. As of Wednesday, Coco will be on the island."

Without another word, Buckhunter walks away from the table as if he hasn't just heard that his half-sister will be there in three days. Holly can see from the way he shakes his head as he wipes down the bar that they're on the same page: this is most definitely *not* good news.

6

Tuesday is a long day. Kitta Banks has called the B&B office and texted Holly no fewer than eighteen times, and Bonnie has made several calls to every craft and fabric store in Key West in hopes that someone carries the very specific shade of creamy yellow tulle that Kitta wants everything from the flower arrangements to the trunks of the palm trees on the beach wrapped in.

"Want to just order dinner from the Jingle Bell Bistro?" Holly asks, chewing on a pen as she taps the keys of her computer. "I can see if Iris or Jimmy will run it over here."

"I can go and pick it up," Bonnie offers, already getting out of her chair. "What do you want?"

"Anything. Seriously. We skipped lunch, so I'd eat anything that landed in front of me right now." She's harried and exhausted, and the realization that this is her last night in her own bed for at least a week is weighing on her mind. After Holly gets up in the morning, she'll need to change the sheets and give everything a once over before Coco arrives, but for tonight, all she wants to do is finish working, shove some dinner in her face, and go home and collapse.

Bonnie takes her purse from the hook by the door. "I'll be right back with whatever Iris and Jimmy want to throw into a to-go box for us, okay doll?" Without waiting for a response, Bonnie bustles down the hall and out into the night.

The sun has been gone for almost an hour, and Holly can see her own reflection in the window of the B&B's office. She looks tired. There are three lamps on in the room and no overhead lights, and Holly pushes back from the white wicker desk and stands, stretching her long arms overhead. As usual, she's kicked off her shoes near the door, and she walks around the room barefoot, stopping to look at the list of dates and times that she and Bonnie have written on the white boards to keep track of all the wedding details.

She's checking and double-checking the notes in front of her when her cell phone buzzes in her back pocket. She pulls it out and glances at it: Kitta Banks. With a deep, exaggerated sigh, Holly accepts the call.

"Hello?"

"Holly!" Kitta's voice is shrill and panicked. "What the hell is going on there?"

"Um," Holly spins around the office, looking for clues. She has no idea what the hell is going on there. Nothing has changed since she spoke to Kitta just an hour or two earlier. "I'm not sure. What's going on, Kitta?"

"I'm emailing you something right now. Look at it and call me back. WITH AN ANSWER." Kitta ends the call and leaves Holly standing there in the center of the office with a silent phone in her hand. She hurries over to the computer and refreshes her email. Sure enough, there in her inbox is a message from Kitta with no subject line.

"I want an explanation," the email says. There is no signature, just a hyperlink under the words. Holly clicks on it, and it takes her to the homepage of *Glitter and Stars*, a popular weekly magazine that focuses on the lives and activities of even the most marginal celebrities.

The homepage is splashed with a series of photos that Holly recognizes instantly: they're all of Christmas Key. She leans in close, examining the front door of Christmas Key Chapel. In one photo is a close-up of Cap walking out of Mistletoe Morning Brew with Marco on one shoulder and an iced coffee in his hand. Another photo shows Holly's hot pink golf cart parked in front of the B&B. A tiny smile plays at her lips as she realizes how good her island looks in full color on the homepage of *Glitter and Stars*. But the smile fades almost immediately when she realizes why it's there.

TOP SECRET WEDDING LOCATION OF KITTA BANKS AND DEACON AVALOY REVEALED!!! a headline screams. The short article that accompanies the photos provides a brief blurb about the island and its residents. Holly reads it with interest, even as her heart is plunging down to the soles of her feet. She swallows hard. When she calls Kitta back, she'll need an explanation for how this happened. And she doesn't have one.

Holly knows she can't put Kitta off much longer. Her iPhone is on her desk and she's sitting in her chair again, staring at the way the lamp casts a ring of light on the white ceiling. Her arms are folded, and she's slumped back in her chair, thinking. Someone had to have sent the photos to *Glitter and Stars*—but who? Were the pictures recent? There's nothing in them to indicate a day or time, and no one new has been on the island recently except the construction workers. None of them strike her as the type to race around the island and snap photos for a celebrity gossip rag, but at this point, anything is possible.

Holly reaches for her phone and slides it across the desk, unlocking it with her thumbprint. She goes to 'recent calls' and touches Kitta's name. The phone rings in her ear.

"This better be good," Kitta says without preamble. "I'm listening."

Holly inhales and lets her eyes close. "I don't have an explana-tion," she blurts. "But I *will* get to the bottom of it."

"How are we supposed to keep this wedding a secret if someone on your island is TELLING THE WORLD that it's about to happen?" Kitta shouts down the line. "I want to know who's doing this, Holly. I can't believe how much trust I've put in you and Bonnie. This is going to be the most important day of my life, and someone there is making a mockery of it."

"Kitta," Holly says, hoping to placate the actress with her calm tone. "I promise you that no one is making a mockery of your wedding. And you were right to put your faith in me and Bonnie. We've worked incredibly hard to meet all of your requests, and I swear to you I'll find out who sent the pictures to the magazine."

Kitta makes a noise, but says nothing.

"But," Holly goes on. "Has it occurred to you that maybe someone else knows about it, and that these are old photos? I mean, we had a reality show film on our island for several months—those could be stock photos from the television network or things people have posted anywhere. There's really no way to know for sure."

Kitta isn't about to admit that her ire might have been misplaced, and Holly doesn't really expect her to, so she forges ahead. "How about you look at it as a simple teaser that will get people interested in the real wedding photos? I know you have one of the best photographers lined up for the event, and no doubt you have plans for how you're going to distribute those first pictures." Holly is banking on the fact that Kitta will take the celebrity route of selling her own photos before anyone else can cash in on it. "This will just get people more interested in seeing the pictures from the big day."

While Holly waits for Kitta's response, Bonnie walks through the door, her hands full of white bags and paper cups. The strap of her purse slips off her shoulder and catches on her elbow, nearly causing her to drop the things she's carrying. Holly puts the call on speaker and sets it on the desk, then hurries over to grab the bags of dinner from Bonnie.

"Well," Kitta's voice comes through the phone. "I see your angle, Holly, and there may be a grain of truth to that. I'm still monumentally unhappy about this new leak," she adds, "but maybe it will pique people's interest, as you say."

Holly opens one of the bags and peers in. She smells French fries.

"Good! That's a really positive way to look at things," she says, craning her neck so that her voice carries in the direction of the phone. "I think if you just keep taking deep breaths, going to yoga, maybe get a massage," Holly adds, reaching an arm into the bag and pulling out a box of fries, "you'll stay calm and focused on your wedding day. Because really," she shoves a fry in her mouth, "that's the most important thing."

"Am I on speaker?" Kitta asks. "And are you *eating*?"

"No, no," Holly lies easily. "I mean yes, you are on speaker. But I just dropped a pen under my desk and I was trying to find it."

"Oh." Kitta inhales and exhales. "Okay, well, I'd still appreciate it if you did some digging to find out if this is coming from your people."

"Yes, Kitta. I definitely will," Holly assures her. "Now enjoy your Tuesday evening, okay? In just a few days, you're going to be here and we'll have a margarita and celebrate that we've pulled this off, okay?" It's a bold move, as nowhere in her imaginings of this event has Holly pictured herself knocking back a margarita with an Oscar winning actress. There's the very real chance that Kitta Banks sees her as nothing more than hired help, and that the thought of drinking with the help might be enough to send her into fits of hysterical laughter.

Instead, she just gives a relieved sigh. "A margarita sounds good. I'll talk to you tomorrow," Kitta says. "Oh, unless anything else comes to mind tonight."

Bonnie and Holly reach out and grab one another's hands in silent prayer that this will be the last call of the night. "Of course, Kitta," Holly says, forcing a smile to her face that she hopes will come across in her voice. "You let us know if anything else comes up tonight."

She ends the call and they sit in silence for a moment, contemplating a time in the near future when their lives won't be monopolized by this wedding. "Shall we eat?" Holly finally asks, breaking the silence.

"We should definitely eat." Bonnie rips open the bags and pulls out two boxes of fish and chips, handing Holly a small container of tarter sauce and a wedge of lemon.

"I need to keep my energy up for tomorrow," Holly says, bending over her to-go box and dunking a piece of fish in the chunky tarter sauce.

"What's tomorrow?" Bonnie is daintily unfolding her paper napkin and setting it in her lap as she sits across from Holly at their shared desk.

"Coco will be here tomorrow," Holly says around a mouthful of fried grouper.

Bonnie pushes her box of French fries in Holly's direction with a sympathetic grimace. "If you're going to stockpile enough energy to survive your mother, then you're gonna need these more than I do, sugar."

7

THE BOAT CARRYING COCO AND THREE CASES OF CHAMPAGNE FOR THE wedding arrives at five o'clock on Wednesday. Holly wages an internal debate all day long about whether she should be there to greet her mother at the dock and ferry her around the island, and the good angel on her shoulder finally wins out just before the boat arrives. She shuts down her computer and walks the short distance down Main Street.

"I was half expecting you to pawn me off on Jake or one of the other old timers around here," Coco says, stepping gingerly off the boat as she waits for the captain to unload her bags.

"I would never do that to Jake." Holly is already annoyed with herself for coming to the dock. After all, Coco knows this island and its residents as well as she does, and surely someone would have taken pity on her and driven her over to Holly's house.

"Oh, come on—I offered, and he didn't accept. Get over it." Coco tosses her dark hair and gives Holly an eye roll that makes her seem like a teenager. Coco is alluding to the fact that she'd gotten drunk the previous summer and made a move on Jake that had been rebuffed, but Holly isn't ready to laugh at the situation just yet. After all, her mother is still married to Alan (though how long it'll last given Coco's current unrest is a mystery to Holly), and knowing that she hit on Holly's ex adds a level of discomfort to their already strained relationship.

"Let's get you over to my house so you can relax," Holly says, taking the handle of her mother's suitcase from the captain with a nod. She walks up to the paved road and sets the wheels down, walking and dragging it behind her as she makes her way to the B&B's parking lot.

"I'm not tired," Coco insists, following close behind on wedged sandals that look like they're made from red bandanas and twine. Her legs are bare and her white denim skirt is short. She towers over Holly as she strides down Main Street, a purse held over one shoulder with her hand like she's strolling the Champs Elysees. "I want to roll up my sleeves and dig into wedding planning with you and Bonnie."

Holly stops walking when she realizes that her mother is approaching the back door of the B&B. She's obviously ready to enter the office and see what they've been working on with Kitta Banks these past few months.

"I don't think that's a good idea," Holly says, lifting her mother's brown Louis Vuitton case onto the back seat of her pink golf cart. "We've got everything handled at the moment."

"Holly, you know that I have every right to be as involved in this wedding as you and Bonnie are. Hell, I have even more right than Bonnie does to plan this thing. I'm here and I'm not going to just sit on the sidelines while Kitta Banks and Deacon Avaloy throw a first class wedding on our little island."

Holly sits on the edge of the driver's seat of her cart. By the middle of October, the sun is setting earlier, but there's still no chill to the air to bring down the humidity of the afternoon. A bead of sweat runs between Holly's shoulder blades and she shifts in her seat, one arm resting on the steering wheel as she contemplates the upcoming wedding.

"Well, 'first class' is kind of a stretch," she says, thinking of the plans that she and Bonnie have been privy to.

Coco frowns and purses her lips. "What do you mean?"

Holly isn't sure how much she wants to divulge to Coco, but she's been working so hard and keeping so many irons in the fire that there's a part of her that wants to just let go of it all and share the details—even if it's with her mother.

"You're not going to believe it," Holly says, resting one foot on the running board of her golf cart. "But Kitta Banks wants a yellow, fairy-themed wedding."

"Wait, what?" Coco's head tips to one side as if she isn't sure she's hearing things correctly. "Fairies?"

"Yep. With glitter and yellow icing on the cake and sunflowers everywhere."

"No."

"Yes."

"No." Coco shakes her head vehemently. "You have to stop her, Holly."

Holly laughs openly. "And how do you think I'm going to stop Kitta Banks from putting her bridesmaids in yellow dresses and fairy wings?"

"You're going to call Deacon Avaloy and let him know that he's marrying a woman of dubious taste," Coco sniffs. She's clearly offended by the aesthetic of the wedding, but even more than that is the thought that a man of Deacon Avaloy's breeding and status is being wasted on a woman whose tastes are so base, so crass, that she'd even *consider* putting grown women in fairy wings on her big day.

"I can't do that," Holly says, shaking her head. "And besides, I'm sure he already knows."

"He can't possibly."

The door to the B&B opens and Bonnie steps out, purse in hand. "Well. Look what the cat dragged in," she says with a forced smile. "Welcome back to the island, Coco."

There is no love lost between Holly's mother and the woman who she obviously would have chosen to be her mother if fate had been kinder, and the air between them is charged with distrust and mutual dislike.

"Hello, Bonnie." Coco walks around to the passenger side of Holly's cart and sits on the bench seat possessively. "Holly and I were just going to head over to her house. But I'll be in tomorrow to help out with wedding plans, so I'll see you in the morning."

Holly and Bonnie exchange a look as Holly processes her mother's sudden change of heart. She'd been gung-ho to get into the B&B's office and start digging through the wedding details, but now all she wants is to show Bonnie that she can monopolize Holly all evening if she wants to.

Never one to be outdone, Bonnie tightens her grip on her purse and smiles the crafty grin of a true Southern belle who is about to win the war. "Fine," she says, shifting her weight and repositioning her hourglass hips as her eyebrows shoot up innocently. "I'll see you tomorrow, Coco." She turns her attention to Holly. "And when should I expect you this evening, sugar?"

"I'll be over in a while," Holly says, flipping her tank watch over on her wrist and consulting the time. "Just let me get Coco settled in and Pucci dropped off at Jake's."

With a click of the park brake as it releases, Holly backs up and pulls out of the lot, waving at Bonnie as she goes. She can feel her mother tense up on the seat next to her and she's dreading what comes next.

To her credit, Coco maintains an icy smile all the way down Main Street, nodding at people as they pass by neighbors and friends. "You know," she says through gritted teeth, a smile still on her face as she makes eye contact with one of the triplets, "you don't have to vacate your own house just because I'm here."

Holly bumps onto Cinnamon Lane, leaving the only paved road on the island behind as they disappear into a thick cover of foliage. They pass under palm trees and through patches of scrub pine, passing by Alligator Pear trees heavy with fruit. Holly thinks of what to say.

"Mom," she finally says, tucking her loose hair behind one ear, "it's not good for us when we spend too much time together." It's the understatement of the year, and Holly keeps her eyes on the road as her words settle around them.

"How do you think it will ever get better between us if we *don't* spend any time together?"

Holly considers this. She's never imagined that her relationship with Coco will be anything other than what it is...than what it's always been. She was born to a restless, pampered sixteen-year-old, and then handed over to her grandparents to raise. They'd brought her up wild and free on a tropical island, with drop-in visits from a mother who'd always felt more like a petulant older sister than a maternal figure.

"I'm in my thirties," Holly says by way of explanation. "I don't expect us to change. Either of us."

Coco holds her purse in her lap, tightening her grip on it as if it's a life preserver and she's going down. "So every time I come to Christmas Key, you're going to either put me in the B&B and run away, or stick me out at your house and go crash somewhere else?"

Holly shrugs. In actuality, this was always kind of her plan. "I guess," she says.

"I just don't see how we can present a united front to this island if you refuse to spend any time with me." Holly slams on the brake, skidding to a stop. She turns to look at Coco, who is making a face and holding the back of her neck like she's just gotten whiplash. "What in the hell was that for?" she shouts.

"A *united front*?" Holly's mouth is gaping in disbelief. "How are we supposed to present a united front? Well, first of all, we don't *have* a united front. How many months has it been since you last tried to sell this island out from under me?"

"Now, Holly—"

"No, stop." Holly holds up a hand and shakes her head. "Stop right there. We see eye to eye on *nothing*. You don't like the way I run this island, you don't like the fact that I'm single, you hate my dog, and you think you can do everything better than I do it."

Coco listens to the list of accusations. "I do hate your dog," she admits, arms folded across her midsection once again.

"You hate everything I do," Holly says accusingly. "And you always have. So in no way am I concerned about presenting anything to our neighbors. They all know the score here, and no one expects us to have a rosy mother-daughter relationship. Trust me."

Coco flicks her dark brown hair out of her eyes with one manicured hand. "It's nice to know that the people of Christmas Key have an opinion on my mothering."

Holly snorts. "How could they not, Mom? They all pitched in and helped to raise me."

"You know what?" Coco turns to face her daughter, eyes narrowed. "I'm done talking about this for today. Why don't you just drop me off at your house and run over to Bonnie's so that you two can talk about what a horrible mother I've been to you."

It's Holly's turn to roll her eyes. "Come on. Bonnie and I have better things to talk about than that." She takes her foot off the brake and touches the accelerator again, causing the cart to lurch forward. "We also talk about how rude you are to Buckhunter." She says it with a smirk, meaning to follow it up with a "just kidding," but before she can, Coco lets out a disbelieving sound.

"Oh, please! Why should I be nice to him?" Coco is notoriously frosty towards the half-brother that her father had given her via a fling with a young nurse the same year his wife had been pregnant with Coco.

"Because he's your brother," Holly says quietly. "And he's my uncle."

"He's my half-brother," Coco corrects unnecessarily.

Holly pulls into the driveway that leads back to the two houses that her grandparents had built on the west side of the island. One house is her own private bungalow, and the other is Buckhunter's, rented out to him by Holly's grandfather shortly before he'd passed. Frank Baxter had moved his son onto the island and planted him next door to Holly with the promise that Buckhunter would look after her, and he had—even before she'd known they were related.

"Let's get you inside," she says calmly, switching off the cart. "And don't worry, I'll be taking Pucci over to Jake's in a few minutes so you won't have to deal with him."

Holly walks up the steps to her house and throws open the front door so that Pucci can rush out to greet her. She leaves her mother's suitcase on the backseat of the golf cart and flips on the front porch light, disappearing inside her house to get her overnight bag. Outside, Coco exhales through her nose and then steps onto the sandy lawn in her wedge heels, wrestling with her suitcase as she tries to lug it up the front steps.

"Is there anything to eat here?" Coco calls out, kicking off her shoes in the front hall. "Holly?"

There's no reply, but the sound of Holly opening and closing drawers in her bathroom rings through the house.

Coco turns on the light in the kitchen and opens the refrigerator to examine the contents.

"Oh, no, there's nothing to eat here," Holly says, materializing in the doorway. "But the Ho Ho is just a walk away." She smiles tersely. "And tomorrow you can have the extra B&B golf cart, but the construction workers are still using it right now."

"Excellent." Coco closes the refrigerator door with more force than is necessary. "I don't suppose you'd drop me off at the Ho Ho on your way to Bonnie's," she says in a pinched voice. "I've been traveling all day and I want to get something to eat. It wouldn't have killed you to consider that before dumping me off here."

"Get your purse," Holly says as she clips a collar onto her dog. "I'll drop you."

Without waiting, she walks through the front door and out into the rapidly darkening night.

"I LITERALLY HAVE *NO IDEA* WHY I TOLD HER ABOUT THE WEDDING," Holly confides to Bonnie later that evening. They're sitting on

Bonnie's screened-in lanai, stemless glasses of red wine in their hands.

She'd dropped her mother off at the bar on the beach and kept driving, heading directly to Jake's to leave Pucci with him, and then on to Bonnie's where she gratefully dropped her bag in the guest room and kicked off her shoes.

"Who knows, sugar. Maybe you know how bad this whole corny event is going to be, and you were just dying to see Coco's face. After all, there's almost no one on the planet who'd hate a yellow fairy-themed wedding more than your mother. There's pleasure in getting that kind of response from someone." Bonnie lifts her wineglass and looks out into the darkness behind her lanai.

"Maybe..." Holly swirls the red wine around before she takes a sip. The women are both sitting in outdoor rocking chairs, gliding easily by the light of the moon. "But what about her telling me we need to spend more time together? Bon, that cannot happen. It just can't."

Bonnie wisely stays silent as they sit in contemplation. There's really nothing she can say about Holly and Coco's relationship that will be helpful anyway. It's always been fraught and difficult, and Holly has navigated it like any other minefield that might present imminent danger: with equal parts tentative tiptoeing and bull-headed survival instincts.

"I feel like every time something important comes up here, she's on the first plane down," Holly says. One of her feet is pulled up on the seat of the rocking chair, and with the other, she's using her toes to make her chair move. "It's like she couldn't care less about this island until something interesting happens."

"Mmmm," Bonnie agrees. She's squinting out into the blackened night beyond the screen of her lanai.

"And now that we've got famous guests showing up on Friday, she's here and ready to care about—" A loud noise makes Holly jump and her hand flies to her heart. "What was that?"

Bonnie sets her wineglass on the small, round table between the rocking chairs. She stands up and walks to the screen, peering out at the tall grass. There's a miniature swamp behind her house, and the only sounds she usually hears are marsh rabbits and all manner of birds squawking and talking to one another.

"Let's go see what the fuss is," Bonnie says. She's already pulled open the sliding door that leads back into the house and is slipping her feet into open-backed shoes. Holly sets her wineglass down and follows Bonnie.

They creep around the side of the house together, Holly falling back just slightly as she holds the tail of Bonnie's white shirt. She isn't completely familiar with the terrain around Bonnie's bungalow, and in the dark, she worries that she'll trip over a garden gnome or a plastic flamingo.

"Hey!" Bonnie calls out, waving a flashlight with a weak beam in the direction of the little swamp. "Who's out there?"

"Mrs. Lane," comes a young male voice. "It's me, Logan. And my friend Owen."

"Boys?" Bonnie says, her shoulders dropping about three inches as she realizes that it's just two sixteen-year-olds wandering around in the dark. "What on God's green Earth are you two doing out here?"

"Hi, Holly," Logan says, giving a small wave. He's standing at the edge of the swamp with Owen, who is holding an expensive-looking camera in front of his face. "We're just getting some night shots of the birds and of the moon reflecting off the water."

Bonnie frowns at the muddy puddle behind her house. "Of the moon shining on this old thing?" She waves a hand at the swampy water. "I've seen prettier catfish," she says. "Why don't you go and try to take a picture of the moon over the ocean? Now *that* would be a shot to get."

"Here." Holly steps closer to the boys. "Let me see what you have so far."

"Uhhh, no." Owen drops the camera and looks at Logan. "We don't have anything yet. We were just getting set up."

There is nothing but the sound of cicadas and birds quietly chattering in the distance.

"Yeah, we were scouting this location," Logan says in an official tone. "But I think we should go to the beach. That's a better idea."

"Definitely. The beach." Owen puts the lens cap back on the camera and follows Logan onto the unpaved street.

"Alright, well you boys be careful. Watch for golf carts and stay out of the water unless there's someone else around, you hear?"

"Sure, Mrs. Lane," Logan says, giving a casual salute. "We will."

The boys disappear down the street, their long, lanky frames fading into the darkness as Bonnie retrains her weak flashlight on Holly's face.

"You look spooked, sugar." She reaches out a hand and puts it on Holly's arm. "Just a couple of boys out nosing around in the dark for lack of anything better to do."

"Right," Holly says, smiling at Bonnie. "They're just looking for a little excitement—I know there's not much here for teenagers to do once the sun goes down."

"Let's get you in and make sure you've got everything you need for the night. We've got one more day to get things ready before Kitta and Deacon arrive." Bonnie steers them to the front porch and gives Holly a light shove to move her towards the door. "And I need you fit as a fiddle for that."

"Not to mention," Holly says, turning around and holding up a finger. "That our last day of prep will involve having my mother in our office with us all day."

"Oh, lordy, child. You do know how to rain on a girl's parade." Bonnie rolls her eyes dramatically and pushes Holly with both hands into the guest room. "Let's go—get on with you. Tomorrow will be here before we know it."

8

BONNIE LEAVES HOLLY ALONE AT THE HOUSE TO TAKE A LONG, HOT shower the next morning and promises to get things started at the B&B without her.

Holly is tugging a wide-tooth comb through her light brown hair in front of the mirror in Bonnie's guest room, making eye-contact with herself as she runs through her conversation with Coco one more time. What was her mother thinking, trying to enforce more togetherness? Holly can't think of a worse idea than spending more time in Coco's presence. That never does anything but aggravate the both of them.

She tosses the comb onto the dresser and pulls on a pair of white Levi's that she's chopped off at the ankle. Under them, she's wearing a red and blue striped one-piece bodysuit. She slips her feet into her well-worn Birkenstocks and sets her Yankees cap on top of her wet hair. Out of habit, she nearly whistles for Pucci to join her on the short drive over to the B&B, but then she remembers that he's at Jake's.

Bonnie's kitchen is clean and the coffee pot is empty, so Holly grabs her woven purse from the couch in the living room and leaves through the front door, not bothering to lock it. She isn't even sure why the bungalows on Christmas Key *have* locks, but it's probably not a bad idea. The night before when the boys had been out prowling around looking for photo opportunities was the first time in a long time that Holly felt frightened, but it did happen occasionally. There were moments when she was home alone and everything around was pitch black and a noise got to her. Those were the moments she'd always relished having Jake around.

The seat of her golf cart is already warm from the morning sun, and Holly slides in and backs out of Bonnie's driveway smoothly, waving at Gwen and Gen as they power walk down Pine Cone Boulevard together, their strides and smiles completely identical.

"Hi, Holly!" calls Gen. "Sorry to hear about Coco!"

"It's okay. She'll only be here for a week," Holly shouts back. She drives on.

Main Street is already busy, and Holly parks in front of A Sleigh Full of Books. She grabs her purse and walks right up to the front door of the bookshop.

"Morning, Vance." Holly pokes her head through the door and takes a peek at the progress he's made.

Vance is behind the front counter, bent over at the waist. He stands up straight and smiles. "Hey, Mayor."

"How are things going?"

"Well, I've got my books sorted," Vance says, waving at the full shelves along the walls. "And I'm waiting on my cash register and some of the supplies I'll need to get the back deck in shape."

"It looks great." Holly lifts her Yankees cap off her head and resettles it, tossing her wet hair over both tanned shoulders.

"Thanks." Vance moves a small fan on the front counter and points it at his face. "I heard through the grapevine that we've got something in common."

"What's that?"

"Our mothers are both on the island."

Holly groans. "Don't remind me. I stayed at Bonnie's last night because Coco's got my house for the next week...or for however long she's going to stay."

"Sorry." Vance runs a hand over his forehead, wiping away a layer of sweat. "Too bad she can't stay at the B&B."

"I don't know how you do it," Holly says, shaking her head. "Your mom actually *lives* with you."

"Well, my mom takes care of my kids and makes a mean pot roast, so I'm planning on keeping her around."

"Valid points. My mom *acts* like a kid and would turn her nose up at anything I cooked, so...yeah. I can't think of any good reason for her to stay."

Vance shakes his head sympathetically. "I feel for you, Holly. But this wedding is going to be great, and maybe having her around will actually work out—maybe she'll pitch in."

Holly can't help herself; she breaks out in a wild, untamed laugh. "Oh," she says between fits of laughter. "Oh, Vance. No."

He looks puzzled. "No?"

"No. Just definitely *no*." Holly switches her purse from one shoulder to the other. "But that's sweet of you to look for the silver lining. I appreciate that."

"Hey, anytime," Vance says. "It's one of the things Calista both loves and hates about me: my unflagging optimism."

"Don't lose it." Holly pats the doorframe twice and walks back out onto the sidewalk. Mistletoe Morning Brew is just steps away, and she needs coffee.

"Holly!" Maria Agnelli is sitting on a chair at one of the bistro tables. "You've gotta try this drink." She holds out her iced coffee. "Ellen, what did I get again? Make one for Holly, will you?" Mrs. Agnelli turns her small body around in the chair and shouts across the coffee shop.

Holly is in desperate need of caffeine at this point, and she'll be happy with anything that has the word "coffee" in it. "Okay, I'll bite. What am I ordering?" She sets her purse on the front counter like she's bellying up to the bar.

Ellen points at a hand-written sign next to the register: *Today's Special—Veruca Salt(ed) Caramel Iced Coffee.*

"I'll take it," Holly says definitively. She pulls her wallet out of her bag.

Without a word, Ellen turns and starts making her drink. Today she's wearing a yellow t-shirt with "We are the music makers and we are the dreamers of dreams" printed across the back. She holds up two different sized cups and raises her eyebrows.

"Uh, large, please," Holly says, eyeballing both cups. "Wait, are you not talking today?"

"She lost her voice," Carrie-Anne Martinez says, stepping behind the counter and standing hip-to-hip with her wife. "Madonkey got out of her pen last night and we ended up searching all over for her. Ellen shouted until her voice was gone."

"That damn donkey," Mrs. Agnelli says, shaking her head as she takes a long pull on her coffee through a straw. "Makes more mischief than Vance and Calista's boys, and that's really saying something."

Everyone within earshot nods knowingly. It's true: Mexi and Mori Guy are whirling dervishes; twin hurricanes racing around the island looking for scrapes to get into and people to pester. But Madonkey is giving them a run for their money with her Houdini act, escaping her pen at Ellen and Carrie-Anne's and winding up in people's yards all over the island.

"She's cute, though," Holly says, counting out dollar bills and sliding them across the counter to Ellen. "And Mexi and Mori are, too."

Holly pulls the paper wrapper off a straw and jabs it through the lid of her drink. She takes her first sip and nods at Mrs. Agnelli.

"It's better than dessert, right?" Mrs. Agnelli gives a pleased smile.

"Mmmhmm," Holly says, pulling a napkin from the dispenser on the counter and wiping her lips. "It's amazing. I feel like I should skip breakfast if I'm going to drink this."

"Maybe lunch, too," offers Wyatt Bender helpfully. He holds up his mug of black coffee and goes back to reading the newspaper that's spread out on his table.

"Hey, just a heads-up," Carrie-Anne says, walking Holly to the door of the coffee shop. "Your mother was in extra early this morning and she took a box of pastries over to the B&B. She said you all had a busy day ahead of you."

Holly blinks slowly. "She's here for the wedding."

"As a guest, or a gawker?"

"Who knows." Holly takes another drink of the iced coffee. "And this really is delicious, by the way."

"Thanks, hon." Carrie-Anne opens the door for Holly. "And let us know if we can help out in any way."

Holly gives an over-the-shoulder wave as she hits the sidewalk again, determined to go straight to the B&B and face Coco head on.

"One more day!" Fiona calls from across the street, walking towards Poinsettia Plaza in her unbuttoned white lab coat. It flaps in the morning breeze, revealing a short summer dress beneath. She's smiling at Holly as she pulls a keyring out of her pocket to unlock the door to her medical office.

"I think we're ready," Holly shouts back to her as she walks up the steps to the B&B. "Are you free tonight?"

Fiona pauses, key in hand. "Yeah, I should be free. What's up?"

"We need to wrap the palm trees with this yellow taffeta ribbon stuff that Bonnie managed to get overnighted from Key West. Wanna help?" Holly is afraid for a second that Fiona has gone back to feeling morose about the wedding stuff, but after a pause, she nods eagerly.

"Sure, I'd love to."

"Good. I'll text you later!" With a wave, Holly opens the door and steps into the lobby. The wood of the front desk shines in the morning sunlight, and the whole lobby smells like lemon cleaner. The chairs in the corner are angled just so, and a pile of magazines is fanned out on a small end table.

"Sugar? Is that you?" Bonnie's voice calls out from down the hallway. "I saw you coming down the sidewalk. Come on back here!"

Holly takes another drink of her coffee and picks up a stack of envelopes from the front counter. They've been so busy the past few days that she hasn't even opened the mail yet.

The doorway frames the exact scene that Holly has been dreading, and she pauses there, taking it all in for a moment. Bonnie is in her own desk chair, a frown plastered on her pretty face as she tries not to openly glare at Coco, who has taken over Holly's spot. An aggressive dance mix blares from the speaker next to Holly's laptop.

"We've got everything moving here," Coco says, swinging her bare legs around in the chair and standing. "Kitta's already called three times, and she isn't happy that your cell phone is off."

"My cell phone isn't off," Holly says, setting her coffee on the edge of the desk so that she can dig through her purse. She fishes out her iPhone and clicks the home button. Nothing. "Wait, how is it off?"

"Who knows, but you'd better get that figured out," Coco says with a smirk. "I gave Kitta my number in the meantime, and she's going to revise the menu for the rehearsal dinner and get back to me."

Holly drops her purse on the floor with a *thud* and pulls her baseball cap off her head. "We can't revise the menu," she says helplessly, totally aware of the rising panic in her voice. "They arrive tomorrow, and we have it all planned out. We've already got all the food, and it would cost an arm and a leg to order a special delivery before Saturday night."

"If they change the menu, we'll send Cap to Key West to pick up whatever we need." Coco walks to the white board on the wall and uncaps a marker. She turns her back to Holly and scrawls "Saturday Rehearsal Dinner—Menu Under Review" in her neat handwriting.

"Who told you to give Kitta Banks your phone number?" Holly demands, walking over to her mother and snatching the marker from her hand. She picks up an eraser and wipes away the words her mother has just written. "And we're *not* changing the menu. Kitta already agreed to it."

"And when I saw the menu, I suggested a few changes," Coco sniffs. "There is no way that Kitta Banks and Deacon Avaloy should be serving potstickers and meatballs on toothpicks for their rehearsal dinner. What were they thinking?"

"They were thinking that it's their wedding and they should be able to do whatever they want," Holly says, sitting down in the chair at her desk. It's a move that's meant to let Coco know that she isn't welcome in the office, but it fazes her even less than having her words erased from the white board.

"Of course they should," Coco says mildly. "As long as it reflects good taste and makes us look like we know what we're doing. Can you imagine how tacky it would seem if we were featured in an article about the wedding and it said we served meatballs and finger food for dinner?" She wrinkles her nose. "We can do better than that."

"We *could* have done better than that," Holly corrects. "If it's what the bride had wanted, and if we'd ordered different food several days ago."

Coco takes her purse off the hook by the door. "Buckhunter has loaned me his golf cart until the construction workers are done with the B&B's spare," she says, taking her sunglasses case out of her bag and snapping it open. From it she pulls an oversized pair of Chanel shades. "I'm going to run around and do a few things that Kitta's asked me to do." Coco puts the sunglasses on top of her head and tosses the case back into her purse. "There are croissants and scones in the box," she says, pointing at the pink pastry box on the windowsill. "You should eat something, Holly. You get crabby when you haven't had food." She's halfway down the hall when her voice rings out one more time. "Oh, and turn on your phone!"

The bells on the front door of the B&B jingle in the distance and Holly puts her forehead on the edge of her white wicker desk and holds onto her thighs with both hands like she's on a plane that's going down and she's bracing for impact. "I can't do this. She's been on the island for eighteen hours, and she's already trying to kill me."

Quietly, without words, Bonnie crosses the small office and picks a chocolate croissant from the box. She sets it on a napkin and walks it over to Holly. "Honey, she's not trying to kill you. She's just being Coco. Now eat something and pull it together, because in a little more than twenty-four hours, we're going to have *two* divas on this island to deal with."

Holly lifts her forehead off the desk and looks at Bonnie as she takes her own purse off the other hook by the door. "Are you leaving?"

"I need to run a few errands. I'll be right back." She blows Holly a kiss. "We got this, doll. I promise you. But for the love of all that's holy, turn on your phone, will you?"

As soon as Bonnie is gone, Holly tears off a chunk of croissant and shoves it in her mouth. She reaches for her phone and plugs it into the charger that's connected to her computer. As tempting as it is to go back to bracing for impact, she's got work to do.

"HOLLY!" KITTA'S FACE COMES TO LIFE ON THE PHONE SCREEN. SHE'S taken to Facetiming Holly and this is their fourth video call of the day. "Is your phone still fully charged? We're taking off from LAX and I'm going to need to talk to you when we land."

"It's charged, Kitta. I told you, I stayed at Bonnie's last night and I just forgot to plug it in."

"Thank god your mother has been available all day," Kitta says. Her eyes are focused on the upper corner of the screen where she can see her own face. "She's fabulous."

"Mmmhmm," Holly says blandly. She tries to keep her face blank.

"I can't wait to get there!" Kitta's eyes light up. "Deacon has some work to do right away, but I'm ready to start talking wedding stuff the second we get there. Hey, you have a strong wifi connection, right? Deacon will probably want to send some emails and make phone calls from the B&B."

"We've got it covered. I mean, we are on an island that's about fifty miles from the mainland, but unless there's a storm, we get really good coverage."

"Perfect. And did your mom talk to you about the menu changes for Saturday?"

As Kitta is speaking, the small group of construction workers appears outside of Holly's window on Main Street.

"She did, and we're working on it," Holly promises. She stands up and tries to hold the phone steady as she keeps her eyes on Kitta. "I'll do my best to have mini quiche and tiny yellow cupcakes by Saturday night."

"Her ideas are just *so* classy," Kitta says. Her white teeth gleam when she smiles. "I can't wait to meet her. You're so lucky to have such a cool mom."

"I am lucky in a lot of ways," Holly agrees. "Listen, I see Bonnie outside with her golf cart full of the yellow tulle you want wrapped around the palm trees on the beach, so I'm going to head over and get that project going," she lies easily, waving at the construction crew.

"Okay, sounds good. I'll call you when I land. And when I get wifi on the plane, I'll email or text you anything I can think of."

"Wonderful. Safe travels." Holly raises a hand next to her face where Kitta can see it and wiggles her fingers before ending the call.

"Looks like we're ready to head out for the weekend," the head of the construction crew says as Holly steps out onto the B&B's front porch. She slides her phone into the back pocket of her white jeans. "Here's the key to the golf cart," he says, holding out a dirty, rough hand and dropping the key into Holly's open palm. "And we're going to grab our stuff from the dining room and jump on that boat. You want us back Tuesday, right?"

"Tuesday would be perfect," Holly smiles gratefully. "Our weekend guests will be gone by then, and it'll give us a chance to clean the B&B and have your rooms ready again."

The foreman gives the other men a nod and they file up the stairs past Holly to grab their bags from the dining room. Bonnie had wisely asked them to leave their things downstairs before they started work for the day so that they could start washing linens and cleaning the rooms, and consequently, by four o'clock most of the rooms have been made up and are ready for the wedding guests' arrival.

"So Kitta Banks, huh?" The foreman wiggles his eyebrows. He's got smudges of grease and dirt along both cheeks and on his forehead. "She's a real looker."

Holly lifts the brim of her hat and sets it on her head again. "Yes, she is beautiful." It doesn't even amaze her that the gossip about Kitta and Deacon has reached the workers. They've been on the island long enough, mingling, eating, and living amongst the locals, and it was only a matter of time before they overheard the big news.

"One of my guys is pretty handy with his phone camera—he's gotten some nice shots of the island to send back to our wives and girlfriends. It's a gorgeous place you've got here."

"We like it," Holly says with a smile.

The other men are back with their duffel bags and backpacks, ready to catch the boat to Key West. They're all as dirty as the foreman, and Holly suddenly wishes she'd been thoughtful enough to let them shower before they left.

"I'm sorry we don't have bathrooms for you all to clean up in before you head home," she says, pressing her palms together. "I didn't even think about that."

"Well, don't think about it now," the foreman says, taking his own bag from another guy. "The wind'll blow the stink off us on the water and our wives and girlfriends will be happy to see us anyway. See you on Tuesday." The foreman raises one meaty hand and then turns and starts walking down the sidewalk. The other men follow, each saying good-bye to Holly as he passes.

"See you later," she says, nodding at each of the guys. "Have a safe trip. Bye."

Holly stands on the steps and appreciates the rare moment of silence after they've all gone. She looks up and down Main Street, watching as a golf cart turns the corner and disappears. A soft breeze blows over the island and it feels like fall for a second, with the afternoon light shifting in the way that indicates a change of season. She breathes in deeply, waving at Calista Vance as she stands at the window of Scissors & Ribbons across the street, holding a long-handled broom. Calista waves back.

The ebb and flow of life on the island sometimes escapes her, as

Holly lives so entirely in the thick of it. But things *are* changing, bit by bit. New businesses are cropping up and new islanders are arriving. Change is inevitable, and rather than fight it, as someone so attached to her home might do, Holly has chosen to embrace it. There's really no other choice.

9

THE WOMEN HAVE LIT TIKI TORCHES ON THE BEACH TO LIGHT THE AREA where the wedding will take place. There's happy chatter amongst them as they wrap palm trees in tulle and prune back the bushes that line the path where the bride and groom will emerge.

"Holly!" Emily Cafferkey shouts. She's walking fast across the sand, both arms waving in the air. "Kitta is coming tomorrow!"

Holly stops what she's doing and stands up straight. She puts her hands on her lower back as a grin spreads across her face. "I know, she's going to be here before you know it!"

Emily and Holly had grown up together on Christmas Key, roaming the island and searching for dolphins as they'd played on the beaches and run through the trees. Because she has Down Syndrome, Emily's sweet, optimistic personality has stayed the same, and seeing her enthusiasm for life always brings Holly joy.

"Can I get her autograph?" Emily is standing in front of Holly, breathless. "And can I take a picture with her?"

"I'm sure you can," Holly says, holding out her arms to hug her friend. "She'll be here for days."

"Jake said he would be my date to the wedding." A blush creeps up Emily's neck and onto her cheeks. "I'm wearing a dress."

The other women wink at each other, tickled by Emily's enthusiasm and her unabashed love for Jake. It's an open secret that Emily has a crush on Holly's ex-boyfriend, and he's always been so good about taking her places and being a friend to her.

"What color is your dress?" Holly asks mildly, bending over again to unwind a length of tulle from the spool so that she can tie bows around the two trees that flank the path.

"Yellow," Emily says proudly. "Because my mom said Kitta loves yellow."

"It seems like she does." Holly looks around at the trees as she nods. Fiona is busy trimming the ends off sunflowers and wrapping them together with thick yellow ribbons. "I think it's her favorite color."

The sun is nearly gone and the sky over the water is the bright blue of sapphires, with a thin orange band hovering at the horizon. The waves crash on the shore with the regularity of a metronome.

"Can I help, Holly?" Emily kicks off her sandals and falls to her knees next to the lengths of tulle.

"In fact, you can." Holly sinks to the sand next to her oldest friend, handing her a pair of scissors. "We need about twenty shorter pieces of this fabric, okay? About a foot long each." She shows Emily how much to cut by doing the first one for her, and soon Emily is hard at work replicating the length of tulle and cutting each piece carefully.

"Next thing you know we'll be setting up the beach for Fiona and Buckhunter's big day," says Iris Cafferkey, smiling down at her daughter and watching as she focuses on the task that Holly's given her. "We'll be decorating the chapel and talking about cake and *hors d'oeuvres* for another wedding!"

Holly's eyes cut to Fiona to see how this discussion sits with her. Fiona's face is placid.

"Maybe Fiona will want to do something different," Bonnie offers. She's well aware that the topic of weddings has set Fiona's teeth on edge.

Fiona stops snipping the sunflower stems and looks up. "I'm not sure what we're doing," she says, pasting a smile on her face. "We're still thinking about it."

"Don't overthink it!" Gwen advises, tossing one end of the tulle to her sister Gen. Gen catches it and they unspool the fabric and start wrapping the nearest palm tree in yellow. "I was so ready to tie the knot that all I did was find a dress and rush to the chapel."

"Oh, you did not," says Gen. "You were head over heels with the idea of being a spring bride. I distinctly remember you requesting daisies in your bouquet and a cake with thick, white frosting and lemon filling."

Gwen's face goes dreamy as she remembers. "You know, you're right. I did put a little time into my wedding daydreams, and it was all worth it."

"Well, it got you married, and that's really the end game, isn't it?" Gen raises an eyebrow.

"It is, but it should be a *little* fun," Gwen says.

"Fiona will make it a little fun," Gen counters. "She's got wonderful taste, and I'm sure she's got her eye on a lovely color scheme. She's probably even picked out her cake and her brides-maids already."

Holly is dragging one piece of the white wood arch that they'll put together for the bride and groom to stand under. She's got another piece strapped to the roof of her golf cart, and with luck, the women can pitch in and get it all set up before it's too dark.

Fiona's completely given up on the sunflower stems and Holly sees her face change by the light of the torches. "Hey," Holly says lightly. "Can I get a hand with the other part of the arch? I need someone to help me drag it over here."

"I'll help," Fiona offers. She follows Holly up the sandy path and over to the golf cart where they stop to assess the part of the arch that they'll need to untether from the roof and carry down to the beach. The women stand side-by-side in the near darkness, hands on hips. "Thanks for the save, by the way."

"No problem." Holly chews on her lower lip. "But you're going to have interest from the other women, so just know that I won't be able to step in and redirect them every time."

"Oh, I know it." Fiona's hands fall to her sides and her shoulders drop. "I get asked at least five times a day what my plans are, and the truth is, I *just don't know.*"

"You don't have to have it all worked out. We talked about this."

"I feel like maybe we should ask you to get ordained online or something and marry us in the middle of Jack Frosty's one night." There's a mix of humor and resignation in Fiona's voice. "I kind of just want to get the whole thing over with, and that doesn't seem like the way a happy bride should feel."

Holly doesn't have a ton of insight into how a bride should feel, so she stands on the running board of her golf cart and reaches for one of the bungee cords that's holding the arch in place. With one long arm extended overhead and a leg outstretched behind her, she loosens the cord and lets it snap free.

"I want to be *excited* about planning this thing. I want to feel like Kitta Banks obviously feels, you know?"

"Mmmhmm," Holly agrees, keeping her back to Fiona. She has zero desire to ever feel the way that Kitta Banks obviously feels. Slathering the island in yellow and feeding people unappealing finger foods while a photographer captures it all? No thank you.

"But I'm getting to where I don't even want to talk about it with Buckhunter. I took your words on the beach to heart, but I feel like maybe I should have kept my mouth shut in the first place. Maybe proposing to him was a huge mistake."

The cicadas chirp around them in the darkness. "Was proposing what was in your heart?"

Fiona thinks about it for a minute. "Yeah," she finally says. "It was in my heart. It felt right."

"Then don't let some overblown wedding make you feel inferior about whether you do or don't have plans, or whether your ceremony will be big or small. Come on, Fee. None of that matters!"

Fiona puts both hands in her wavy hair and makes a face like she's drowning or choking. "I can't believe how obsessed I've gotten with this whole thing!" She laughs self-consciously. "I need to just get over it."

"Or talk to Buckhunter and come to some sort of agreement about what you both want," Holly says, tugging the piece of arch slowly so that it will come off the top of her golf cart. "And if you really want me to get ordained, you know I will. Cap might be a little offended, but..."

"Oh, you're right!" Fiona's mouth forms an O as she remembers the fact that Cap is ordained to marry and bury at will and has done both in the little chapel on the island. "I totally forgot about Cap."

"Well, you can consider all those details later," Holly says, pointing at the other end of the arch so that Fiona will help her. "Right now, we have a gaudy wedding to throw for an actress and a politician, and I don't think we have all of the fake butterflies or all the spray paint we'll need to turn this arch gold."

"Then by all means, let's get cracking."

Fiona and Holly heave the arch off the roof of the cart and tote it down to the beach together, stepping carefully over fallen palm fronds and foliage as they march their way back to the other women.

10

"IT'S JUST GORGEOUS!" KITTA BANKS SQUEALS. SHE TAKES THE hand that the boat's captain offers her, stepping gingerly onto the sand in a pair of shiny gold Grecian sandals that wrap around her ankles and up her toned calves. "I swear to you I feel like I found paradise!"

Behind her, Deacon Avaloy is waiting patiently in a pair of aviator sunglasses that show off his chiseled cheekbones, his thick, dark hair windswept like he's posing for the cover of a J. Crew catalog. He has both hands in the pockets of his khaki shorts, and the collar of his golf shirt is turned up rakishly.

"Holly!" Kitta waves her hands and bounces up and down on the sand. She's wearing a one-piece jumpsuit that ends at the tops of her tanned, toned thighs, and her long blonde hair is curled into camera-ready waves that hang down her back. The giant stone on her left ring finger glints in the sunlight. "Hey!" Kitta opens both lean arms and reaches out for Holly as she approaches. "It's so good to finally meet you!"

Holly hugs her back, realizing that this is the kind of surreal moment that she'll probably never repeat in her life. An Oscar-winning actress of Kitta's magnitude just doesn't wash up onto

Christmas Key's shores everyday, and in her wake is a young, dashing politician who will most likely make a very plausible bid for the Oval Office at some point.

"Welcome to Christmas Key," Holly says, hugging Kitta back. After Kitta has finally released her, she stretches out an arm and shakes Deacon's hand. "It's nice to have you both here."

Deacon waits as the captain unloads their luggage and garment bags, nodding and smiling as he hands over each item. Kitta is already gliding up to Main Street from the dock, and the beaded bracelets on her wrists clink together as she points at everything she sees.

"The coffee shop!" she shouts, clapping both hands together. "I'm going in right now." Without waiting for Deacon or Holly, Kitta crosses Main Street and pushes open the door of Mistletoe Morning Brew. She disappears inside.

"She's a hurricane," Deacon says, laboring under the load of luggage on his own as he tries to balance it all in both hands.

"Oh, here," Holly says, stepping over to him. "Let me help you." She takes one of the suitcase handles and two garment bags and leads the way to the B&B. "Let's get your stuff over to the B&B and I can check you in while you go get a coffee with Kitta, if you like."

Deacon follows Holly gratefully, using his free hand to pull his phone from one pocket and scroll through his messages. "Strong WiFi," he says, head down as he trails behind Holly.

"Yes, you'll have good coverage while you're here. Kitta wanted to make sure you could work as much as you want to."

"She'll kill me if I work too much," he says, locking his phone and sliding it back into his pocket. The easy smile of a seasoned politician creases his handsome face. "But I feel like she has this whole ceremony under control, so all I really need to do is show up, right?"

Holly laughs. "Sure. Just put on a tuxedo and roll up to the arch on the beach. We've got the rest."

"Am I wearing a tuxedo?" He frowns as Holly steps up to the front door of the B&B and opens it for them. "I was assuming she'd have me in a yellow sequined muscle shirt and hot pants or something."

Holly turns to look at him and sees the smirk on his face. He winks at her. "I'm kidding, of course. It's a traditional tux."

Holly hangs the two garment bags she's carrying on a coat rack in the lobby and stands the suitcase upright before she steps behind the counter and moves her mouse to make the computer screen come to life.

"We've got you two in the Palm Tree Pagoda," she says, clicking on an item and pulling up their reservation. "And the other rooms are all set for your guests, who should start arriving in the next couple of hours."

"We've got people coming on their own boats, right?"

"Some." Holly nods. "And others have chartered a boat from Key West to deliver them today and pick them up on Monday. But we've got a full house here and they're all your guests."

"Cute place you got here," Deacon says, scanning the lobby and walking over to the doorway that leads into the hall. He admires the banana leaf wallpaper and rubs the doorframe with one hand like he's checking to see if it's been sanded. "I like it."

"So do I." Holly smiles at him and pulls a room key from the drawer under the desk. "I opened the B&B after college and I've been running it ever since."

"How long have you been on Christmas Key?" Deacon puts one hand in his pocket and leans the other elbow on the front counter.

"My whole life. My grandparents bought the island when it was nothing more than a bunch of seagrass and overgrown scrub pine, and they slowly turned it into their version of paradise. Over the past thirty years we've grown and become what you see here today." Holly lifts her chin at the front window and looks out at Main Street. "I've been other places, but there's no place like home—at least for me."

The back door to the B&B slams loudly and footsteps grow closer in the hallway. "Holly?" Coco calls out. She peers into the lobby. "Oh!" she says, pausing where she is. "We've got company."

Holly's heart sinks as she watches her mother's whole demeanor shift. Not only is she in the presence of a man—and an attractive one at that—but she's in the presence of a well-known, powerful politician who oozes charisma and sex appeal. Coco slithers to the front counter and leans against it with one hip, holding out a thin hand to shake Deacon's.

"Coco," she says coyly. "Welcome to my island."

"Your island?" Deacon asks. "So you and your sister co-own Christmas Key?" He looks back and forth from Coco to Holly.

The disgusting taste of bile fills Holly's mouth as she tries not to gag. Coco laughs uproariously, putting one manicured hand on her artificially inflated chest. Her augmented breasts have been the cause of Holly's dismay on many occasions.

"Well, Deacon," Coco says, taking a step closer as she slides her hip along the front counter. "You really know how to flatter a girl. That made my day."

Looking puzzled, Deacon watches Coco. It's obvious that he's intentionally flattering her, but he has a convincingly unaware expression on his face. "Is this not your sister?" He hooks a thumb in Holly's direction, not looking at her. "I see a strong resemblance...but it might be my mistake. In which case, you have my sincerest apologies."

Coco sweeps away the hair on one side of her face with her hand. "No, Deacon. There is a resemblance, but it's because Holly is my daughter." She waits for the usual flood of disbelief to come her way, and she is not disappointed.

"No!" Deacon says. "That's not possible. No way." Now his eyes return to Holly as he assesses the two women. "You had her when you were eight, right?"

"Twice that," Coco admits sheepishly. "But I was quite young."

"My uncle is also part-owner of the island," Holly interjects, wanting to say something that will annoy her mother. This comment works.

Coco's eyes narrow almost imperceptibly as she turns her chin slightly in Holly's direction. "Yes," she admits. "My half-brother Leo is also part-owner of the island. I'm sure you'll meet him. He'll be the one with an abundance of chest hair showing and a spatula in one hand as he flips your burger at Jack Frosty's." From her tone, Holly can tell that Coco would have pinched her arm or kicked her with one sandaled foot had they been on the same side of the front counter.

"A real family operation. I like that." Deacon's phone buzzes in his pocket and he pulls it out. "If you'll excuse me," he says, putting it to his ear. "Hi, Kitty-cat," he purrs into the phone. "I'm at the B&B. Mmmhmm. It's just like you said. Very charming. Okay. Be right there." Deacon ends the call and smiles at Holly and Coco. "I'm wanted at the coffee shop. Apparently the locals are all as welcoming as the two of you and Kitta's already made new friends."

"Here's your key," Holly says, pushing the room key across the counter at him. "Everything is ready for you, and there'll be someone at the front desk twenty-four hours a day. If it's not me or Bonnie—"

"Or me," Coco interjects, wiggling her fingers as she waves at Deacon.

Holly suppresses an eye roll and continues. "If it's not one of us, it'll be a lovely lady named Maggie. One of us will always be available to help you with anything you need."

"And Kitta's got your number," Deacon says with a knowing grin. "And she has no problem using it." He's got one hand on the doorknob. "Thanks again for such a warm welcome."

"Of course!" Coco says excitedly, taking another two steps closer to Deacon as he walks through the door. "Just let us know what we can do to make your stay as comfortable as possible."

Deacon waves as he pulls the door closed behind him. The women's eyes follow him as he makes his way down Main Street to Mistletoe Morning Brew.

"Wow," Coco breathes, craning her neck as she watches him disappear from sight. "Just wow."

"Put your tongue back in your mouth there, old girl." Holly purses her lips and closes the screen she's opened on the computer. "He's here to marry a woman half your age. And I should probably remind you that *you're* already married."

A cloud passes over Coco's face as her daughter reminds her of Alan.

"For now I am," Coco says, still staring out at the street. "But that won't stop me from admiring anything that washes up on these shores."

Holly slaps the desk with an open palm, making Coco jump. "Pull it together, Coco—I need your help, since you're here." Holly reaches into the drawer and pulls out a master key that opens all the suites. She tosses it to her mother, who catches it with both hands. "Go check all the rooms and make sure they look perfect, will you? Make sure there are enough towels, that the mini fridges are stocked, the works." Without waiting for Coco's reply, Holly walks toward the front door and out onto the porch. She knew having her mother on the island would be an added chore for the weekend, but now she knows she'll have to step up her game and keep Coco away from Deacon Avaloy until Kitta slides a ring onto his finger.

She starts counting down the hours in her head.

THERE'S A HINT OF ANTICIPATION IN THE AIR ALL UP AND DOWN MAIN Street, and Holly can tell that her neighbors are on their very best behavior. Eyes follow Deacon and Kitta everywhere they go, but the moment an islander comes face-to-face with them, the local's awestruck gaze softens into an easy smile, and they greet Deacon and Kitta like they would any other visitors to Christmas Key.

"Hi, there," Deacon says to Maria Agnelli as he stands in front of A Sleigh Full of Books. Vance is inside listening to Kitta talk about why he needs a metaphysical section and a wind chime in the doorway that represents all seven rainbow-hued chakras.

"You got yourself a real looker there," Mrs. Agnelli says to Deacon as she pauses in front of him. She narrows her eyes at him, sizing him up. "And you aren't too hard on the eyes yourself. You ever had a real Italian woman?"

"Mrs. Agnelli!" Holly reaches them just in time. She puts a hand on the older woman's shoulder. "How are you today?"

"I'm fine, Holly. Right as rain. No need to treat me like an invalid--
I still live on my own and manage my own affairs, you know."

"Of course you do," Holly says, trying to keep the patronizing tone
out of her voice. "I was just going to introduce you to Deacon Avaloy."
In one smooth move, Holly lets the hand on Mrs. Agnelli's shoulder
snake around so that she's got a firm grip on the woman; she gives
Mrs. Agnelli's bony body a warning squeeze.

"Well, I've met the boy already," Mrs. Agnelli says, keeping her
eyes on Deacon's handsome face. "I was just asking him whether he'd
ever enjoyed the company of an Italian lady. Thought I'd make the
offer before he says 'I do' to that one." She nods at Kitta's long, lean
figure through the front window of the bookstore.

Holly's cheeks flush and she looks at Deacon apologetically.

With an easy smile, Deacon saves the situation. "I've never had
the pleasure of dating a woman from 'the boot,'" he says with a smile
that reaches his eyes. "But I'm afraid I'm off the market completely.
I'm a one woman kind of man." He winks at Mrs. Agnelli.

Maria Agnelli gives a shrug and shakes off Holly's arm in the
process. "I figured you'd turn me down anyway, but Coco is going to
be disappointed to hear that there's no wiggle room."

Holly's stomach lurches at the mention of her mother as Maria
walks over to Mistletoe Morning Brew. Inside the bookstore, Kitta is
pulling titles from a shelf and rearranging books. Vance looks
somehow both dismayed and totally charmed.

"The next boat is approaching," Deacon says, nodding at the
water. On the horizon, they can see a mid-size vessel cutting through
the sparkling waves. "On it, my brother, my best friend, and the
insane people I'm about to call my in-laws." His words are muttered,
but it's obvious that he meant for Holly to hear them. "You're not
married, are you, Holly?"

"No. I've never taken that particular plunge."

Deacon nods, his face in profile, sunglasses firmly in place. "Just
remember—when and if you do—the family is a package deal."

"Got it." Holly turns her attention to the boat and feels the tiny kick of nervous anticipation that she always feels when new people are approaching the island. "Who else is on this boat?"

"Oh," Deacon says, putting one hand to his lightly stubbled chin and rubbing it thoughtfully. "Probably an actress or two, a director, maybe a politician. Who knows." He shrugs in the same way that Maria Agnelli had just moments before. "God forbid a person wants to just tie the knot without an audience, right?"

Holly chuckles nervously and keeps her eyes on the boat. It suddenly seems like all she's doing lately is listening to disgruntled wedding talk, and a part of her wishes she could just introduce Deacon and Kitta to Fiona and Buckhunter and let them kick around ideas and expectations. It's definitely *not* her area of expertise.

"I'm going to run back to the B&B and make sure the rooms are exactly the way I want them," she says, rubbing her lips together as she thinks. "Why don't you greet your guests and send them my way whenever they're ready to check in, okay?"

Deacon's jaw clenches and unclenches as he nods. "Sure. You got it, boss."

He doesn't turn to look at her, so Holly backs away from him, watching his strong shoulders as he looks out at the water. There's a resigned aura to Deacon that makes her think of someone who's been roped into something, though it's clear that he's smitten with his bride-to-be. Maybe this is the way all grooms feel as they watch their soon-to-be wives spin out of control with ideas for color schemes, bite-size desserts, and cutesy photo ops. She suddenly feels a bit more sympathy for Buckhunter's reluctance to dive into wedding talk headfirst.

As Holly walks the short distance back to the B&B, she catches sight of two people standing at the mouth of Cinnamon Lane, their backs to the tree-lined street that leads to Holly's own property. One of them has a camera stuck to his face; the other is wearing a baseball cap pulled low over his forehead. Their camera is trained toward the dock.

"Hey!" Holly calls out, waving as she approaches. It's Logan and Owen, and the sound of Holly's voice gets their attention.

"Holly," Logan says. He clears his throat. "I'm learning a lot about photography from Owen. We're trying some daylight shots now."

"I'm hoping to get extra credit in the fall if I put together a digital photo album of my trip," Owen says with a dimpled grin. All that's missing is the addition of the word "ma'am" at the end of the sentence.

"Okay," she says, watching their faces closely. "But we've got guests on the island who definitely won't want their pictures taken. So maybe focus your shots elsewhere, okay? Try some nature shots along December Drive or something." Holly makes a wide, sweeping circle with her arm. "There are plenty of gorgeous shots you can get on Christmas Key—I guarantee it."

Logan elbows Owen and they turn to head down Cinnamon Lane. "Got it, Holly," Logan says, leading the way into the dense bushes. "See you later!" The boys pick up their pace, disappearing into the dark arms of the trees.

She wants to be wrong, but Holly is almost certain that Logan had been framing a shot of Deacon Avaloy with his hands as Owen had taken the shot of the politician waiting near the dock. But her hands are full keeping the women of the island away from Kitta's groom and making sure that everything about the wedding is perfect, so she pushes the thought to the back of her mind.

What harm is there in a couple of teenage boys taking a bunch of pictures for a school project? Not much, she thinks, pulling her phone from her back pocket as it starts to buzz. It's Kitta. Holly springs back into action.

11

"AND THIS ONE IS FOR HOLLY," KITTA SLURS, HANGING FROM DEACON'S neck with one arm as she holds her drink in the air. "We've worked our butts off to get this thing pulled together, but I know I couldn't have done it without her." Kitta puts the glass to her lips as Deacon leans in and whispers in her ear. "And Bonnie!" she shouts as an afterthought. "We needed Bonnie too!"

"I'm touched," Bonnie says quietly through her teeth, a smile plastered to her face. Holly elbows her in the ribs lightly.

Most of the island is gathered at the Ho Ho Hideaway that evening, drinking and laughing with the guests of honor and the new arrivals who've come to celebrate with the happy couple.

Wyatt Bender is on Bonnie's other side, watching her from the corner of his eye as she laughs and makes wisecracks with Holly. Fiona and Buckhunter are sitting at the tall tables along the wall, taking in the festivities as they share a pitcher of beer. Jake is sitting with Mrs. Agnelli at the bar, talking to Joe Sacamano as he mixes drinks, and Cap and Heddie are kicking off their shoes to take a walk on the sand together as the sun sets. Joe's put on a CD of steel drum and guitar music, though Holly is hoping he'll get out his own guitar and play for them once everyone is on their second round of drinks.

"Your mother is a hoot," Kitta says in Holly's ear, nearly falling into her arms as she lets go of Deacon. "She asked me today if I knew the average length of time a politician stays married without cheating."

Holly forces an amused grin. "Yes, she is a hoot." Speaking of Coco, Holly's eyes scan the crowd and land on her mother, who is leaning over the back of Jake's chair at the bar as she orders a drink from Joe. Her tank top is tight and it's obvious that her chest is pressed against Jake's shoulder intentionally. He looks wildly uncomfortable. "Actually, I need to talk to her now. Excuse me," Holly says, redirecting Kitta and giving her a tiny push in the direction of her groom.

"Mom," Holly says. She steps up behind Jake's other shoulder. Coco stands up straight. "Alan called my phone today looking for you. He said he's been trying you and it's going right to voicemail."

"Huh." Coco reaches for the frosty drink that Joe's mixed for her. There's a wedge of pineapple stuck on the rim and she pulls it off, putting it between her full lips and sucking the alcohol from it. "That's strange. I swear my phone is on."

Without caring how it looks, Holly wraps a hand around her mother's bicep and pulls her aside. "I don't know what you're running away from at home, Coco, but I haven't got the patience to watch you self-destruct this weekend. In fact, I haven't got the patience for anything that pertains to you, really."

"I figured that out when you kicked me out of your house today and moved me to that dump on White Christmas Way," Coco says with annoyance.

"I just wanted my house back." Holly isn't in the mood to explain to her mother again that things are simply easier this way, so she changes her tack. "Can you please just go back to the bungalow and sleep this off?" she hisses. "And quit flirting with Jake and—for God's sake—*do not go near* Deacon Avaloy."

A wicked smile crosses Coco's face as she toys with the straw in her drink. "Is it bothering you, Holly? I know how much you hate it when your mother gets more male attention than you do."

STEPHANIE TAYLOR

"No." Holly shakes her head. "No, no, no. That has nothing to do with anything. I've told you to stay away from Jake because it's just creepy and wrong. And as far as Deacon, he's about to get married on our island. He is off limits. Not on the market. Unavailable. Forbidden. So knock it off."

Coco shrugs and rolls her eyes in a way that tells Holly that this drink isn't her first. "You're no fun." She pouts.

"Well, you're a real carnival ride," Holly shoots back. "But seriously, Mom. I'm done babysitting you. Pull it together."

Sitting outside the bar in his mother's golf cart is Logan Pillory. He's taken it upon himself to start a chauffeuring service, and he specializes in trips to and from the Ho Ho Hideaway on Friday nights. Next to him on the bench seat is Owen, who is staring at the LED screen of his digital camera as he scrolls through his photos.

"Hey, Logan," Holly says, taking the steps down from the bar and onto the sand of the parking lot. Logan looks at her and waves. "You ready to make a few bucks?"

"Sure. I'm always ready." Logan smiles at her and runs his hand through his sun-bleached hair. The burn that had colored his neck and cheeks upon his arrival on Christmas Key has turned into a constant bronze tan. He looks like a real islander after only being there for a few months. "Whatcha got in mind?"

"My mother," Holly says, walking up to the cart. She's still got her drink in one hand. "She needs a ride back to that blue house next door to the Vances, but more importantly, she needs to *not* come back here. You think you can get her lost for...let's see," Holly reaches into her back pocket and pulls out a wad of crumpled bills. "Can you take her on a long tour of the island for nineteen bucks?" She shoves the cash in Logan's direction. He stares at it.

"You want me to just drive her around for a while?"

"Sounds like she wants you to drive her mom to the dock and push her off. She did say to get her lost..." Owen adds helpfully. He doesn't look at Holly.

"Not lost-lost," Holly clarifies. "No one needs to go off the end of the dock wearing cement shoes. I just want you to let her drink in the back of the cart while you take every turn you can and loop all the way back around December Drive. Drop her off at the house when you're done. You got that?"

"Yeah," Logan says, looking at Holly with trusting eyes. "Of course. Whatever you want, Holly."

"Great." Holly pats the frame of his golf cart and turns back to the bar. "Let me refill her drink and get her in the back of the cart for you."

The boys look at each other and shrug. Nineteen bucks is nineteen bucks.

Inside, Holly asks Joe for another of whatever her mom is having in a to-go cup, then steers Coco away from Kitta Banks, who has caught her attention. They're chatting amiably by the stairs that lead out to the beach, and as Holly approaches, she can hear Coco asking Kitta whether either of them is signing a prenup.

"Because you never know when things might go south," Coco is saying wisely, one talon-like claw wrapped around Kitta's tanned forearm. Kitta's eyes are wide. "A woman has to protect herself. Think of it as an *investment*."

"Kitta," Holly interrupts. "I'm sure Joe would love to mix you another drink whenever you're ready." She puts a hand on Coco's shoulder. "But I really need to borrow my mom right now, if you'll excuse us." Without waiting for Coco to acquiesce, Holly steers her away from Kitta. "I got you a fresh drink," she says to Coco in a cheerful voice.

"I can get my own drink," Coco says, trying to pull away from her daughter. "I was having a good time with Kitta."

"I was hoping you'd try out our new ride service and see how it is." Holly puts the to-go cup in Coco's hand and links her arm through her mother's. "Logan Pillory is trying to get it up and running, and he and his friend want to test it out. They asked for most fun person I could come up with, and of course I thought of you."

Outside, the boys are idling in the cart as Holly guides her semi-drunk mother down the steps. Coco snorts. "No way you thought of me."

"Honestly," Holly says in a sincere voice. "I wanted to find someone who would entertain them and give them a run for their money. And who better than you?"

Coco lets Holly help her onto the bench seat in the back of the cart. She still looks unconvinced.

"Hi, ma'am," Owen says politely, turning to greet Coco. In response, she swings her legs around and tries to step out of the cart.

"He called me ma'am," she says, pointing an accusing finger at Owen.

Holly shakes her head. "Don't call her ma'am. Coco is fine."

"Got it," Owen says, giving Coco a smooth smile. "So you're going to show us the ropes, right?"

"Honey, I could show you ropes you've never even heard of," Coco says, slurring her words slightly as she tries to stick the straw into her mouth and misses.

"They're sixteen, Coco," Holly says under her breath as she shoves Coco onto the center of the bench seat. The last thing she needs is for her mother to fall out of the golf cart and hit her head as the boys drive her around in the dark.

"Right. Sixteen." Coco finally manages to get the straw between her lips. "The same age I was when I got pregnant!" Her eyes light up as she remembers. She reaches a hand out for Holly. "Sixteen is a fun age," she says, reminiscing.

"Uh huh." Holly pats her mother's bare thigh. "Sixteen is fun." She moves to the front seat and leans into the cart so the boys can both hear her. "She's a handful. Listen to about a third of what she says, and make sure you don't stop anywhere long enough for her to wander out of the cart and into the ocean. Drinking too much sometimes makes her want to skinny-dip." The boys' eyebrows shoot up simultaneously. "She's pushing fifty," Holly says plainly. "She could almost be your grandmother." Their eyebrows go down.

"We'll get her home safely," Logan assures Holly. "Don't worry."

"Thanks." Holly pats the cart's frame again to send them on their

A Little Nonsense   89

way and watches as the boys pull out of the lot carefully. The cart lumbers over the bumpy, unpaved terrain of December Drive.

"Holly!" Kitta is leaning through one of the open windows of the Ho Ho Hideaway. "Come have a drink with me! Let's do body shots!"

Holly takes one last glance at the taillights of Logan's golf cart before scanning the bar for Kitta's fiancé. Deacon seems to have abandoned his bride-to-be in favor of talking to the local men about fishing and sports, and it's up to Holly to keep Kitta from laying on the bar and letting people lick salt out of her bellybutton.

"Coming," she says halfheartedly. They've got a rehearsal dinner to put on the next night and a wedding to pull off on Sunday, and Holly's already exhausted.

"This place is so much fun!" Kitta shouts through the open window, holding a drink in each hand.

"Yes," Holly agrees to herself, kicking at a seashell in her path as she walks back into the Ho Ho. "It usually is."

12

"Oh, Holly, why did you let me drink that much?" Kitta Banks is standing on the opposite side of Main Street on Saturday morning. A giant pair of black sunglasses shields her eyes from the bright morning light.

Holly stops in front of the B&B with her iced latte in one hand. "You feeling a little under the weather?" she asks, putting one hand over her eyes as she takes in Kitta's wet hair and baggy olive green shorts. Kitta is standing in front of Scissors & Ribbons, one arm looped through Deacon's as he holds her upright.

"I told you on the phone we were having *one* margarita together, but I'm pretty sure I killed a whole pitcher by myself last night!" Kitta makes a gagging face. "I'm getting a massage right now from Calista to see if I can release some of the toxins."

Holly nods knowingly. "Good call." She takes a drink of her latte as she watches Deacon pull open the door of the salon for Kitta. *And maybe take a hard pass on the alcohol tonight at the rehearsal dinner*, she thinks in her head as she waves at the couple and keeps walking. She's got a kitchen full of hors d'oeuvres to check on and enough on her to-do list to keep her busy for days.

"Buckhunter," Holly says as she walks into her uncle's bar. He's taking the chairs down off the tables in the empty restaurant and listening to Jimmy Buffet on the jukebox. "Any chance you've seen your sister this morning?"

Buckhunter raises one lazy eyebrow. "Is that how we're referring to her now?"

"Until she can stop hitting on every man on the island, I'm not claiming her." Holly pulls out a chair that Buckhunter has just set on the floor and drops into it wearily.

"Jake again?"

Holly rolls her eyes and takes another drink of her coffee. "Yeah, but not overtly. Mostly Deacon Avaloy at this point."

Buckhunter gives a low whistle as he flips up the counter of his bar and walks behind it. "That's a solid Coco move," he says, nodding his head as he considers it. "Yeah, that's right up her alley."

"But it's not okay," Holly says emphatically. "We've got to stop her from doing something stupid."

"No we don't." Buckhunter rinses a dish rag in his bar sink. "Everyone involved is an adult here. They'll make their own choices."

Holly purses her lips. "But she could—"

"Nope." He flips a switch and the overhead fans start to spin. "Take your list out of your purse." Buckhunter nods at the straw tote she's set on the table.

"What list?"

"The list of things you need to do before the wedding tomorrow."

Holly smirks. "How'd you know?"

"Take it out."

Without another word, Holly pulls a folded piece of yellow legal paper from her bag. There's a ballpoint pen clipped to the paper.

"Now open it," he orders as he starts to wipe down his already clean bar, "and cross 'Babysit Coco' off the list. That's not in your job description."

Holly looks at the paper sheepishly. Sure enough, off to the side she's written "Keep Coco out of trouble" in blue ink. She uncaps her pen and holds it over the words.

"Cross it out," Buckhunter says. "Do it."

Holly scribbles over the item and recaps her pen. "There. Happy?"

"I was already happy," he says with a shrug. "And now you can be, too. Let go of her and her actions. That's not your responsibility right now."

Holly nods as she listens to Buckhunter's wisdom. He's right and she knows it.

"Hey," she says after a pause. With careful consideration of her words, she folds the paper slowly and slips it back into her bag. "What's going on with you and Fiona?"

Buckhunter continues to wipe the bar down without looking at her. "Not much."

"I mean," Holly says, hemming and hawing a little as she wonders how much to say without breaking her best friend's trust. "About the wedding. Have you made any plans? Talked about what you both want?"

Finally, Buckhunter stops cleaning and looks at his niece. "Did she send you to get a read on me?"

"What? No!" Holly holds up both hands, waving them back and forth. "Definitely not. I'm just curious. You know how women talk…"

"I've heard tell that they talk," he allows. Buckhunter rests one hand on his hip as he watches Holly intently.

"Well, the women around here are trying to get details out of her —just out of curiosity and excitement—and she never has much to say." Holly shrugs, hoping he'll fill in the blanks.

Instead, Buckhunter takes the rag in hand and starts wiping the counter again. "Maybe she's not one of those over-the-top brides," he says. He doesn't make eye contact with Holly. "Or maybe she's not ready to start planning it."

"Hmm," Holly says. She chews on the inside of her cheek, but doesn't say more. "Okay. I was just wondering."

"Hey," Buckhunter says as she stands to leave. Holly is sure he's going to add some tidbit about Fiona and the wedding, but instead he points a finger at her and narrows his eyes. "I'm serious about your mother: let it go. You have to."

"You got it," Holly says with a smile. There's no use admitting to Buckhunter or anyone else that she'll never be able to let Coco do as she pleases. "I've got bigger fish to fry today anyway."

"Go get em, girl." He winks at her and whistles along to the next song that starts playing on the jukebox.

THE KITCHEN OF THE B&B IS JUMPING WITH ACTION. IRIS CAFFERKEY IS at the center of it all, pointing out different work stations and giving orders to the group of volunteers who've assembled there on Saturday morning. She's got Bonnie and Fiona getting metal trays of canapés ready for the oven at the last possible second so that they come out hot and ready during cocktail hour.

The triplets are busy putting together cheese platters and polishing martini and champagne glasses, and Maria Agnelli is holding court near the sink, demanding that someone help her wash the mushrooms that Iris is going to stuff with a parmesan, parsley, and breadcrumb mix.

"Morning," Holly says from the doorway. She's still got her iced latte in one hand and her purse looped over one shoulder.

"Hi, sugar," Bonnie calls out, waving with an elbow as she sorts hors d'oeuvres onto baking sheets.

"Anyone seen my mother?" Holly pushes her sunglasses up on top of her head and scans the faces gathered in the kitchen. Faces are blank and heads shake all around. No one has seen her. "Okay. I'll be in my office if anyone needs me." With one hip, Holly bumps the swinging door open and heads back towards the lobby of the B&B.

"Good morning," Coco says from behind the front counter.

Holly nearly jumps out of her skin. "I just walked by and Maggie was standing there."

"And now she's gone." Coco's smile is tight. "She worked overnight, so I thought it would be the right thing to do to send her home."

Holly glances at her silver tank watch. Ten-thirty. That does make sense; Maggie Sutter works from midnight to eight o'clock when they have guests, so having her there until after ten is really a stretch.

"I really enjoyed the unnecessary grand tour of the island that my parents created from nothing—thank you for that," Coco says drily. "I figured out after the third trip down Main Street that something was going on, and those damn kids wouldn't stop and let me out."

"You're welcome." Holly gathers her composure and walks past the front desk. "There've been so many years when you barely visited the island that I thought you might want to see it all in one go."

"Are you trying to keep me out of your hair during this wedding, Holly?" Coco places both hands on the front counter and taps it with her long nails.

"I'm trying to keep you out of Deacon Avaloy's pants. Keeping you out of my hair is just a bonus."

Coco sighs deeply. The drinking from the night before has barely marred her well-preserved face, and she's clearly taken the time to apply her usual make-up and to do her hair. In contrast, Kitta Banks looks as if she's been put through a meat grinder. Holly isn't sure how her mother pulls it off at her age.

"I'll man the front desk," Coco says sarcastically. "Don't worry about me."

"Perfect." Without a glance back at her mother, Holly heads to her office and sets down her coffee and purse. Her computer boots up quickly and she pulls the list out of her bag and smoothes it with one hand. It had been a nice thought on Buckhunter's part to get her to stop worrying about Coco, but as always, one interaction with her mother leaves Holly feeling like she's got to stay on the defensive. She takes the cap off the pen and writes across the top of the paper in bold block letters: GET COCO OFF THE ISLAND ASAP.

HOLLY IS WHIPPING AROUND THE ISLAND AT THREE O'CLOCK THAT afternoon, a pencil shoved through the haphazard bun on the top of her head as she takes corners at full speed in her pink golf cart. She's got her cell phone between her thighs and a can of Diet Coke wedged into the drink holder near her knee. Her phone rings and its buzzing jolts her bare skin. She pulls it from between her legs and answers it.

It's the number for the front desk of the B&B. "Hello?" Holly says, letting her sandaled foot ease up on the accelerator just a bit.

"Holly? It's Maria."

"Mrs. Agnelli?" The golf cart slows to a complete stop as Holly veers to the right and takes her foot off the pedal completely. "What's wrong?"

"What *isn't* wrong?" Mrs. Agnelli asks in a loud voice. "We've got a bride in tears in the middle of the ballroom and your mother is trying to convince her that the butterfly wings will turn up somehow. But they won't, because I know where they are and there's no way they'll be here before tomorrow."

"Wait. Slow down." Holly reaches for her Diet Coke and lifts the can to her lips. "What butterfly wings?"

"The ridiculous glittery ones that this wack-a-doodle actress wants her girls to wear at the wedding."

"Oh, the *fairy* wings," Holly says, catching up. "Okay, so they lost the wings?"

"Not lost," Mrs. Agnelli says, drawing out a long pause. "More like they were intentionally vanished."

Holly puts the cart in park and gets out. She stands on the side of December Drive, one hand on her hip, the other holding the phone to her ear as she surveys the long, empty stretch of sand before her. "Who intentionally vanished the wings?"

"Let's just say that if the Mafia was involved, Coco would be the *capo di tutti*, the maid of honor would be the *consigliere*, and these other nitwits would be the associates."

"I don't speak fluent gangster, Mrs. Agnelli. Can you break this down for me?"

Mrs. Agnelli lets out a stream of words that Holly assumes are Italian expletives and then takes a deep breath. "Coco and the maid of honor cooked up a scheme to get rid of the wings. They're gone. It's done. *Finito.*"

Holly kicks at the ground with her right foot and is rewarded with a shoe full of sand. She's tempted to let loose with a couple of four-letter words herself. "Please tell me," she says calmly, "exactly how my mother arranged to permanently get rid of a portion of the wedding party's attire."

"I don't know and I didn't see anything," Mrs. Agnelli assures her, though not convincingly.

"Maria Agnelli. You tell me what you know right now." Holly is rarely this forceful with her elders and especially not with Mrs. Agnelli, but the time is right for her to exert some mayoral control over the island.

"What I know is that snitches get stitches," Maria says knowingly. "Now, I gave you a heads-up on this one, and that's all you get. Plus I got customers here at the front desk wanting pool towels, so I gotta go."

"Mrs. Agnelli! Are you manning the front desk?" Holly is aghast at the thought of the eighty-six-year old woman running B&B errands and helping guests. Not only is she not an employee, she's not even someone Holly would consider as a front desk volunteer during a busy weekend like this. "Mrs. Agnelli? Are you there?" She holds the phone away from her ear and sees that the call has already ended.

In under three minutes, Holly is back in the sandy parking lot of the B&B, screeching to a halt near the back door to the office. She leaves her Diet Coke and sunglasses in the cart and flings open the door, storming down the hallway towards the front desk.

"Where is she?"

Maria Agnelli looks up from her perch on a chair behind the front desk. She's got the latest issue of *People* magazine open in front of her on the counter. With a slow shake of her head, Mrs. Agnelli gives Holly a pitying look. "If you're looking for your mother, she just went up to the suite with the bride-to-be. You want me to call up there and see if you can join them?"

Holly brushes past the front desk without another word, hitting the stairs and taking them two at a time. At the door to the Palm Tree Pagoda she pauses and holds her fist in the air for a second. She needs to compose herself before someone other than Coco opens the door and sees her standing there looking like a wild banshee. After two deep, cleansing breaths, she raps on the wood and then straightens her shirt with both hands.

"Hi," says a short, muscular brunette in a turquoise sundress. She's tanned and has the body of a gymnast. "I'm Nylie." Her smile is huge and white.

"Nylie, it's nice to meet you. I'm Holly." Holly smiles at her. "I'm the mayor of Christmas Key. Welcome to the island." Even to her own ears it's amazing how cool and collected she sounds. "Is Kitta here?"

Nylie makes a face that's half squint and half chagrined smile. "She's in the bathroom with Coco."

"Excuse me." Holly walks through the doorway without invitation and makes a beeline for the suite's bathroom. "Kitta?" She knocks at the door gently. "It's Holly."

Coco opens the door swiftly and fills the crack with her face and upper body. "I've got everything under control here," she says quietly. Coco is about to shut the bathroom door again when Holly puts a hand out to stop it from closing. "Kitta is just a little upset about the fact that we can't find her bridesmaids' fairy wings."

"I bet I know someone who knows where they are." Holly lowers her chin so that she's looking directly into her mother's eyes.

"Hmmm," Coco says noncommittally. "Maybe. But hey, I hear there's a little fire you need to put out in the kitchen."

Holly frowns. "What fire?"

"The edible glitter that Kitta wanted on her yellow mini cupcakes tomorrow accidentally spilled everywhere. I think we're going to have to go a different direction on dessert…"

Rather than calling her mother out right there in the Palm Tree Pagoda suite in front of an upset bride and three guilty-looking bridesmaids, Holly inhales so sharply that her nostrils flare. "Kitta?" she asks in the most patient voice she can muster. "I want you to know that I'm going to do my very best to make sure that tonight and tomorrow go exactly the way you want them to, okay?"

Loud sniffling comes from behind the bathroom door.

"I don't know how we'll replace the fairy wings and I'm not sure how we'll substitute something else for edible glitter, but I'm on it. So don't worry about a thing."

Much to Holly's surprise, the door opens. Kitta stands before her in a white robe with the words 'Christmas Key B&B' embroidered on the chest in lime green thread. Her eyes are rimmed with red and she's holding a tissue to her nose. "This was sup-supposed to be a fu-fu-fun and whim-whimsical wedding," she says through little hiccups. "I wanted Deacon to be su-su-surprised."

Coco puts one toned arm around the bride's shoulders. "Shhh," she coos. "Don't you worry about a thing. He'll be surprised by how gorgeous you are as you walk down the aisle tomorrow, and he'll love that the wedding is classy and simple. Trust me, Kitta."

It takes all of Holly's willpower not to scream at her mother. Coco's idea of "classy and simple" might be very different from Kitta's idea of "fun and whimsical," but ultimately, this is Kitta's show and it should go the way she wants it to.

"Why don't you wash your face and get ready for the rehearsal," Holly suggests, "and I'll go handle everything in the kitchen."

Kitta nods and dabs at her eyes with the crumpled tissue. "Okay." She hiccups again.

"Mom, I really need you down there to help out with food," Holly adds. "Now."

Coco's going to have to acquiesce to Holly on this one in order to appear graceful, so she does. "You got it," she says with a close-mouthed smile. "I'll be right down."

"You ladies are going to be stunning no matter what," Holly assures the three bridesmaids. They're all sipping cans of Diet Coke through straws. Their eyes skitter around the room guiltily. It's clear that they're all in on Operation Disappear the Fairy Wings, so Holly leaves it at that and exits the room.

In the kitchen, she finds Iris sweeping up the last of the edible glitter with a resigned look on her face.

"Your mother knocked this off the counter entirely on purpose," Iris says as she turns the dustpan over an empty garbage can. Glitter flutters into the wastebasket, catching reflections of light from the window as it falls. "She suggested that we serve the cupcakes with one edible pearl in the center of each one."

"Do we even have edible pearls in this kitchen?" Holly frowns as she opens a cupboard and moves around jars of spices. "And if so —why?"

"You bought them for the pirate weekend, remember?" Bonnie offers. They make eye contact briefly, each recounting the weekend that Christmas Key had been taken over by a band of pirate enthusiasts who liked to dress and act the part. The event had led to a brief and ill-advised romance for Bonnie, something they rarely bring up at this point.

Holly shuts the cabinet. "We can't use stale cake decorations!"

The women in the kitchen go silent as they all consider this.

"Why don't we see what Ellen and Carrie-Anne have at the coffee shop?" one of the triplets says. "They have tons of candy since it's Willy Wonka month, and they redecorate that place every time we blink. I bet they'd have something we could use."

"That," Holly says, pointing her finger at the triplet in question, "is a great idea. Would you three mind frosting the cupcakes while I go and talk to them?"

"You got it." Gwen and Gen slide the rack of cooled cupcakes to the center of the island and start transferring them to waxed paper so they can start frosting.

"When my mother gets here, just lock her in the pantry or something, would you?" Holly says over her shoulder as she rushes out the door to head over to Mistletoe Morning Brew. "Whatever you do, don't let her harass the bride anymore."

"Your mother is uncontrollable, Mayor, you know that." Maria Agnelli puts one gnarled fist on her hip as she lowers her chin. "She's always been that way, and she always will be."

"Don't I know it." Holly sighs on her way out the door.

Outside, the groom and his groomsmen are standing on the sidewalk laughing with half-empty cups of beer in their hands.

"Hey, Holly," Deacon says, motioning for her to stop and join them. "These are my buddies."

"We're here to witness Avaloy sign his life away," says a tall, angular man who looks like he could be a member of the extended Kennedy clan. He puts one large, square hand on Deacon's shoulder chummily. "I'm Darren Kennedy," he says, holding out the other hand to shake Holly's.

Of course he's a Kennedy, she thinks, trying not to let the recognition cross her face. "Holly Baxter," she says, sticking her hand out and shaking firmly. "I'm the mayor of Christmas Key."

Darren and the other guys eye the hot pink strings of her bikini, which tie around her neck. Her cheeks go crimson as she realizes that her tank top is white.

"Have you talked government policy with Avaloy yet?" Darren asks her, letting his eyes skim her from head to about mid-thigh before he drags his pupils back up to hers. "He was the mayor of a small town once."

Deacon reaches out and punches his friend on the shoulder lightly. "I was not. I was the governor of Maine before I ran for the Senate."

"I'm sure Deacon has no interest in what it takes to run a small island," Holly says, smiling at the group as she starts to walk away. "He's got much bigger fish to fry."

"*I'd* be curious to hear more about it," Darren says. He takes a step away from the other men as if he's making a move to follow Holly. "I've got some politicians in my family—I think it's in my blood."

"Let's get you another beer, Kennedy." Deacon grabs hold of Darren's elbow and pulls him towards Jack Frosty's. "You're not nearly drunk enough to get through a rehearsal dinner with my sister."

"Your sister is here?" Darren's eyes light up. "Didn't we...?"

"Probably." Deacon makes a face. "She talks about you every time she calls. I think she's planning on catching the bouquet tomorrow."

"Okay. Well, you guys have fun," Holly says with a wave as she makes her escape. She mentally thanks Deacon's sister for pulling Darren's attention in her direction. "I'll see you later."

The door to Mistletoe Morning Brew is just closing as Cap walks out. Marco is waiting on the bistro table outside for him, hopping from taloned foot to taloned foot as he watches his master nurse a hot cup of coffee.

"What's cookin', Mayor?" Cap reaches out to let Marco walk up his arm and perch on his shoulder. "Coffee break?"

"No time for coffee," she says, pushing past him. "We've got a cupcake emergency!"

Cap gives a long, slow shake of the head and watches through the window as she rushes up to the front counter of the shop.

"Ellen, I'm in a pickle." Holly places both palms down on the counter and drops her chin to her chest. "I need candy."

"Well, you can help yourself to anything on the tables, Holly. I don't want to deprive a girl of gobstoppers and licorice whips," Ellen says with an amused look like an eight-year-old has just asked her for a peppermint stick. She continues to clear off the nearest bistro table.

"No, I mean we need something specific. The glitter for the cupcakes spilled, and now all we have are yellow-frosted mini cakes. No decoration. No flair. And that's not what the bride wants."

Ellen stops cleaning and looks at Holly. "Candy for the cupcakes?"

"What's happening?" Carrie-Anne comes from the back room holding a tray of clean coffee mugs. She sets it down on the counter and it rattles. "What cupcakes are we talking about?"

"For the wedding," Ellen says breathlessly. "We need to help decorate them for Kitta Banks and Deacon Avaloy." She's clearly starstruck.

"We need to help decorate them?" Carrie-Anne parrots back. "Now?"

"If you had anything that would look good on top of yellow cupcakes, it would be a total lifesaver," Holly says. "It's supposed to be kooky and fun."

"Kooky and fun," Carrie-Anne repeats.

"We need to stop repeating everything and start coming up with solutions," Ellen says to her wife, shooting her a lovingly annoyed glance.

"We've lost the fairy wings for the bridesmaids, and we had a mishap with the edible glitter...things are looking less and less whimsical with every passing second."

"Willy Wonka is pretty whimsical," Carrie-Anne points out. "Why don't we use some of this stuff?" She motions around the shop. "Give every guest a t-shirt for tonight—we're never going to sell all of these anyway."

"Oh, that's a brilliant idea!" Ellen says, rushing over to the pile of shirts they have for sale behind the front counter. She picks up a stack of pink and mint green shirts with various quotes from the movie on them. "Here, give one of these to every guest tonight. They all say 'Mistletoe Morning Brew' on the back, so we're also advertising the island."

"I love it." Holly reaches for the stack of shirts gratefully. "I'll write you a check for everything as soon as we get it all sorted out."

"Worry about that later." Ellen waves a hand, which makes the bangles on her wrists jingle merrily. "We've also got golden tickets to hand out. We've been doing that all month so far and people love them."

"The ones with the coupons for free drinks and pastries in them?" Holly takes the golden ticket that Ellen hands to her.

"We just printed those out and put them inside the tickets. You could easily do something else." Ellen pushes a stack of them across the counter. "Here, take them."

Holly examines the gold foil. Her mind is racing as she considers the possibilities. "We could put in a free night's stay at the B&B for another visit. Or free dinner at the bistro. Maybe something from Cap's store."

"Well, darlin'," Carrie-Anne walks over and puts an arm around Holly's shoulders. "Given that you only have a couple of hours here to pull this together, why don't you narrow your focus a bit?"

Holly frowns and tucks her hair behind her ears. "How?"

"Maybe just give away a package to the B&B to one lucky winner?

Or two? Put the golden tickets underneath the chairs at the reception or something," Ellen offers.

"Ohhh, that's a great idea!" Holly nods as she imagines that. She could probably convince Iris and Jimmy to do a free dinner and get Calista to give away a massage with the package to make it more enticing.

"Now," Ellen says, putting a stack of golden tickets on top of the pile of t-shirts. "How about those cupcakes?"

By four o'clock, there's a cake stand in the B&B's kitchen that's laden with bright yellow cupcakes covered in rainbow-colored candies. Ellen and Carrie-Anne have come through with all kinds of confections, and although the color scheme has shifted slightly from just yellow to everything in the spectrum, it looks nothing short of fun and whimsical.

"Are you serious?" Kitta is sitting across from Holly in the B&B's office, her tanned legs sticking out of a short white skirt as she perches in a wicker chair. She laughs in a way that almost sounds like disbelief. "You came up with this?"

"I did." Holly does her best to sound certain of the direction things have gone. "You were crying and you told me you wanted things to be lighthearted, so I came up with everything I could."

Kitta nods. She's looking out the window at Main Street as Deacon and his groomsmen cross the road with cigars in hand from Cap's shop. "I definitely want lighthearted. And yellow. And zany. It's who I am." Her eyes narrow as she watches Darren Kennedy jam an unlit cigar between his lips and follow Deacon to the B&B side of the street. "Some of Deacon's friends think I'm too...California. Not East Coast enough. Not classy." She pauses briefly and then sighs. "But Deacon loves me the way I am. And I like to have fun."

"Then you should," Holly says carefully, watching Kitta's face. All trace of her earlier tears have gone, and she seems pleased with the work Holly's done to turn things around. "Your wedding should be everything you want it to be."

"You've never been married?" Kitta crosses her legs and leans back in the chair. Her attention has shifted from the guys out on Main Street to Holly.

Holly starts to move papers around on her desk, dropping a stack into her wooden in-box and setting two pencils in the cup between her computer and Bonnie's. "Me?" she asks casually. "No, I've never been married."

"I bet you'll get married someday," Kitta offers kindly. "You're young and beautiful. Plenty of guys would be thrilled to marry a girl who owns an island and looks like you."

Holly blushes. "Oh, thanks." She tucks her hair behind one ear self-consciously. For a second, she's unsure of what to say. "Hey, want to go over the details for tonight?"

Kitta looks at the ceiling like she's considering it. "You know what?" she says. "I really don't." Kitta stands and smooths her white skirt over her thighs. "I trust you, Holly. You saved the day with this funky idea when everything seemed to be falling apart. Whatever you come up with will be amazing. I believe that."

Holly blinks twice, three times. This laid-back Kitta is a night and day transformation from the control freak Bridezilla that she and Bonnie have worked with for the past several months. How had she gone from demanding specific shades of yellow for everything to being blasé about something as major as the theme for her whole wedding?

"Are you sure?" Holly stands up from her own chair to face Kitta. "I want you to be comfortable with my ideas."

Kitta waves a hand. "I am. I'm here now and Deacon is here," she says, glancing out the window again. "Our family and friends are here, and this is going to be amazing."

Holly nods. "Okay, as long as you're sure."

Kitta runs a hand through her loose, salt-air tousled hair. "I'm sure." She starts for the door. "I think I'm going to go for another swim at the beach before I have to get dressed and ready for the rehearsal dinner," she says, glancing back at Holly. "Thanks again for everything."

Holly watches Kitta go, wondering what's gotten into her. After the meticulous planning, the demanding insistence that no photographs be leaked, the tears over the missing fairy wings—after all of that, how was Kitta now floating around like a 60s housewife on Valium?

She wondered for just a moment, but then suddenly she knew: Coco.

13

"Coco!" Holly shouts, pulling to a stop on the side of the sandy street. Coco is talking to Kitta's mother in the informal parking lot next to the Ho Ho Hideaway. Beyond the two women is the sparkling blue of the Gulf of Mexico, winking in the distance like an invitation. Holly feels the pull of it briefly and remembers that she's wearing a bikini under her shorts and tank top, but she quickly pushes the thought from her mind. "*Mother!*" she says loudly, stepping onto the sand. "I need to speak to you."

"We'll serve the drinks right over there," Coco is saying, pointing at the sand in front of the bar. They'd planned on having cocktail hour on the beach and mixing the drinks at the Ho Ho as guests mingled and enjoyed the sunset after the wedding rehearsal. The actual dinner would take place at the Jingle Bell Bistro.

"Oh, your daughter is here, Coco!" Kitta's mom says, clapping her hands together. She looks at Holly with a big, open grin. "Kitta's said nothing but wonderful things about you." She opens her arms to hug Holly in a tight embrace. "Thank you for helping her plan this." Kitta's mom is quintessential California, just like her daughter. She's wearing a flowy caftan and several bangles on her wrists, and her skin has the light tan of someone who gardens and walks on the beach under a thick layer of sunscreen. The only lines on her face are faint crow's feet around her blue eyes that show when she smiles.

"Of course," Holly assures her, accepting the hug. "It's been my pleasure. I only hope it turns out to be everything she wants it to be."

"It will," Kitta's mother says. She puts her hands on Holly's arms and looks at her. "My daughter can be a pill sometimes, but that's just because of the time she's spent in Hollywood. I promise you, at heart she's a wildflower, not an orchid."

"She's been fun to work with," Holly says, trying to forget all the maddening texts and phone calls that Kitta has made to her in the past four or five months.

"Good." Kitta's mother lets go of Holly's arms. "Now, if you'll excuse me, I'm going to head back to the B&B and freshen up a bit."

"We'll see you in a while, Margaux," Coco says, giving a wave as Kitta's mom climbs behind the wheel of the B&B's golf cart that she's borrowed.

As soon as they're alone, Holly's smile fades. She turns to Coco. "What did you give her?"

Coco looks at the back of the golf cart as it disappears around the bend of December Drive. "Nothing," she says simply. "We were just talking about this evening."

"Not her," Holly says, lifting her chin in the direction that Margaux has gone. "Kitta. Why is she acting like she just binged on Scooby snacks?"

Coco lifts an eyebrow and makes a face to let Holly know that she thinks she's being a prude. "Scooby snacks? As if I would do that. I just gave her a couple of Xanax. She needed to calm down." Coco starts to walk over to the golf cart that one of the triplets has loaned her.

"No," Holly says. "No you didn't." She follows Coco across the sand. "You gave the bride *Xanax*? She's so chill now that she'd be happy to marry a sea lion."

Coco shrugs as she sits on the sun-warmed seat of the golf cart. "Well, if she marries a sea lion, then that would free up Deacon Avaloy to be with someone who actually deserves him."

"You're unreal," Holly says, standing in one spot as her mother turns on the cart and starts rolling away. "You really are."

"Hey," Coco calls over her shoulder. She cranks the steering wheel as she prepares to pull out onto December Drive. "Did you hear that one of his groomsmen is a Kennedy? I'm going to try to wrangle you an introduction later."

"Don't do me any favors!" Holly yells, her words lost in the crunch of golf cart tires on shell-strewn sand. "I don't want your help with *anything!*"

But Coco doesn't hear her as she pushes down on the gas pedal and speeds away.

THE SMALL CHAPEL ON THE CORNER OF HOLLY LANE AND WHITE Christmas Way is strung with yellow lights. There's been a last minute change of rehearsal venue after Kitta has decided that she might prefer the wedding to take place inside the chapel rather than on the beach, and Holly's spent the afternoon scrambling to relocate everything, but she's done it. The doors of the chapel stand open now, and inside, Deacon and his groomsmen are gathered around the tiny altar, laughing and cracking jokes.

Cap is standing on the front steps as the bridesmaids arrive, shaking the hand of each woman and making small talk with the fathers of both the bride and groom.

Holly parks her cart on the sandy lane and waits patiently for the guests to wander into the church and take their seats in the pews. Kitta has been clear that the rehearsal is supposed to be fast and casual, and as people climb the steps in flip-flops and loose, tropical shirts, Holly knows that her wishes have been honored.

"Any sign of the bride?" Holly asks quietly, standing next to Cap with their backs to the church.

Cap shakes his white head and consults his watch. "Not yet."

"Okay." Holly nods and thinks about this. Suddenly, a jarring thought occurs to her and she reaches out and clamps down on Cap's left arm with her hand. "I don't want to get worried about it yet, but she was acting a little off this afternoon, and the last thing she said was that she wanted to go for a swim."

"Pool or beach?" Cap frowns.

"Beach."

"You should go and look for her." Cap's face is serious. "Everyone is here," he says, peering through the open doors, "and they're going to want to get this show on the road and do a run-through so that they can go eat and enjoy themselves."

"You're right." Holly bites her lower lip. "I'll be back."

In less than three minutes, she's whipped through the forested side of the island, passed her own property, and is taking December Drive slowly enough to peek at the stretches of sand where a person might leave their clothes and shoes and head out into the water. Why had she let Kitta go off alone when she could tell that she wasn't acting like herself? Even before knowing about the Xanax, she never should have let Kitta out of her sight. She should have forced the bride to stay with her and talk about the plans for that night or something.

Holly rounds the bend of December Drive and the early evening sun shifts so that it's over her shoulder. She scans the beach frantically for signs of Kitta as she reaches for her phone.

"Bonnie?" she says into the receiver as soon as her friend picks up. "Any chance you've seen Kitta around in the past hour or so?"

"Hey, sugar. Nope. Haven't seen the blushing bride. Why? She get cold feet and disappear on us?"

"No, nothing like that," Holly says. "I just need to find her and I'm not sure where she's hiding."

"You try her cell phone?" Bonnie suggests.

Of course she hasn't tried anything that simple. Holly slows to a stop. "That would have been too obvious, wouldn't it?"

"Go call her, doll. Get back to me if there's something I need to do."

Holly hangs up and dials Kitta's number. There's no answer. She's about to panic as she ends the call when she notices two figures stepping over the low sand dunes. Their arms are bronzed, and their long, youthful strides match one another. It's Logan and Owen.

"Hey!" Holly calls. She jumps out of her cart and approaches them on the soft sand. "Logan! Owen!"

The boys stop walking and look at Holly guiltily. Owen flicks a switch on the camera that's hanging around his thin neck and lets go of the device.

"Have you seen Kitta?" Holly asks them. She puts a hand up to shield her eyes as she scans the beach.

Owen makes a face that Holly can't quite read. His eyes cut to Logan.

"Yeah," Logan finally admits. "We just saw her."

"Where is she?" Holly grabs Logan's arm and shakes it without meaning to be as firm as she is. "Is she on the beach?"

"She's over there," Logan says, pointing at the hard-packed sand where the tide has washed in and then out again. "She's totally out."

Holly wants to ask what they mean, but instead she kicks off her Birkenstocks and breaks into a run. She can see Kitta lying on the beach, her white skirt wet and sandy, her shirt pushed up to reveal a patch of stomach. She's got her sunglasses on, and her hair is wet and tangled around her. Her feet are bare.

"Kitta!" Holly screams, falling to her knees next to Kitta's unmoving body. "Hey," she says, putting her hands on the woman's shoulders and shaking her gently. "Wake up."

The boys have followed Holly back to the shoreline. "She's okay," Logan says. "We saw her come out here and lay down, and we stayed close by while she caught a few winks."

"Wait," Holly says, standing up. The waves are rolling in, and a rush of water comes up to them, stopping just inches from Kitta's body before it retreats again. "You sat here while she laid in the waves and nearly drowned? And you didn't call for help?"

The boys look at each other with raised eyebrows. Neither seems to know how to answer this.

"She wasn't going to drown, Holly," Logan says. "We were here. And see how her head is away from the water," he says, pointing at the fact that her body is angled so that her head is farther up the beach than her feet. "She was totally fine. She just got a little wet."

Holly puts both hands on her hips. "So she just laid down here and fell asleep?"

Logan and Owen look at each other again.

"Yeah," Owen says, answering the question. "That's what she did. And we didn't think it was right to wake her up if she needed a nap, so we just stayed here in case anything bad was going to happen to her."

Holly processes this, pacing around Kitta's still figure as she imagines the teenage boys standing guard over the body of a sleeping actress on the beach. "Okay," she says, considering her next move. Kitta is wet and sandy and clearly in no place to be standing before her guests and her groom at the Christmas Key Chapel, doing a dry run of her wedding. "We need to get her into my golf cart. Can you help me?"

The boys spring into action. Logan puts his hands under Kitta's armpits and Owen picks up her feet. Holly notices that they studiously avoid glancing at the skin of her stomach or at the way her skirt is hiked up to the tops of her thighs. Like nice young men, they carry her to the cart and lay her gently on the back seat, head at one end and feet at the other.

"What's wrong with her?" Logan asks, stepping back to assess the gorgeous blonde passed out in Holly's golf cart. "Is she drunk?"

"No, she's not drunk." Holly grinds her teeth, silently cursing her mother for giving Kitta whatever medication has turned her into a zombie bride. "She's just really tired. I need to get her back to the B&B." She makes a quick decision. "Can you guys do me a favor and run over to the chapel and let Cap know that Kitta isn't feeling well, and that she'll meet everyone at the dinner later?"

Logan nods. "Yeah, we can do that."

"Thanks. I'll see you later. Thanks for making sure she didn't drown." Without waiting for a reply, Holly pulls back onto the road and punches the gas. She needs to get Kitta cleaned up and awake as soon as possible. As she drives, she calls Bonnie again.

"Whoa, sugar." Bonnie is standing in the lobby when Holly walks in with Kitta draped over one of her shoulders. The actress is able to walk with assistance, and she's alert and talking, but her words are loopy.

"I love sugar," Kitta breathes, blinking heavily.

Bonnie and Holly exchange a look.

"I'm sure you do, doll." Bonnie reaches out both arms and takes Kitta's weight off of Holly for a second.

"Let me get the key to the Palm Tree Pagoda," Holly says, yanking open a drawer under the front desk. She finds the master key and shuts the drawer. "Here, I'll take half of her." Holly puts her shoulder under Kitta's armpit again, slinging the woman's limp arm around her neck. "We need to get her upstairs," she says to Bonnie. "Fast."

In short order, Holly and Bonnie have Kitta changed and sitting on the edge of the bed sipping a Diet Coke from the mini-bar.

Holly kneels in front of Kitta, gently combing through the wet hair on the side of Kitta's face. She hopes that her light make-up application and the motion of pulling a brush through her hair will make it look like the bride has just emerged, fresh-faced, from a shower.

Kitta puts the silver can to her lips. "Your mom is the best. She gave me something while I was getting ready because I wouldn't stop crying." She shrugs. "It definitely made me stop crying."

"Mmhmm," Holly says, twisting Kitta's long, blonde hair and setting it behind her shoulders. She's hoping it will dry in waves and not look like she's just spent the past hour comatose on the beach. "Well, no matter what she says going forward, my mother is not a doctor and should not be prescribing you anything. Don't take a single pill from her, okay?"

Kitta rolls her eyes like a petulant teenager. "Okay, Mayor," she says, giggling.

Bonnie is hanging Kitta's wet clothes in the bathroom and she sticks her head out to look at Holly. "We almost ready to get this young lady to her groom?"

"I think so." Holly stands and takes one more look at Kitta. It would be hard to make such a beautiful woman look unattractive, and even with minimal interventions, Kitta looks stunning. The yellow sundress Holly found hanging in the closet skims Kitta's curves nicely, and her sun-bronzed skin shines. "We should probably get over to the rehearsal dinner." She tosses the hairbrush onto the rumpled bed and stands back to assess her handiwork. "You ready, Kitta?"

Kitta nods and stands, but the Xanax is still very much in her system. She weaves from side to side unsteadily, and Holly reaches out to grab her.

"Whoops-a-daisy," Bonnie says, coming up behind Kitta and putting out her hands to catch her.

"I'm fine," Kitta insists. She puts her hands on Holly's shoulders and looks her in the eyes gravely. "Holly," she says, her voice serious. "I want to thank you for everything. I'll never forget you or this day. You're like a sister to me."

Holly nods and keeps both hands on Kitta's narrow waist. "Of course. It's my pleasure," she says, not taking a word of what Kitta is saying to heart. She's still hopped up on whatever Coco's given her, and there's no way she'll ever remember any of this.

"Come on, let's roll," Bonnie says, picking up Kitta's purse and grabbing a lipgloss from the vanity to put inside of it. "I've got your stuff, doll."

The three women make their way back to Holly's golf cart and, with some finagling, manage to get situated and over to the Ho Ho Hideaway just as the guests are all mingling with their first drinks.

"Kitta!" Deacon shouts, handing his Mai Tai to Darren Kennedy. He rushes over to the cart and holds out his hands to pull his bride-to-be to her feet. "What happened? I've been calling your cell and panicking." Deacon looks at her closely, examining her face and body to make sure that she's whole. "But everyone promised me that you were with Holly and everything was fine."

"And everyone was right," Kitta says, swatting at Deacon and missing his shoulder entirely. She stumbles just a bit as she puts one foot in front of the other. "I need a drink." She points at the colorful Mai Tais in everyone's hands. "I want one of those."

"Um, Deacon?" Holly grabs his elbow and motions for him to step to the side with her while Bonnie guides Kitta into the fray of guests. "So, there's been a slight situation."

Deacon's brow furrows. "I figured." His eyes follow Kitta closely. "When she didn't show up for the rehearsal, I thought maybe she'd gotten cold feet. You can't imagine how humiliating that would be for me at this point in my career."

Holly reaches up and pushes at the loose hair that's falling out of her haphazard bun. "No, I can see that," she agrees, wondering why his concern is about his career when his bride is clearly in need of some assistance. She shakes that thought off and pushes ahead. "So, what happened was that the fairy wings all went missing—"

"I don't give a damn about the fairy wings," he says, looking around to make sure no one is listening. "I just want this wedding to go off without a hitch."

"And it will," Holly says, holding out a hand to slow him down. "But Kitta was pretty upset by the missing wings, and I'm afraid my mother—though well-meaning—isn't the best person to soothe a panic attack. She offered Kitta a Xanax, and, well..." Holly's eyes drift over to where Kitta is hiking up her yellow sundress and wading out into the water.

"Sweet Mary and Joseph," Deacon swears under his breath, watching as the water laps over Kitta's thighs and wets the edge of her dress. She's laughing and splashing around, swatting water at her father and at Cap Duncan as they wade in after her. "One Xanax did *that*?"

Holly clears her throat. "It might have been slightly more than one."

"We've got party gifts for everyone!" Millie says cheerfully, circulating through the small crowd with two of the triplets in tow. They're handing out goody bags to the guests, smiling and making small talk in hopes of distracting everyone from the spectacle that Kitta's making in the water. "T-shirts and candy," Millie says, thrusting a bag at Kitta's confused mother.

Holly watches as two of the guests pull out the colorful t-shirts and read the Willy Wonka quotes that Ellen and Carrie-Anne have designed for this month's shirts. There are mildly amused smiles as people compare the giant lollipops in their bags and gamely trade chocolate buttons for licorice whips.

With everyone occupied and Deacon following Kitta into the water himself, Holly takes the opportunity to rush up the steps to the Ho Ho and lean across the bar. "Joe," she says hurriedly, patting the counter to get his attention. He switches off the blender.

"What's up, Mayor?" Joe sets three glasses on the bar and waits to hear what Holly has to say before he pours the drink he's been mixing.

"Buckhunter is here," she says breathlessly, tilting her head towards the sand. "Would you mind if he took over behind the bar while you got the music going? We desperately need a distraction out there."

Joe follows her gaze. "Why? What's going on?"

"The bride is hopped up on Xanax that Coco gave her, and the groom is mad that she missed the rehearsal at the chapel. We've resorted to handing out goody bags."

Joe watches the scene on the beach from the corner of his eye as he pours the frozen drinks into the glasses. "You definitely need music," he agrees. "Get Buckhunter up here to man the bar, and I'll grab my guitar." Joe sets the blender down and wipes the condensation from his hands on the sides of his shorts.

Holly finds Buckhunter on the edge of the crowd, talking to Vance Guy. They're on standby for the evening to help with moving guests and items from the beach to the Jingle Bell Bistro when it's time to relocate for dinner, and as Holly approaches, they're discussing baseball and the World Series.

"I know!" Vance says, giving Buckhunter's shoulder a light punch. "Did you see that run?"

"Hey, guys." Holly is out of breath as she approaches. "I need help. Buckhunter, can you fill in for Joe and make a few drinks?"

"Sure." Buckhunter shrugs. "Just go take over for him?"

"Yeah." Holly turns to Vance. "And would you mind helping Joe set up the speaker right over there?" She nods at a stool already sitting beneath a lone palm tree that's wound with strings of lights that blink merrily in the fading light. "He's going to play for a bit while everyone mingles."

"You got it," Vance says, giving a sloppy salute. The men disperse and Holly stands there for a second, looking around. A couple of the guests are eating the candy from their goody bags, and Deacon has successfully coaxed Kitta out of the water. He's currently got her under his arm, and he's steering her around, making small talk with their guests as she laughs too loudly.

Joe has his speaker set up in no time, and before Holly knows it, he's strumming the guitar softly, picking out a tune that fills the air and mixes with the crashing waves. The drinks keep coming from the bar courtesy of Buckhunter, and everyone looks happy and relaxed.

Holly relaxes. For the moment, it seems that crisis has been averted.

14

THE SUNDAY OF KITTA AND DEACON'S WEDDING IS OVERCAST. A LIGHT, misty rain is falling over Main Street, and Holly is standing behind the front desk of the B&B, closely monitoring the updates from the weather service when Kitta comes flying down the stairs.

"Holly!" she says in a loud, commanding voice. *Uh oh,* Holly thinks, *the old Kitta is back.* "Did you see this?" She skids to a stop in front of the desk. Her hair is in giant Velcro rollers. She thrusts her iPhone at Holly.

"What is it?"

"It's *Glitter and Stars* magazine again." Kitta's face is suddenly darker and less inviting than the weather outside. "Who did this?"

Holly takes the phone and puts it closer to her face. Sure enough, there on the screen is a photo of Kitta laying in the waves on the beach, her eyes closed as the water laps over her.

"This headline says *Kitta Banks Gets Drunk and Passes Out Before Wedding Ceremony.*"

Holly's stomach plunges. Suddenly she knows what's happened. All of it: the pictures of the island, the information leaked to the press...she gets it now.

"I was *not* drunk yesterday, and this is *not* right before my wedding ceremony!"

"I know," Holly agrees, handing the phone back. "I know what really happened."

"But the rest of the world doesn't!" Kitta is livid. "How do you think this makes me look?"

Holly tries to think of something more flattering and more charitable than the thoughts that are running through her head.

"It makes me look like a *drunk* who can't even stay sober for her own wedding!" Kitta looks down at the phone again and shakes her head. "I want to know who did this, Holly. This is not okay."

Holly walks out from behind the desk and puts a hand on Kitta's shoulder. "No, it's not okay. I hear you. And we will figure out what's going on. But right now, our focus should be on the wedding."

"Oh, the wedding?" The panic in Kitta's voice rises as she turns to the window. "The wedding that's going to take place on the rainiest day of the century?"

"It's definitely not the rainiest day of the century," Holly says mildly, hoping to bring the high-strung bride back to reality. She walks over to the window and tilts her head up to look at the sky. "But it's a bit cloudier than we'd hoped for."

Kitta folds her arms across her chest and stares at Holly. "Nothing is coming together like I'd hoped it would."

"It really never does," Holly says quietly, keeping her back to Kitta.

"Did you find out?" Deacon's voice forces Holly to turn around as he comes down the stairs and into the small lobby.

"No," Kitta says, her face still frosty. "Holly says we'll figure it out though."

"This is unacceptable," Deacon says, holding up his own phone and showing Holly the same image of Kitta passed out on the beach. "We're going to have to do some major damage-control on this."

"I'm sorry." It's all Holly can think to say, and she does mean it. Especially now that she's figured out what's going on with the leaked photographs. "I really am. We're doing our best to handle things as they pop up, and for now, all we can do is get you ready for the wedding. I can't control the weather, and I can't control the press. But you're going to be beautiful, and your groom is obviously here to love and take care of you."

Kitta's eyes soften just a bit at the mention of Deacon. She turns to him.

"You are going to be beautiful," he says, smiling at her.

Before they start kissing right there in her lobby, Holly walks over to the couple and puts a hand on each of their arms. "Why don't you two go and get ready, and I'll make sure that everything is coming along for the ceremony and the reception."

Reluctantly, Deacon leads his bride back up the stairs. Holly watches their retreating backs, Deacon dressed in sweatpants and a t-shirt, and Kitta in a short, satiny white robe with "Mrs. Avaloy" stitched across the back in blue. She has to admit, things have gone off the rails a bit for Kitta, but doesn't every wedding include some sort of build-up and let-down cycle? Don't they all have some sort of variation on unpredictable weather, drunken guests, and wedding day blues?

Holly forwards the front desk phone so that it will ring on her iPhone and walks down the hallway to the side door. It's still only nine in the morning, but she wants to head off any more ill-gotten wedding photos before they come to pass.

She parks her pink golf cart in front of Hal Pillory's bungalow and sits there for a minute, watching the quiet house. Katelynn walks past the front window inside the house and Holly gets out of the cart.

Standing at the front door, Holly considers how to broach this topic with Katelynn. She knocks and waits.

"Holly." Katelynn is surprised. "How are you? Come in."

"Smells like breakfast. Guess I'm just in time." Holly inhales the scent of bacon and waffles and fresh coffee.

"Oh, I'm cooking," Katelynn says. "Do you want to stay?" The offer is awkward and not quite sincere.

"No, no—I'm kidding," Holly assures her. "I came to talk to the boys."

"Logan and Owen?" Katelynn frowns. "Why, what's up?"

"I'm not going to take you up on breakfast, but could I maybe steal a cup of coffee from you?" Holly asks, trying to buy herself a couple of minutes.

"Yeah, of course." Katelynn leads the way into the kitchen and hands Holly a steaming mug of coffee before they sit at the table.

Hal's late wife, Sadie, had decorated the entire bungalow in simple, frilly white curtains, plain but comfortable furniture, and walls adorned with framed family photographs. Holly sips her coffee as she glances up at a picture of a much younger Sadie and Hal on the wall next to the table.

"I feel kind of bad about showing up here and lobbing accusations first thing on a Sunday morning," Holly says, setting the coffee mug down on the round wooden table. "But there have been more photographs leaked to the press lately, and it flies directly in the face of everything we discussed at the village council meeting about keeping this wedding quiet."

Katelynn frowns and moves the napkin holder on the center of the table to one side. "But what does this have to do with the boys?"

Holly laces her fingers through the handle of her mug. "I think they took the photos and sold them to *Glitter and Stars*. Kitta found a new one online this morning from when I found her on the beach yesterday during the rehearsal."

"What are you talking about?" Katelynn pushes back her chair and stands up to pull the bacon off the burner. "I'm totally lost here."

"Yesterday when Kitta went missing, I found her passed out on the edge of the water. The only two people on the beach were Logan and Owen, who I've also seen around taking photos of other things."

"So they like to take photos," Katelynn says defensively. "How does that make them savvy enough to photograph Kitta and sell the photos to some trashy website overnight? They're just sixteen-year-old boys, Holly." When she sets the spatula on the counter, it's with such force that it sounds like she's dropped something.

"Katelynn," Holly says calmly. "It was them. Trust me."

Just then, the doorbell rings. Katelynn puts one hand on her hip. "Let me get that and wake the boys up."

Holly waits in the kitchen while Katelynn answers the door. A familiar man's voice fills the entryway, and Holly looks around the corner to see who's there.

"Jake?" Holly steps out of the kitchen and stares at him. "Is everything okay?" Her mind immediately starts turning over the reasons why Jake might be there at nine o'clock on a Sunday morning. Has something happened? Did he see her golf cart out front and track her here to tell her something important?

"Yeah, everything is fine," he says, exchanging a look with Katelynn. "I'm just here for breakfast."

"For—" Holly's mouth keeps moving even as her mind processes this information. "Oh, for breakfast." Katelynn has invited Jake for breakfast. She isn't sure what to say next.

"Mom?" Logan appears at the end of the hallway, hair messy, a wrinkled t-shirt pulled on over his narrow frame. "Who's here?"

"Hi, buddy," Katelynn says to her son. "Jake is here to eat with us, but Holly dropped by and she has something she wants to talk to you about."

Logan looks at Holly expectantly.

"Hey, Logan," Holly says, smiling at him like she's about to deliver bad news. "Listen, you and Owen were the only people on the beach yesterday when I found Kitta, and somehow a photo of her ended up on the *Glitter and Stars* website this morning. What do you guys know about that?"

Logan shrugs.

"This isn't the first time that wedding related information or photos of the island have been leaked in conjunction with Deacon and Kitta getting married here." She stops talking and waits to see what Logan will say.

He nods thoughtfully. "Okay," he says.

"Okay, what?" Holly has expected more—like an admission or an apology.

"Okay, so someone leaked pictures." Logan shrugs.

"After I specifically asked at the village council meeting for all talk or information about the wedding to stay here on the island."

Logan nods again and looks at his mom.

"Do you and Owen know anything about that?" Holly is a little more perturbed by the whole thing than she'd thought possible. Initially, her only desire was to get to the bottom of the whole thing to make Kitta happy, but now that she's looking at Logan and seeing his casual, unapologetic attitude, she's feeling annoyed on a personal level. "Because I'd be really disappointed if I felt like you had done something like this knowing that it was the wrong thing to do."

"Okay, Holly," Katelynn interrupts. "That's enough for this morning. Logan hasn't given you any indication that he knows what you're talking about, so let's just drop it for now."

"Oh, then I'll just go and question Maria Agnelli and see if she's the one leaking the information to *Glitter and Stars,* because that seems more likely."

Jake steps up to the women then, risking the obvious awkwardness that will arise from Holly being reminded of his presence there first thing in the morning. "Hol, why don't you go back and handle the wedding stuff, and I'll talk to both boys when they're up and dressed." He puts a hand on Holly's shoulder blade and gently guides her to the door. It's clear that the two women have quickly come to an impasse, and if there's any way for Jake to intercept a potentially messy situation, then he will.

Holly wants to argue, but she knows he's right. There is wedding stuff to handle, and a bride who's about to enter into a downward spiral over the weather. There are guests on the island and all kinds of details that will only come off without a hitch if Holly has her head in the game.

"I'll be busy all morning, but I want to hear what the boys have to say by the end of the day," she says as she takes two backwards steps towards the door. "This was a totally irresponsible and wrong thing to do."

"Holly," Jake says. The tone of his voice is a warning. He opens the door for her and stops just short of grabbing her by the elbow and physically marching her out to the golf cart. "I've got this."

As she leaves, Holly can hear Katelynn whispering urgently to Logan, and she knows that she'll have her answer by the end of the day. As fiercely protective of a mother as Katelynn might be, she's also smart enough to know that there's nowhere to hide from the truth on Christmas Key.

BACK AT THE B&B, KITTA IS STANDING IN THE MIDDLE OF THE DINING room amidst all of her attendants. They've got a photographer snapping candids of their last minute preparations, and several of the local women are bustling around, gluing things together and fussing over flower arrangements and wedding accoutrements.

"What is this?" Nylie, Kitta's tiny brunette friend, takes a bouquet from Ellen and Carrie-Anne and frowns at it. "It's got lollipops in it."

"It's Willy Wonka themed," Kitta explains, watching as Iris and Maggie and Calista stick giant rainbow-colored lollipops on sticks into the bouquets of colorful flowers. Her wedding dress is a slim column of yellow sequins, and her hair is falling in casual waves dotted with tropical flowers. The whole look is a feast of colors for the eyes.

"Willy Wonka?" Nylie's eyes shift to the other bridesmaids; it's clear they're now regretting the part they played in losing the fairy wings.

"I said fun, I said festive, I said zany," Kitta says, smiling at Holly. "And when things started to go wrong, Holly jumped in and got creative."

"It's really Ellen and Carrie-Anne," Holly demurs, thinking of the women who have stripped their coffee shop bare to give Kitta the kind of off-beat wedding she desires. "They had all this stuff."

Nylie and the other women can hardly conceal their disapproval. "It's definitely...unexpected," one woman says. "Does Deacon know about all of this?" asks another.

"If I'm happy, Deacon is happy." Kitta takes a giant bouquet dripping with glittered ribbons in every shade of red, yellow, green, and blue. "And as long as it doesn't rain today, I'll be happy."

Holly quickly steps into the lobby and peers outside at the sky: still gray. But as of yet, no rain.

"Is my lovely bride hiding around here somewhere?" Deacon comes down the stairs straightening his bowtie. His groomsmen follow close behind.

Darren Kennedy looks almost more dashing than the groom in his suit, his hair slicked back to reveal his sharp cheekbones and icy blue eyes. "Hello, Mayor," he says smoothly, adjusting the cuffs of his shirt.

"You guys all look great." Holly avoids looking at any one of them for too long, instead focusing on Deacon. "Kitta is in the ballroom, so stay away from there. It's bad luck if you see her, you know."

"So I've heard." Deacon stands next to Holly and gazes outside. "Think we'll keep the rain at bay?"

"I'm hoping," Holly says. She's watched Kitta's attitude shift perceptibly as the morning has gone on, and the misty weather seems to be lower on her list of concerns at the moment. "As long as we can get you guys to the chapel without rain, then I think it's going to be just fine."

Deacon nods and rocks back and forth on the heels of his shiny dress shoes, hands in the pockets of his tux pants. "Listen," he says in a low voice. "I know Kitta's been hard to handle, and I know this thing with the leaked photos has been a lot, but we really do appreciate the way you all have welcomed us to the island."

Holly is taken aback. She expected him to be more put off by the way she's taken charge of the wedding and moved it even further away from the classy affair she would have imagined he'd want. "Of course," she says, still watching Main Street in front of them through the window. "We're thrilled to have you here."

Deacon takes a hand from his pocket and rubs his chin. "You know," he says, "some people think I'm insane for marrying Kitta. They don't think she has what it takes to potentially be First Lady someday." Deacon looks over his shoulder and scans the lobby to make sure they're alone. "But that's not why you marry, you know?"

"No, of course not," Holly agrees.

"You marry because someone makes you smile," he goes on. "You marry because you can't imagine your life without the humor and love they bring to you. You marry because, when you look into their eyes, you can see forever."

Holly nods at this because she isn't sure what else to say.

"So I don't much care that my bride is wearing yellow instead of white." Deacon's eyes crinkle at the corners as he turns to face Holly. "And whether her friends wear fairy wings or not is no concern of mine. I want her to be happy. Do you think we can make her happy today?"

Holly is looking into his eyes, and she feels like she's being hypnotized by his melodic voice and flawless grin. "Yes," she says without thinking. "I do."

"Good." Deacon claps a hand on Holly's shoulder. "Then let's see if we can run between these raindrops and get this wedding underway."

As if on cue, the groomsmen walk into the front lobby and start ribbing Deacon good-naturedly.

"You ready to sign your life away?" one of them goads, punching Deacon's bicep.

"Let's get you hitched, huh?" Darren Kennedy says. He throws an arm around Deacon's shoulders and leads him out the front door. It's a short walk to the chapel, and the men head that direction as Holly watches.

"Hey," Bonnie says, interrupting the temporary quiet. She's standing in the doorway with a multi-colored pinwheel in her hand. "What am I supposed to do with this?"

"I think we're putting that on the golf cart." Holly reaches out a hand and takes it from Bonnie, examining the long stick with the shiny spokes. "Let me go and make sure it's ready."

In the B&B's parking lot sits Holly's own pink golf cart. It's draped with every shade of ticky-tacky thing imaginable: ribbons; tassels;

pom-poms dangling from strings; twinkling Christmas lights. "Wow," she says under her breath, standing there to admire it. The women of the island have really stepped up to the plate with this one, and Holly takes a moment to appreciate her friends and neighbors in a way she doesn't normally have a reason to do. "I think this is all going to come together somehow."

"Of course it is, sugar," Bonnie says, standing behind her. "Have we ever *not* pulled things together when you needed us to? Tell us to turn this island into a pirate's paradise, we get it done. Convince us that we belong on a reality show, we play along. You want a *Willy Wonka and the Chocolate Factory* themed wedding? You got it."

Holly turns to Bonnie and smiles. "Thanks for always being my right-hand woman, Bon."

"It's my pleasure," she says, walking around the cart and examining the decorations. "I can't imagine what would make an otherwise sane woman want to turn her wedding into a circus like this, but hey, if it's what she wants, then we'll make it happen."

Just then, the bride and her attendants emerge from the side door to the B&B. They're holding up the hems of their dresses and carrying high heels in their hands while they wear flip-flops on their feet.

"Oh," Kitta says. She comes to a stop and her bridesmaids nearly rear-end her. "This looks awesome!" She drops the hem of her yellow sequined gown and rushes over to the golf cart. "It's perfect."

"Let's get you into your chariot and over to the chapel," Holly says, putting one hand under Kitta's elbow and helping her into the front passenger seat. She takes a look at the sky overhead and feels a sliver of hope break through when she sees that the formerly gray sky is now broken with swirls of yellow and blue. This weather may pass yet.

"Are you ready to be Mrs. Deacon Avaloy?" Nylie holds her own dress up so that it doesn't drag in the sandy parking lot as she bustles around the bride, tucking the edges of her gown around her on the seat of the golf cart. She hands Kitta her giant bouquet.

"But more importantly," Coco asks, stepping into the group seemingly from nowhere, "is he ready to become Mr. Kitta Banks?"

The women all turn to look at Coco.

"It's not going to be like that," Kitta says with a confident smile. "We support each other. Neither of us overshadows the other."

"Mmm," Coco says, looking unconvinced. "I heard he and the groomsmen talking about it earlier." She glances back at the B&B confidentially. "He sounded worried."

"Let's head over," Holly says. She hurries two of the bridesmaids into the back of her cart and slides behind the wheel. "Bonnie, can you bring up the rear with the other cart?"

Bonnie is quick to get into the B&B's cart and motion for the other bridesmaids to follow. The islanders have decorated this one as well, but it's slightly more understated (if one can ever call a golf cart strung with twinkling Christmas lights and ropes of silk flowers "understated").

"But I'm sure everything will be fine," Coco says, watching as they load into the carts and pull out of the lot. "I'll see you all over at the chapel."

Holly completely ignores her mother as she drives carefully over the bump of the driveway and turns onto Main Street.

Kitta puts one hand over her heart. "I'm a little nervous," she says. "Now I wish I'd made it to the rehearsal last night."

"Hey," Holly says with a force that's meant to bring Kitta down to Earth. "You've got this. Ignore everything my mother said. All you have to do is keep your eyes on Deacon and remember that you're about to say 'I do' to the man you love."

Kitta turns to look at Holly. Her face is serious beneath the light layer of foundation and blush that the make-up artist has applied. She looks beautiful.

"You're right," Kitta says. She gazes at the bouquet in her lap. "Of course you're right."

As they pull up in front of the chapel, the bridesmaids give little gasps of amusement. "No way!" one says, stepping out of the cart that Bonnie's driving as soon as she comes to a stop. "Kitta! Look!"

But Kitta is already out of the cart, dress in hand as she stands on the sand. "It's wild," she says under her breath.

And it is. The women had worked tirelessly the night before, waiting until the rehearsal was over and the chapel emptied. Holly is awed by the result: the decor of Mistletoe Morning Brew has been completely moved over from the coffee shop and repurposed as wedding decorations. Next to the steps leading up to the front door are the oversized papier-mâché mushrooms that Ellen and Carrie-Anne had spent hours making for this month's *Willy Wonka* theme. There are red mushrooms with white polka-dots and orange mushrooms with yellow dots. There's a tall, bent tree wrapped in red and white like a candy cane that Holly recognizes from the corner of the coffee shop, and the whole church has been draped in colored lights. There are oversized flower pots filled with sand that hold giant lollipops on sticks standing up like flowers. And standing at the top of the steps with a huge grin on his face is Cap Duncan, his shoulder-length white hair pulled back and tucked under a top hat. He's wearing a long, purple velvet jacket with a bow tie, which Holly knows that Ellen has ordered in specifically for him to wear to a special event they've been planning to hold at the coffee shop that month anyway. It's all perfect.

Kitta slides her feet out of her flip-flops and holds her arms out as her bridesmaids help her into her sparkly yellow heels. They look remarkably like Dorothy's red slippers in *The Wizard of Oz*, but rather than the color of blood or roses, they're in a hue more reminiscent of butter or sunshine.

Cap comes down the steps and offers a hand, which Kitta takes. "Your father is waiting just inside the chapel," he says quietly, smiling at the bride. With strong, certain steps, Kitta walks up to the door of the chapel and drops the hem of her gown. The heavy sequins and beads of the dress land on the wood.

In short order, the four bridesmaids have put on their own heels and followed suit, standing behind Kitta as she takes a deep breath.

"We should let them go first," Cap says to Kitta, giving gentle direction to the dazed bride. She steps aside so that the other women can make their entrance.

Holly comes up behind Kitta and bends forward to straighten her dress and make sure it's hanging just so. "You look incredible!" she says to Cap as she reaches out and touches the sleeve of his purple jacket.

Cap winks at her. "Let's get this show on the road," he says. The soft guitar music inside the chapel pauses, and as Holly peers through the open doorway, she can see Joe Sacamano sitting on the edge of a stool in white linen pants and a red and white striped boat shirt. He's wearing a newsboy hat and white suspenders with red polka dots. With a wink in her direction, he shifts gears and starts an instrumental version of "Going to the Chapel." Holly smiles at him.

Kitta's father steps up to the threshold and offers an arm to his daughter, his eyes filling with happy tears as he escorts her down the short aisle. The pews are filled with the wedding guests, and most have gotten on board with the impromptu change in theme. The men are wearing the silly, patterned bow ties that Ellen and Carrie-Anne have been selling all month at Mistletoe Morning Brew, and the women have all borrowed from the pile of crazy scarves and hats that the islanders have pitched in for the occasion. Everyone looks zany and colorful as they turn to watch Kitta's smiling face.

Cap has made his way to the front of the chapel by walking up the side of the small room, and now he stands before the wedding party and guests. Deacon and his groomsmen are at one side, and Kitta's bridesmaids are at the other as the bride approaches. Her father delivers her to Deacon with tears in his eyes and he puts a kiss on his daughter's cheek before going to sit with her mother in the front row of the chapel.

Joe plays the rest of the song and then lets it trail off.

"Welcome, welcome," Cap says in his deep voice, looking around at each person in the chapel. "Today we have the pleasure of witnessing the joining of two lives. Of taking part in the start of a magical adventure between two beautiful people..."

Holly stands near the entrance to the chapel, watching from

outside. The photographer that Kitta's hired to capture the wedding is kneeling on one side of the chapel, quietly getting shots of the bride and groom as they face one another and hold each other's hands. The whole scene is framed by the doorway, which is ringed in colorful lights.

All the work that Holly and Bonnie have put in to make this wedding happen may have been sidelined by the leaked photographs, by Coco's meddling, and by a drastic, last minute theme change, but in the end, it's clear from looking at the happy couple that this—this moment right here—is the most important part of the whole thing. As Holly watches Kitta's beaming face and feels her love and joy, she realizes that all of her controlling, demanding behavior leading up to the event was just her way of trying to manage the emotions that go along with marrying the man of your dreams.

Will I ever have this? Holly wonders. She folds her arms across her chest as an unexpected breeze sweeps up from behind her and touches the bare skin of her arms and legs. Her short sundress billows around her tanned thighs. *Will I ever stand at that altar and look into the eyes of someone who completes me?* It's a lonely feeling to know that it might never happen for her, and Holly swallows the lump that rises in her throat as she tries to imagine herself holding the hands of a man she'll love forever as she pledges herself to him. Maybe it'll happen. Maybe it won't. She shifts from one sandaled foot to the other as Deacon says his vows to Kitta.

Cap is about to ask Kitta to pledge her vows when the sound of sudden, driving rain comes out of nowhere. Holly turns in surprise to look behind her. The sky has closed up again, the clouds folding in over the sun breaks she'd seen not long before. From the gray comes a downpour so torrential that the papier-mâché mushrooms immediately start to wilt and fall apart. The rain falls onto the sand and pelts the palm trees strung with holiday lights. The decorations on the golf cart drip with rain, and the pinwheels fixed to its sides spin uncontrollably like windmills in a hurricane, spitting off water as they turn frantically.

Holly wants to laugh at the way things are turning out, but she's too afraid of Kitta's response. She peers back into the church, hoping that the rain hasn't interrupted the vows. But it has, and the entire wedding party and its guests are turned to face the doorway. Their faces are amused and mirthful as they watch the rivers of water stream from the eaves of the chapel.

When Holly sees their smiling faces, she releases her own breath and laughs out loud. In a way, it's perfect. All of it. And with their guests turned to the doorway to point at the sudden storm, Kitta and Deacon lean in to sneak a kiss before Cap has even pronounced them husband and wife.

Holly smiles to herself. It *is* perfect—crazy and fun and unexpected and perfect. Just like Kitta wanted it to be.

15

THE BEACH RECEPTION HAS QUICKLY BEEN MOVED TO MAIN STREET. Holly's got to hand it to Coco: in a pinch, she makes rapid decisions and carries things out, and for that, Holly is grateful.

The tiki torches from the beach have been moved and set up under the heavy shelter of the palm trees, and the rain has let up enough to be re-classified from a storm to a light drizzle. The guests have been ferried the short distance from the chapel to the sidewalks of Main Street, and the proprietor of every shop on the street has switched on the holiday lights that decorate their buildings year-round. Most of the wedding party is standing around inside the open bar of Jack Frosty's, and the women have changed back into their flip-flops.

"Holly!" Kitta calls out with a wave. She's got a cold drink in one hand, and her hair had been swept up into a damp bun after she got caught in the rain with Deacon during a post-ceremony photograph.

Holly makes her way through the crowd of people still wearing bowties and colorful scarves. "Congratulations," she says, leaning in to hug the bride. "I wish you both all the best."

"This is perfect," Kitta says into her ear as she holds her close, embracing her with one thin, toned arm. "I love all of it."

As the women stand there, a group of wedding guests and groomsmen make their way across the street, hopping over puddles on the way to Cap's shop to buy a few celebratory cigars. Kitta's mom and her aunt are strolling down the sidewalk with linked arms, each holding a cup of coffee from Mistletoe Morning Brew, which Ellen and Carrie-Anne have opened so that guests can drop in as they please for non-alcoholic drinks. The yellow cupcakes covered in candies are on a tall, multi-leveled silver cake stand inside Mistletoe Morning Brew, and several of the guests are holding the tiny cakes with the paper peeled back as they bite into the lemon and raspberry flavored confections.

"I'm just so happy we pulled this off." Kitta holds up her hand with her impressive wedding ring turned towards Holly as proof. The giant yellow diamond on a gold band glints under the lights of Jack Frosty's. "We did it!"

Deacon drapes an arm around the newly minted Mrs. Avaloy's shoulders as he comes up behind Kitta. "We did, my love. We did it," he confirms, planting a kiss on her cheek. "You got your fun wedding and I got my gorgeous wife."

Holly is about to congratulate them again when she spots Kate-lynn and Jake walking into Jack Frosty's with Logan and Owen in front of them. The boys look chagrined.

"Excuse me," she says, touching Deacon lightly on the arm of his rolled-up dress shirt. He's already taken off his jacket and lost his tie. "I see someone I need to talk to."

"Hi," Holly says to the foursome as they walk up the steps to the bar. "How are things?"

Katelynn gives her son a sharp look. "Logan," she prompts. Jake wisely stays silent and stands to the side.

"Holly," Logan says, not meeting her eye. "It was me and Owen who took the pictures."

"And?" Katelynn says. She puts both hands on her hips.

"And we're sorry. We didn't think it through."

Owen runs a hand through his hair. He looks guilty as sin. "Yeah, sorry," he adds. "We were just having fun."

Holly looks back and forth between the two boys. "How much did *Glitter and Stars* pay you?"

Logan can't bring himself to meet Holly's gaze. After an awkward moment, his mother puts a hand on his shoulder and squeezes. "A thousand dollars for each picture they used," he admits.

Holly tries to add up the number of photos she's seen of the island, but before she can come up with a total, Owen clears his throat.

"Nine thousand so far."

"Nine thousand dollars?" Holly looks back and forth between the boys. "Are you serious?"

"Yeah." Logan looks at Kitta and Deacon across the room. They're busy laughing with some of their guests. "I'm supposed to apologize."

Holly knows how lucky the boys are that Kitta and Deacon are currently basking in a rosy post-nuptial glow, and that the wedding came off without a hitch. "You probably should," she agrees.

With deep reticence, the boys cross the bar together. They approach the bride and groom and stand in front of them with their backs to Holly and Jake and Katelynn.

"I had no idea," Katelynn says to Holly. There is an apology in her voice.

"Hey, they're sixteen." Holly shakes her head. "At a certain age, kids do what they're going to do and they get smart enough to do it without their parents knowing."

A smile spreads across Katelynn's face. "Remember that summer we snuck out and got drunk on the beach with Mrs. Agnelli's grandsons?"

The memory comes flooding back to Holly and she laughs at the image of her fifteen-year-old self lying on a moonlit beach with Katelynn Pillory and Henry and Brock Agnelli. They'd shared a pilfered bottle of rum from the Agnelli's unlocked bar cabinet. Holly had drunk enough rum that night to float a ship full of pirates all the way from Australia to Antarctica. It was years before she'd ever touched rum again, no matter what it was mixed with.

"I do remember," Holly says, watching the boys as Deacon looks at them gravely. They are clearly explaining the situation, and Kitta's face reflects her emotions as she listens to their confession. "There are so many bad choices to make when you're young, aren't there?"

"And fortunately, so many opportunities to live them down," Katelynn adds.

"Wait," Jake says, finally speaking up. He's got a wry grin on his face. "You two snuck out together and got drunk with *Maria's grandsons*?"

The women laugh, remembering the sloppy kisses they'd shared that night with Henry and Brock. Neither had been terribly enamored of the younger Agnellis, but they'd been the only boys available on an island with very little chance of visitors, and the girls had drunkenly kissed them like they were a couple of young Hollywood stars who'd been shipwrecked on their shores.

"Yeah." Holly's face is almost disbelieving as she remembers Henry Agnelli asking if she'd be his first kiss. "We did. And when my grandpa found us on the beach at sunrise, I'd thrown up twice, and Katelynn and Brock Agnelli were—"

"Oh, let's not go down that path," Katelynn interrupts, waving both hands in warning to make Holly stop talking. "Gross, gross, gross. He had braces. Just no."

"Wait..." Jake is entirely amused. "You two *made out* with these guys?"

Holly is about to answer when Logan and Owen walk up to them, mercifully interrupting this impromptu trip down memory lane.

"How'd it go?" Katelynn asks her son.

Owen speaks first: "They said they were disappointed, but that it wasn't the first time things got leaked about either of them."

"And?" Katelynn asks, watching Logan's face.

"And they said that they would forgive us if we'd promise to take the money and put it into our college funds, and not to take any pictures of today and sell them."

"That's it?" Katelynn frowns. She looks at Holly.

Holly was definitely expecting worse, given Kitta's regular freakouts leading up to the wedding.

"Deacon said he was going to have his financial advisor call you to make sure it actually happens, but yeah, I think that's it." Logan shrugs. Even he looks surprised to have gotten off so easily.

"Wow," Jake says. He gives Deacon a nod from across the room. "Classy. I'm impressed."

Holly is satisfied that everyone is okay with the outcome of the situation, so she delicately extricates herself from the group before Jake can bring up Henry and Brock Agnelli again. That's one memory she's happy to leave in the past.

"Great wedding," says Kitta's friend Nylie. She reaches out a hand and touches Holly's arm as she passes. "This whole thing was just as crazy as Kitta is."

Holly pauses for a second to chat with Nylie and the other bridesmaids. "Hey, she seems happy with it, so that's all that matters."

"How did you ever come up with the idea to turn it into a *Willy Wonka*-themed wedding?" one of the other bridesmaids asks. She puts a straw between her red lips and takes a sip of her mixed drink.

"It was genius. Totally," says another one of the women.

"Well, our resources here are somewhat limited," Holly admits, "but we've got great people on this island. And when we put our heads together, we can usually pull off anything."

Two of the women raise their glasses to Holly in toast, and she smiles as she shoulders her way through the full bar, waving at Buckhunter as she takes the steps down onto Main Street. Now that everything has come together and the wedding is done, she's ready to take off her sandals and call it a day. The revelry has officially veered into "shoes off and third drink in hand" territory, and people are leaning against one another in laughter and sitting on the wet curb in party clothes because they're having a such a good time.

Holly smiles at the triplets as she makes her way to her fully decorated pink golf cart, then slowly cruises up Main Street like she's in no hurry at all. In truth, she can't wait to get home, and as soon as she bumps over the edge of the paved road and onto Cinnamon Lane she presses the gas pedal down, zipping through the thick trees on this quiet part of the island.

Her bungalow appears at the edge of the road and Holly swings her cart onto the long driveway, crunching over shells and fallen leaves. The house is dark and quiet, and Buckhunter's bungalow next door is only lit by his porch light. Holly stops the cart and finds the extension cord in the semi-darkness of early evening, plugging it into the back of her cart so that it'll charge overnight.

"Hey, buddy," Holly says, kneeling down in the grass to greet Pucci as he steps off the porch. "Did you miss me?" The dog rubs his cold, wet nose against her cheek. Holly nuzzles him, running her hands over his silky ears. "I'm home now. Let's get you some dinner."

Inside, Holly turns on lights as she goes. She drops her sandals by the kitchen doorway and pads across the tile floor, feeling the cool stone beneath the soles of her feet. Putting on a wedding—especially a star-studded one—has been overwhelming. She'd basically returned from Europe early in the summer after her ill-fated trip with River and dived headfirst into planning a wedding that had veered so far off course that it barely resembled its earliest incarnations. But it's over now, and that's the most important part.

Holly dumps a can of wet dog food into Pucci's bowl and sets it on the floor next to his water dish. Being home alone after days of swimming through crowds of people and putting out fires is like leaving a concert with your ears ringing. The silence in the bungalow is golden, and Holly walks through the darkening rooms with only her thoughts to keep her company. Packing Coco off to the empty bungalow across the island and taking her own house back is the best choice Holly has made in a long time.

In the living room is a stack of CDs next to her stereo; she picks out an 80s compilation and slides it into the player. A Tears For Fears song comes on. Holly heads down the hall to her bedroom, pulling her dress off over her head as she walks. She hums along to "Head Over Heels" while she picks out a pair of cut off shorts and a stained pink tank top that says KEY WEST across the chest in block letters. It's been a while since she's worked on her shell wall on the lanai, and she quickly decides to do that instead of sitting down to a quiet dinner alone.

With a window open and the music filtering out into the dusky purple evening, Holly mixes a batch of mortar and pulls out the bucket of shells she's always adding to on her beach walks. She pulls out the broken shells and sets them in a pile on the table, then lines up the ones she likes the looks of so that she can affix them to her wall.

It had started as a crazy idea one hot summer evening, but Holly's slowly worked on the project over the past couple of years, adding bits and pieces on nights when she can't sleep. She's gotten more than half of the wall covered at this point, and she doesn't really care how long it takes to finish. It's the process of being outside with her thoughts in the evening that she loves, and she's worked through tons of things in her mind as she's spent nights methodically spreading mortar on the wall and pushing shells into place like puzzle pieces she's trying to connect.

Holly loses track of time as she sings along to the music, and she doesn't even realize when two and a half hours have passed and Pucci's joined her on the lanai. His head is on his paws as he watches her feet moving across the tiles.

"Hey, kid," comes a voice from the darkness outside. "Can I join you?"

"Of course. Come on in." Holly doesn't even turn around from the wall.

Buckhunter unlatches the screen door and lets himself onto the lanai. "You disappeared on us."

When Holly turns to face him, she's got a streak of the cement-colored mixture smeared across her smooth cheek. Her hair has gone frizzy around her damp forehead, and she swipes at her brow with the back of one dirty hand.

"I was ready to be alone for a bit," she says, picking up the glass of water she's brought out with her. The ice has long since melted. "Want something to drink?"

"Yeah," Buckhunter says. "But let me pour. You keep working."

Holly says nothing as he walks through the door into her kitchen.

She picks out another shell and presses it onto the wall, holding it there as she counts so that it'll hold fast to the mortar.

"Arnold Palmers okay?" Buckhunter calls out through the open window.

"Absolutely."

He's back in less than three minutes with two tall glasses of ice tea and lemonade. He sets them down on the tabletop ceremoniously. "For my favorite niece."

Holly gives a quiet laugh as she picks up the cold drink gratefully. "For your only niece."

"That I know of." Buckhunter winks at her over the edge of his glass as he drinks. He's sitting in a chair, one foot crossed over his knee as he appraises her. "I've realized it's never too late in life for surprises."

"Good point." Holly wipes her hands on the front of her beat-up looking denim shorts and sits in a chair across from her uncle. She takes another long drink of her Arnold Palmer.

It's only been a little more than a year since she and Buckhunter had realized they were related, and he's quickly become a hugely important part of Holly's life and her family history. Their formerly antagonistic relationship morphed nearly overnight into one where Buckhunter acts more as protector and friend, and Holly has come to appreciate that he'd been invited to live near her by her grandfather for just that purpose.

"So what's with you leaving a Hollywood wedding to glue shells to a wall?" Buckhunter gazes out into the darkness beyond the lanai, drink held in both hands.

Holly shrugs. "I'd just had enough of it. I did what I needed to do, and everyone seemed happy. I figured someone would call me if they needed me."

"True, true." Buckhunter nods. "Everyone left my bar about an hour ago and moved over to the B&B."

"Oh?" Holly's eyebrows raise. "Are they done for the night?"

"No, there was talk of meeting at the pool for champagne and cigars. I think they were just ready to change out of their dress clothes and party more freely."

Holly sets her drink on the table. "You think I should go supervise? I mean, people are drinking at the pool—that doesn't seem particularly safe."

"I think you're fine," he assures her. "Maggie is at the front desk to make sure everyone has what they need, and Cap went along with the wedding party and said he'd keep an eye on things."

They sit in silence for a moment as Holly decides what to do. Cap's been sober now for a while, and she trusts that he'll be the voice of reason and the eyes of the island in case things get out of hand at the B&B's pool. "Okay," she says. "I can always change and do a drive by in a bit to make sure things are fine."

Another lull falls over the lanai as Holly and Buckhunter eye her handiwork on the shell wall. She takes a drink of her iced tea and lemonade and reaches out with her foot to give Pucci's thick, golden fur a scratch with her hot pink polished toes.

"So what's the plan?" Holly finally asks without preamble.

"The plan?"

"You and Fiona. Wedding plans. I've been so busy that I haven't gotten to talk to her much this week."

"Yeah, wedding plans..." Buckhunter's eyes glaze over as he thinks about the question.

"Last I heard, you were avoiding the topic altogether whenever she brought it up."

Buckhunter looks uncomfortable at the prospect of discussing his wedding plans with his niece again, but he takes a deep breath and sets his drink on the table. "It's just something I've never considered," he admits.

"A wedding?"

"Being married at all. I've been a happy bachelor for fifty years, and I had every intention of staying this way."

Holly isn't sure she wants to pose the question, but she forges ahead anyway. "So why did you say yes?" She asks gently, but the words sit between them like an accusation rather than a simple question.

"Because I love Fiona," he says. "And I want her to be happy."

Holly folds her hands over her stomach and sits back in the chair. "But will it make *you* happy to be married? Be honest."

Buckhunter takes a moment. A look of realization comes over his face and he nods slowly. "Yeah, to Fiona. It would make me happy if she was Mrs. Buckhunter." He smiles widely. "Whoa, I haven't thought of her that way yet."

"Dr. Buckhunter," Holly corrects. "But do you think she'd even change her name?"

"I'm not sure. That's how much I've been avoiding the topic, I guess."

Holly reaches out and puts a hand on her uncle's arm. "You should probably talk to her. Seriously."

"You're right." Buckhunter pushes back his chair and stands up. "I've been acting like an idiot, and Fiona deserves better."

He opens the screen door to the lanai and lets himself out into the dark yard that separates their two bungalows.

"Night," she says to him as the door latches shut behind him.

"Night, Hol." She can hear his voice and his footsteps even though she can't see him anymore. "Thanks, kid."

Holly keeps her hands laced together on her stomach and leans her head back on the chair. The ceiling fan on the lanai spins overhead, stirring the air as she contemplates her shell wall. She'll finish it eventually, but not tonight.

"Come on, Pooch," she says, making a clicking sound with her tongue. "Let's take one more run by the B&B tonight to make sure everything is good there, huh?" The dog stands up on all four legs and follows his mistress with a lazy, lumbering gait as she meanders through the house, slipping her feet back into her shoes. "Then we can put a wrap on this Hollywood wedding business and get back to real life."

16

"SO THEY'RE OFF, HUH?" CARRIE-ANNE HANDS HOLLY AN ICED CARAMEL latte over the counter of Mistletoe Morning Brew.

"Yes, they're off. We got everyone onto the boat just now and we're working on cleaning up the B&B, which will take a good portion of the day."

"You did good work, Mayor," Ellen adds, breezing through the coffee shop with an armful of paper to-go cups in her arms. "That wedding was as fun as a carnival ride at a county fair."

Holly nods and takes a sip of the cold coffee. "Thanks again for letting us use everything—we couldn't have done it without you."

The women have sacrificed a majority of their shop's decorations, and all that's left are a few movie posters, some copies of the book, and an assortment of jars of colorful candy that they didn't use for the reception. Carrie-Anne glances around at the depleted decor with a shrug.

"Not to worry, milady," she says with a wink. "It's nearly November, and we'll start from scratch with something new."

Holly waves at the women as she heads back out onto Main Street. The sun is already high in the sky at eleven o'clock, and she's feeling a deep sense of relief that the wedding is officially behind her.

Of course there's no time for a real break, but she's got her bikini on under her white summer dress just in case the opportunity for a swim in the sea presents itself.

"Holly!" Vance Guy pokes his head out of the bookstore as she walks by. "Good morning!"

"Hey, Vance." She pauses in front of the tall windows to his shop and looks in. "How's business?"

"Not bad," he says, putting both hands on his waist as he looks up and down the street. "I've got regulars stopping by for newspapers and magazines, and I've been moving books at a reasonable clip."

"Glad to hear it," Holly says. "And how are things at home?" She knows that his mother living there is a bone of contention between Vance and Calista, and she bites her lip in anticipation of getting mediocre news.

"Great! No, things are really good." Vance nods. "Calista is thrilled that I'm working because she knows it makes me feel more focused, my mom is glad not to have me underfoot all day while she looks after the boys, and I get plenty of time to work on my novel between customers," he says, nodding at the open laptop on his front counter. "Best of all worlds."

"That's great, Vance. Honestly." Holly swirls her coffee around in its plastic cup before she takes another drink of the sweet, cold beverage. "And I seriously love that we have a bookstore now. You and I should really talk about events together. Maybe we could do something big."

"You got anything in mind?"

Holly tips her head from side to side. "How about inviting a bunch of mystery writers to the island for an author event and turning it into a murder mystery weekend?"

Vance's eyes light up. "That would be *incredible*," he says, running one hand over his face as the idea percolates between them. "Did you just come up with that right now?"

Holly smiles. "Yeah. I saw that new James Patterson on your shelf and it came to mind."

"Brilliant. I love it. Let's do it."

"Okay," Holly laughs. "We'll talk more about it soon, okay?" She walks on past Tinsel & Tidings gift shop, where one of the triplets is sweeping the front walkway. Across the street, Iris and Emily Cafferkey are heading into Poinsettia Plaza for an appointment with Dr. Potts, and Holly blows Emily a kiss, which she returns with an excited wave.

"I'm back!" Holly walks through the empty lobby of the B&B. The washers and dryers are spinning in the distance, laundering the first of many loads of sheets and towels, and Katelynn Pillory appears in the doorway with a box in her arms.

"Hey, Holly," she says. They've hired Katelynn for the day to help get the B&B back in order for the construction workers by the end of the day, and Katelynn has left Logan and Owen in charge of looking after her grandfather.

"How are things?" Holly sets her drink on the front counter and logs into the computer at the desk.

"I'm just refilling all of the soaps and shampoos, and Bonnie and I have all the rooms completely stripped and ready for a deep clean."

"Fabulous." Holly moves the computer's mouse around as she consults the chart on the screen. The workers will be back on the island shortly, and she wants to have everything turned over as quickly as possible. "Let me check my voicemail really quickly and then I'll roll up my sleeves and get to work, okay?"

There's nothing new in her email or in her phone messages, so Holly leaves the office behind and loses herself in dusting, scrubbing, and vacuuming for the afternoon.

At some point, Coco sticks her head into one of the rooms and smirks at her daughter, who is on her knees in the bathroom. "One day you put on a wedding for two world-famous people, and the next day you're elbow deep in toilets. It's a glamorous life you lead."

Holly has a scrub brush in hand as she pauses and looks up at Coco. "Hey, I do what I have to do," she says. "When toilets need to be cleaned, I clean them. When fairy wings mysteriously go missing, I figure out some way to make a distressed bride happy again."

Coco scoffs. "Those fairy wings would have ruined the wedding."

"That's not the point." Holly stands up and pulls off the yellow rubber gloves that cover her hands. "The point is that you would come here under the guise of 'helping' me and then turn around and intentionally make things more difficult. Why would you do that?" She really should know the answer to this by now, but she's genuinely puzzled by her mother's need to make her life more challenging at every turn.

Coco shifts her weight from one foot to the other and folds her arms across her chest. She looks around the room and takes in the open windows, the stripped bed with its stark white mattress, and the basket of fresh linens on the dresser that's just been delivered by Katelynn.

"Well," she finally says. "I don't always think you know what you're doing."

"And how do *you* know what you're doing? You've never spent any amount of time on this island, and when you blow in here and start rearranging my life, all it does is tell the people around me that I'm incompetent. That I need my mother to step in and fix things."

Coco shrugs. "Maybe you do." Her words sound confrontational, but her tone is matter-of-fact.

"No, that's the thing, Coco. I *don't*."

"So we're back to this same tired old argument, huh?"

"What tired old argument?" Holly frowns and tosses the yellow gloves into the bathroom sink.

"The one where you tell me to get off your island because I never do anything for you."

"Mom," Holly says with exasperation. "I wouldn't even call that an argument. You being here always disrupts the flow of things, and you leaving is the only way my life gets back on track."

"Ouch." Coco usually takes whatever Holly throws at her with little to no show of emotions, but this statement actually causes her to visibly recoil. "I know we have our differences, but I always hope that at some point we'll manage to forge some sort of normal mother-daughter relationship..."

Holly's eyebrows go up. "I don't think anything about us is normal."

"True." Coco lets out a breath. "True." The women stand there in the unmade room for a minute, letting this sink in. "So you want me to go?"

Holly sighs heavily. "I just don't think this island is big enough for both of us," she admits.

Coco nods. "You're probably right. I'll head out as soon as I can make arrangements."

Holly watches her mother go, wishing for just a moment that she felt even a twinge of sadness. But she doesn't. Instead, she feels only relief. Her family on the island—including Buckhunter, who is actually family—is all she really needs. She pulls the fitted sheet from the basket on the dresser and holds onto the end as she flings it open and lets it settle on the bed. It's possible that she'll never find love on or off this island, and it's possible that she'll never come to terms with her mother, but doing what she loves in the place she loves most in the world is enough for Holly. It has to be.

"Welcome back!" Holly has purchased two six-packs of soda from the triplets and set them in a cooler full of ice on the B&B's front porch. The construction workers have returned right on schedule to continue work on the dock for Island Paradise Excursions, and after a full day of travel, they're happy to be back at the B&B.

"Holly," says the foreman. "Good to see you." He bends forward and grabs a can of Coke from the cooler, holding it up to her to say thanks. "We've got a new crew member," he adds, raising his chin in the direction of a young guy in a beat-up blue hat that looks a lot like the Yankees cap on Holly's own head. "This is Miguel. He's replacing Todd, who got into a motorcycle accident this weekend."

"Is Todd okay?" Holly's brow creases.

"Yeah, he's fine. Just hurt his back and needs to sit out a few weeks. The worst part is that his wife is nagging him endlessly about selling the motorcycle, but...whatcha gonna do?"

"Well, I'm glad he's okay. And welcome to the island, Miguel." Holly smiles at the guy who's standing at the foot of the stairs. His skin is a rich mahogany from the hours spent in the sun, and from under the brim of his cap, she can see two beautiful eyes the color of amber.

"Thanks," he says, moving his duffel bag from one shoulder to the other. "Glad to be here."

In short order, Holly has the men checked back into the rooms they'd occupied before the wedding. As she's showing Miguel to the suite he'll be staying in, he clears his throat.

"This is a beautiful island," he says, standing behind Holly's right shoulder as she unlocks the door to his room and pushes it open. "The guys tell me that you're the mayor."

"Mayor, majority owner, and longest resident of Christmas Key," Holly says, ticking off the list on her fingers. "My grandparents bought the island when I was a baby and they raised me here."

"And since you're the longest resident of the island, that means they're..." His words trail off.

"They've passed," Holly confirms. "And now my uncle lives here as well and my mother visits occasionally."

"So it's a real family thing. I admire that." Miguel nods firmly. "Family is everything."

His words strike a pang in Holly's heart, especially given the conversation that she just had with her mother that afternoon. "Yes, family is important. And where is yours?" Holly shifts the topic to him, since he doesn't seem overly eager to go into the room just yet.

"All over," Miguel says. When he smiles, a dimple caves in on his left cheek. "I'm from Puerto Rico originally, and my mom still lives in Miami, where she raised me and my siblings."

"Our island's only police officer is from Miami," Holly says, handing Miguel his room key. "I'm sure you'll meet Jake soon."

"Looking forward to it."

There's a lull in the conversation as Holly waits for Miguel to walk into his room. Instead, he just smiles at her, watching her face.

"Well, we're happy to have you on Christmas Key. Everyone here is amazing and we've loved having the crew here. I'm sure once you all shower and change, the guys are probably going to head to Jack Frosty's or to the Ho Ho Hideaway. It's kind of become an evening routine."

Miguel laughs. "That sounds amazing right now."

The sun has already left deep creases in the skin around Miguel's eyes and they make his eyes crinkle merrily.

"Hey, Cruz," another of the construction workers pokes his head out into the hall and addresses Miguel. "You gonna shower, or just stand there stinking up the hallway all night? We're headed over to the bar for fish tacos and beer in ten minutes."

The door closes again and Miguel gives a laugh. "I'm holding everyone up. I better get showered."

"Right. Don't keep a group of hungry men waiting," Holly says, pointing at him and lowering her chin. "They'll push you off the dock and into the water tomorrow as payback."

"Hey, thanks again for putting us up here," Miguel says, finally heading into the room with his duffel bag. "I already feel like I never want to leave."

Holly heads back down the hall, ready to check her email one more time and then call it a night as far as work is concerned. Coco has informed her that she's made arrangements to leave the next day, and every room in the B&B is back in order. Things are starting to feel right in Holly's world again.

"You busy?" Fiona comes into the B&B as Holly is walking back to the office.

"No, I'm actually wrapping things up here."

"Wanna get something to eat?"

Holly flips over her wrist and consults her watch. "Sure. Can I meet you in ten minutes? I have a couple of things to do before I close up shop here."

"You got it, Mayor. See you in ten at Jack Frosty's. I'm ordering a drink while I wait for you."

Holly has everything shut down for the evening and Maggie Sutter is perched behind the front desk with a thick romance novel and a can of 7Up by the time she's ready to head to Jack Frosty's. If any of the construction workers need anything overnight, Maggie is there to see to it.

"Hey, hey," Buckhunter says, lifting a hand in the air when Holly enters the bar. She smiles at him and joins Fiona at a table near the open wall that looks out onto Main Street.

"We're drinking margaritas tonight and eating fish tacos," Fiona says decisively, setting a plastic menu upright and wedging it between the salt and pepper shakers.

"Oh? You've decided for us?" Holly twists her hair into a bun and wraps an elastic around it as she gets comfortable in the chair.

"It's on me tonight, so I went ahead and pulled the trigger. I hope that's fine."

"Of course it's fine, Fee. You know I'll eat pretty much anything." Holly puts her feet up on the seat of the chair across from hers and folds her arms across her stomach. "But what's the occasion?"

"I wanted to thank you."

"For what?" Holly laughs. Buckhunter drops two margaritas off at the table, setting them on square cocktail napkins.

"For getting his butt in gear," Fiona says, leaning forward over the table and talking quietly as Buckhunter retreats. "He said you two had a good long talk the other night and he realized how stupid he's been and how much he's avoided the topic of the wedding."

"Oh, that." Holly slides her drink closer and stirs the frozen margarita with its hot pink straw. "It was nothing, really. Just a little neighborly chat."

"It was more than neighborly, Hol. You know he'd never listen to just anyone. You're family, and you got through to him." She lifts her glass off the table and reaches forward to clink it against Holly's. "And for that, I'm eternally grateful."

"Hey, you're welcome," Holly says. She gets a brain freeze from the very first sip of the margarita. Holly hits her forehead a few times with the heel of her hand as she squints.

"Now, if that drink hasn't killed your brain, I wanted to ask you something else."

Holly stops smacking her own head and looks at Fiona. "What's up?"

A happy flush spreads across Fiona's face. "Would you be my maid of honor?"

"Oh, Fee!" Holly sets her drink down and reaches for her best friend's hands across the table. "You know I will! When is it? What are we wearing? Do you need help planning?"

"It's going to be small," Fiona says, squeezing Holly's hands with fingers that are still cold from holding her margarita glass. "So let's not go crazy."

"You got it," Holly says excitedly. "We'll stay totally sane."

The women are busy hatching a plan and talking possible details when the construction workers walk into Jack Frosty's. Miguel gives Holly a nod as he trails behind the other men. Since it's his first night on the island, he doesn't have the lay of the land quite as well as the other guys, so he quietly follows suit and pulls up a chair at a long table across the room from Holly and Fiona.

"One of those guys is making eyes at you," Fiona says. She's dumping salsa onto her fish taco, but she glances up at Holly from under her lashes. "What's that about?"

Holly's already bitten into her soft taco and she chews before answering. "That's Miguel. He just joined the crew because another of the guys got hurt and couldn't come back."

"Cute," Fiona says, giving him an approving look. "He looks young."

Holly shrugs with one shoulder. "I only talked to him for a few minutes. He said he liked it here already."

It's clear that Fiona wants to keep giving her a hard time, but Jake and Katelynn walk in together and Holly's attention is dragged in another direction. Jake pulls out a chair for Katelynn and waits while she sits down.

"Date?" Fiona asks before she bites into her own fish taco.

"Dunno. No one called to tell me." Holly's words are sarcastic, but her tone doesn't quite match. True sarcasm would have made it obvious that she didn't much care about seeing Jake and Katelynn together again, but there's an edge to her voice that gives her away: she still cares. At least a little.

"Hmmm," Fiona says, taking another bite. She can see on her friend's face that there's something there, but she wisely leaves it alone. "So have you heard from River lately?"

Holly rolls her eyes. "Are you on a mission to make me order a second margarita?"

Fiona laughs and reaches for her drink. "Hey, you've put me on the spot a lot recently with wedding talk, so I thought turnabout was fair play here."

"Ugh." Holly takes a giant bite of her taco and scans the bar with her eyes, ignoring the question that Fiona's thrown out there. There's really not much to say about River anyway. Sure, they've had some contact since she fled Paris and left him there, but what else is there to say, really? They realized that things weren't going to work the way they'd hoped, and it was time to move on.

"Looks like your friend is coming over," Fiona says, motioning with her eyes. She wipes her hands on her napkin.

Holly looks up as Miguel approaches their table. "Hey, sorry to interrupt."

"Hey, Miguel." She smiles and takes a sip of her untouched water. "This is Fiona Potts. She's the only doctor on the island. Fiona, this is Miguel."

"Nice to meet you." Fiona smiles up at him winningly. "Holly told me you're ready to set down roots here and become a permanent resident." Holly kicks Fiona under the table. "I'm kidding," Fiona says with a laugh. "No one decides that quickly that they want to live on an island in the middle of nowhere."

Miguel smiles and puts both hands into the pockets of his shorts. "I'm actually kind of drifting now, and this seems like paradise to me."

"So what else are you guys up to tonight? Headed to the Ho Ho after this?" Fiona jabs her straw around in the slush of her quickly-melting margarita.

"I don't know." Miguel's hair is still wet from his shower, and his deep dimple creases his cheek again when he smiles. "I'm along for the ride."

"If you hit the Ho Ho," Fiona advises, "make sure Joe Sacamano pours you some of his homemade rum!"

"Will do," Miguel says. "Enjoy your dinner, ladies. Nice to meet you, Fiona."

As he walks away, Fiona twists a strawberry blonde curl around one finger and watches him. "Cute. And not shy."

"Young, and a temporary visitor on the island," Holly counters.

"Well, he seems to want to make an impression on you."

Holly shrugs. "He's just being friendly. And so am I."

"Mmmhmmm." Fiona purses her lips like she doesn't quite believe this.

"So," Holly says with a wicked grin. "Let's talk more about your wedding..."

17

"YOU'VE GOT SOME NERVE!" MARIA AGNELLI IS STANDING ON THE CURB in front of Mistletoe Morning Brew, pointing a crooked finger at Idora Blaine-Guy. Idora's fists are on her hips and her chest is puffed out so that it's dangerously close to the maroon-tipped edge of Mrs. Agnelli's fingertip. "You aren't the only widow around here, so you don't get to swoop in and gather up sympathy points from all the men. That's not how it works."

"Mrs. Agnelli!" Holly leaves her purse on the seat of her golf cart and breaks into a jog down Main Street. "What's going on here?" The idea of physically inserting herself between the two women is ridiculous, but from the look in their eyes, it seems entirely possible that fisticuffs are on the horizon.

"This lady comes fluttering down here from *Canada*," Maria Agnelli says, changing her tone when she says 'Canada' to make it sound like a filthy word. "And she thinks she can just have her pick of the men."

Idora huffs and turns to Holly. "I think no such thing," she protests. "There's not a single one of these men I'd take on—even as a gift."

"Oh, so now our men aren't good enough for you?" Mrs. Agnelli's finger finally makes contact with Idora's chest and Idora takes a step back, a look of incredulity passing over her face.

"No, no, no!" Calista Guy comes flying out of the door to Poinsettia Plaza. From her perch at the front desk of the salon, she's spotted the commotion just outside the coffee shop. "You all press pause on this *right now!*" she calls out, looking both ways for golf carts as she crosses the street.

"This woman is crazy," Idora says to her daughter-in-law, pointing right back at Maria Agnelli. "Throwing unfounded accusations around like she has any business with me."

"Mama," Calista says, catching her breath as she slows down. "Now let's calm down." There is a noticeable flicker of disapproval on Idora's face when her son's wife calls her Mama. "Mrs. Agnelli is a sweet woman."

"Sweet, my foot!" Idora frowns. "I've done nothing wrong here and she's poking at me with her finger."

"Where are the boys?" Calista asks, scanning the sidewalk for her twins. From inside the coffee shop, four little fists pound the window. "Oh, there they are," she waves at Mexi and Mori. "Now what's going on here?"

"I got the boys all set up in the coffee shop with a treat," Idora says, glancing at her grandsons. "And I told them I'd be back in a minute."

"And then this harlot swooped right in," Maria Agnelli interrupts, "and tried to steal poor Heddie's man." As she says this, Cap steps out of A Sleigh Full of Books and right into the fray. "Isn't that right, Cap?" Maria presses him. "Didn't she come right up and ask you to carry her box?"

Cap chuckles. "I'm afraid it's not nearly as scandalous as it sounds, Maria," he says, putting a large hand on the older woman's shoulder. "Heddie and Idora are friends, and all she did was ask me to help Vance move a few heavy boxes inside the bookstore. That's all there is to it."

"Mrs. Agnelli," Holly says, putting out her hands and encouraging

Maria to move towards her. "It sounds like a big misunderstanding. Idora isn't making moves on anyone's man, and all Cap is doing is helping Vance set up the bookstore. No harm, no foul."

"Come on, Mama," Calista says, motioning with her hand for her mother-in-law to follow her into the coffee shop. "Let's talk to the boys and see what you all are doing this afternoon." The two women disappear into the shop and the bells on the door tinkle behind them, but not before Idora shoots a mistrustful look in Mrs. Agnelli's direction.

"Things got a bit carried away out here, huh?" Holly says calmly, wrapping an arm around Mrs. Agnelli's shoulders. "I love that you're looking out for Heddie, but maybe there's a better way to approach someone than a showdown on Main Street at high noon."

"Don't you talk down to me, Holly Baxter," Mrs. Agnelli says, shrugging her bony shoulder to shake Holly's arm off. "I've known you since you were knee-high to a bug's ass, and you don't need to tell me how to handle things."

"Okay, okay," Holly says placatingly. "I just don't want Jake to have to come and cuff anyone on such a beautiful day."

"You won't be laughing and telling jokes when she makes off with your friend's man," Mrs. Agnelli says, holding her small, straw purse close to her chest with both hands.

"What are you talking about?" Holly stops walking and turns to face Mrs. Agnelli. Maria is about eight or nine inches shorter than Holly, and the years have forced her knobby frame into a slight stoop.

"I'm talking about Bonnie. That tart," she hooks a thumb in the direction of the coffee shop, "was dancing with Wyatt Bender all evening at the Ho Ho last Friday, and the redhead was nowhere in sight."

Holly scoffs. "Come on, Mrs. Agnelli. Wyatt isn't Bonnie's boyfriend, and he can dance with whomever he chooses."

"Hmph," Maria says, shaking her head. "Don't you be naive, missy. There are some lines you don't cross, and that broad is crossing them."

Holly sighs and gives another glance at the coffee shop. Idora and

Calista are still safely inside with the twins, so Holly steers Mrs. Agnelli towards her hot pink golf cart and settles her into the passenger seat. "Let me run you home, okay? It's about lunchtime anyway."

Maria's tone and mood are far more cantankerous than Holly is used to. "You think I'm cooking lunch for you, young lady? You can drop me home, but I'm not making pasta carbonara for *you* after you butted in and sided with that woman." She folds her arms like a petulant child.

"I'm not siding with her," Holly says, glancing over her left shoulder as she pulls onto the street. "I just don't want to see any blood shed on Main Street over a seventy-three year old man."

"Oh? Now his age has something to do with it? That sounds ageist, and I don't think that's the kind of attitude our mayor should have."

Holly sighs for what feels like the hundredth time. "No, I was just being funny. Or trying to." She swings her cart around a corner and slows down as they hit a bump in the sandy lane. She isn't sure what's gotten into Mrs. Agnelli.

"You can drop me here," Mrs. Agnelli says at the end of her driveway. "Just send an old woman on her way." She steps out of the cart with her purse clutched in both hands again. "Besides, you've got your own mother to deal with, and I hear she's been kicking up a fuss with Buckhunter. You might want to check on that."

"What?" Holly lets her foot off the brake and starts to roll forward. "What kind of fuss?"

"She had her nose right where it didn't belong last time I was at Jack Frosty's. Wouldn't hurt you to focus less on my business and more on your own." With her eyebrows raised, Mrs. Agnelli totters up to her front door while Holly leans on the steering wheel, lost in thought. *What is Coco up to now?* She finally puts her foot on the gas and eases back into the street. No time like the present to find out.

❄

COCO IS HAULING HER WHEELED SUITCASE DOWN THE FRONT STEPS OF the B&B when Holly gets back.

"Leaving?" Holly asks her mother. She parks her golf cart by the curb once again and gets out, taking her purse with her this time.

"The boat gets here in about thirty minutes." Coco gives the hardshell suitcase one more tug by its handle and it bumps onto the sidewalk. She sets it upright and faces Holly.

"So what's going on with you and Buckhunter?" Holly cuts right to to the chase. Not only is Coco's time limited, but there's no point in Holly tap dancing around an issue when it comes to her mother.

"Nothing is going on with me and Buckhunter." Coco pulls her Chanel sunglasses from the case in her purse and slides them onto her face. "Nothing at all."

Holly follows closely behind Coco as she starts to pull her suitcase towards the dock again. "That's not what I hear," she says.

There's no response as Coco shakes out her perfectly flat-ironed bob and holds her head high. She continues her hip-swaying walk down Main Street.

"Mom," Holly says firmly. She's not going to give up and let Coco walk away. "What are you stirring up with Buckhunter?" They're already past Jack Frosty's, and out of Buckhunter's earshot. "Do you want me to go back and ask him myself?"

Coco stops walking and turns around. "I'm not trying to sell the island, if that's what you're worried about." Coco's desire to sell Christmas Key and turn a profit is well documented.

"I'm not even sure whether I'm worried," Holly says. "I'm just curious. I know you and Buckhunter aren't that close, and when someone tells me I better get to the bottom of some discussion you two had, then I take that seriously."

Coco shakes her head and makes a face like she can't believe what she's hearing. "Doesn't anyone on this island have anything better to do than to be nosy and tell tales? Oh, wait—of course they don't. They're all sitting around here on God's doorstep, looking for a little drama to entertain them during their golden years."

"That's unnecessary." Holly lowers her chin and her voice. "We're a tight-knit community, and if someone passes on information like that, it's only because they care."

Coco tosses her hair again and turns around. She continues walking with her suitcase knocking along behind her over the sidewalk. "I had a few things I needed to say to him," she says loudly enough for Holly to hear her even though she's facing the other direction. "He's planning on getting married, and as part-owner of this island, he has assets to protect."

Holly's jaw drops. "Are you *kidding* me?" she shouts. "You're trying to get Buckhunter to have Fiona sign a prenup?"

"Don't be so naive, Holly." Coco stops walking again and yanks off her sunglasses. "Buckhunter's portion of this island is worth something, and if he and Fiona divorce, she could potentially get her hands on it."

Holly shakes her head and tries to find the right words. "You're unbelievable," she finally says. "You come down here and meddle in the wedding of complete strangers, and now you want to get into your own brother's business and try to put your two cents in there, too."

"Half-brother." Coco corrects Holly out of habit, not because she really cares how anyone refers to Leo Buckhunter. In her mind, his illegitimate birth makes him a tenuous relation, at best.

"Fiona and Buckhunter are totally happy and in love," Holly says defensively. "There's no way that she's got her eye on scoring a piece of Christmas Key."

Coco reaches the dock and stops walking again. With her sunglasses in one hand, she looks down at her daughter, who—while not a short woman—is still several inches shorter than Coco in her wedge sandals. "I worry about you, Holly." It could have come out sarcastically, but it doesn't; instead Coco's words are laced with concern. "You have control of something very powerful here, and you seem totally unaware of how to manage it and of how to view the world. You need a dose of reality."

Holly's anger and disbelief ebb and flow throughout her as she breathes in and out before answering. "My dose of reality came when my own mother left me behind to be raised by her parents so that she could roam free. My dose of reality came when I had to adjust to college after growing up on an untamed island. And my reality is continuously delivered to me in small doses as I run businesses and an island that's at least a part-time home to over a hundred people. So I don't need *you* to come down out of your gilded cage in New Jersey to tell me how to live my life."

Coco shields her eyes and watches as the boat approaches on the water. "It's only a matter of time," she says curtly, "before you or Buckhunter marries wrong and loses part of this lump of sand to an ex. One of you will call me begging to help you sell it. Mark my words."

"I'm guessing you don't need any help loading that suitcase onto the boat," Holly says, nodding at her mother's luggage. "So I'm going to just head back to the office. Good visit, Mom." Without waiting for a goodbye, Holly strides back up Main Street and crosses the sandy lot behind the B&B. Her heart is still pounding when she opens the back door and cuts through the air-conditioned hallway that leads to her office.

"Sugar!" Bonnie says brightly, looking up from her laptop. "You get your mom on a boat?"

"Not fast enough." Holly hangs her purse on the hook by the door and kicks off her Birkenstocks. "But I think I can safely say that we've got everyone off the island and that it's time to get back to business as usual." She sits at her desk and opens her own laptop, logging in as she gets comfortable.

"Well, we still have the construction crew here," Bonnie corrects her. "And rumor has it that one of them has taken a shine to you."

Holly stops tapping at the keyboard and laughs out loud. "Are you serious? This island is unbelievable..."

"Come on, doll. You know that news around here travels like a horse at the Kentucky Derby!"

"I checked everyone in and the new guy—Miguel—chatted with me briefly in the hallway."

"And at Jack Frosty's," Bonnie adds.

"Who told you that? Fiona?" Holly reaches for a pencil in the cup on the corner of her desk.

"No, I heard from two other people this morning at Mistletoe Morning Brew that he came right up to your table and made a pass at you."

"*Made a pass?*" Holly wrinkles her nose. "This feels like something out of an old movie. And no, he did not make a pass at me. He was just being friendly."

"Listen, Holly Jean. You can call it what you like, but when a man approaches a woman's table and interrupts her meal to talk, he's taken an interest in her." Bonnie looks at Holly over the top of her reading glasses. "Don't roll your eyes, at me, missy. I wasn't born yesterday."

"Did you hear about Maria and Idora?" Holly doodles on a notepad with the sharp pencil in her right hand. "I stepped in before any hair got pulled."

"Heard about that, too," Bonnie says. "Iris and Jimmy saw the whole thing from across the street and popped by to give me the highlights."

"Maria had some idea in her head that Idora was flirting with Cap just because she asked him to move a box for Vance."

"Mmmhmm." One of Bonnie's eyebrows arches.

"What does that mean?"

"That means she probably *was* flirting with him."

"Bonnie, come *on*," Holly says. She puts the pencil back in the cup and folds her legs underneath her. "Idora is here to take care of her grandsons and to help Vance and Calista get things going with the bookstore. She's not here to steal every man on the island."

"Honey," Bonnie reaches across the table and puts her soft hand on top of Holly's, "you know I love you, right?"

Holly blinks twice and waits.

"I love you like the daughter I never had. But you've got a thing or two to learn about matters of the heart."

"Name one thing I need to learn," Holly says, less to actually learn something about matters of the heart and more to give Bonnie the chance to rattle off some Southern witticism about romance or seduction. Instead, she's hit with a serious look from her friend from across the table.

"When it comes to love, everybody wants some."

18

"YOU WANT ME TO TAKE A FEW INCHES OFF THE ENDS?" MILLIE Bradford offers as she massages Holly's scalp in the shampoo bowl at Scissors & Ribbons. "I could clean this up and do a nice deep conditioning treatment."

"Sure. Let's do it." Holly's eyes are closed as Millie's fingers work circles through her wet hair. Millie could have suggested that Holly pierce her septum with an elephant's tusk at that moment and she would have agreed that it was a fabulous idea.

Millie has slowly gotten back on her feet and continued doing hair and nails and running her salon after her husband's death. Holly's absence during Ray's passing is one of her great regrets, and she still feels deep remorse at not being on the island during a time when her friends and neighbors needed her most.

"You got another booking in an hour, Mil," Calista says as she walks through the salon with a pile of freshly laundered and folded towels. "Heddie Lang-Mueller is coming in at three for a manicure."

"Holly and I won't be but an hour here," Millie says, rubbing a towel over Holly's wet head.

"Hey, Calista." Holly's chin is lowered to her chest while Millie sprays detangler in her hair. "I was wondering what's up with your mother-in-law."

Calista sets the towels on the front counter and leans a hip against the wooden desk. She's wearing a sarong that's knotted on one side of her waist and a sleeveless bodysuit under it that shows off her sleek, yoga-toned figure. "If I had the answers to what goes on in that woman's head, I'd be the queen of my own castle again."

Millie chuckles. "It's hard to run a house with two women both trying to take the lead."

"She shouldn't even be *taking* the lead," Calista says in a pleading tone. "We're talking about *my* house!"

"True, but you're married to her son." Millie waves the comb she's using to work through Holly's hair. "And a woman never truly lets go of the desire to be number one in her son's eyes."

Holly doesn't want to get into a discussion about mothers and sons when she has no experience whatsoever with the topic. "What about that business with Mrs. Agnelli in front of Mistletoe Morning Brew—what's your take on that?"

Calista blows a corkscrew curl off her forehead with a puff of breath. "My take on that?" She thinks about it for a second. "My take is that Idora is probably trying to assert dominance in some way. That does seem like her."

"So you think she was actually flirting with Cap?" Holly winces as Millie works through a tangle in her wet strands.

"Flirting is a strong word...probably testing the waters." Calista moves behind the front counter and starts putting loose pens in the jar by the computer. "Women always have to establish a pecking order of sorts, don't we? Maybe she was trying to let the other ladies on the island know that she's still a viable option."

"I don't know if women always need to try to outdo each other, do we?" Holly asks as Millie gently moves her chin so that she's looking down at her lap. The scissors in Millie's hand open and close a few time as she assesses the amount she'll trim from Holly's hair.

"It's not always a matter of trying to outdo one another," Millie says, slicing through the bottom of Holly's long, light brown hair. "But we do jockey for position." She flicks the inch of freshly-trimmed hair from the black cape around Holly's shoulders. "Lest you should forget, you and your mother are in a constant battle to determine who's in charge around here."

"But that's different," Holly argues.

"Is it?" Millie turns the chair and keeps talking. "I don't know that it is. I think we all figure out where we fit in and what our strengths and weaknesses are. It establishes a hierarchy."

Holly says nothing as the scissors snip through her hair. She considers the fact that there's already an established order on Christmas Key that she's—maybe intentionally—tried to ignore. In her quest to run an island and to develop it to its fullest potential, has she really ignored obvious social norms? Has it completely passed her by that every person on the island is simply looking to be loved in one way or another?

"All I know," Calista says, interrupting Holly's thoughts, "is that my mother-in-law can't stay forever. I appreciate her help with the boys, but it won't be long before we drive each other insane." She picks up a towel from the pile she set on the counter and shakes it out, refolding it as she talks. "I've already told Vance that at some point, it's gonna be me, or it's gonna be her."

Millie arches an eyebrow and stops snipping for a second. "You better be careful with that, hon. I've been down that road before, and when it comes to a man's mother, that might be a battle you *don't* win."

A SLEIGH FULL OF BOOKS IS PACKED WHEN HOLLY WALKS IN LATER THAT afternoon. She pushes her sunglasses on top of her head and looks around the narrow store.

"Wow, it looks like you have every single islander in here right now!" She waves at Katelynn Pillory, who's carrying two books out the back door to the newly completed deck.

"Didn't you see my flyer?" Vance Guy thrusts a lime green paper in Holly's direction. "I hung them up at the coffee shop and at North Star Cigars. One at Jack Frosty's—actually, they're everywhere."

Your first purchase at A Sleigh Full of Books is 25% off! Come to the island's first bookstore—we've got bestsellers, classics, and monthlies for you to enjoy on our back deck. Grab a calendar of events while you're here... we've got exciting things on the horizon!

"This is great, Vance," Holly says, setting the flyer on the front counter. "I have no idea how I missed your advertisements!"

"Well, you're a busy woman, so it's forgiven." Vance smiles at Carrie-Anne as she digs in the pocket of the apron that she always wears at work for a few dollars to pay for her Sunday edition of the *Miami Herald* newspaper.

"You know," Carrie-Anne says, setting her cash on the counter. "I'd be happy to trade you a coffee for a newspaper sometime. A little barter and trade."

"I'd be amenable to that," Vance agrees, nodding as he takes her money and puts it in his till. "Next time I come in, I'll bring the paper with me."

Carrie-Anne tucks the paper under one arm and winks at Holly, stepping around her on her way back to Mistletoe Morning Brew.

"Check you out, already making deals and trading goods and services with your next door neighbors!"

Vance smiles. "I've never run a business before." He closes the drawer to the register firmly. "But it seems like a fair trade."

"Building goodwill is always fair trade." Holly makes an 'okay' sign with her thumb and forefinger.

"Hey, Holly," Gwen says, putting her hands on Holly's shoulders and giving her a squeeze as she passes behind her in the small shop.

"Hi, Gwen," she says. Gwen walks through the front door and waves at one of the other triplets as she passes by with a coffee in hand.

"So," Holly turns back to Vance, "did my order come in?"

"Right." He turns to the back counter and opens a cabinet. "I got it in this morning when the mail boat arrived." Vance pulls a thick manila envelope out and sets it on the counter. "I haven't opened it yet—let's make sure you got what you wanted."

With an envelope cutter, Vance rips through the end of the package and sticks a hand inside. He pulls out a stack of magazines.

"*Island Bride, Tropical Weddings, Bride & Blooms,* and *I Do—Forever.*" He lays out each magazine, reading off the titles as he stacks them next to the register. "Does that sound right?"

Holly nods. "Yep."

"Let's get you totaled and bagged then." Vance punches keys on the register, charging her for each specially ordered magazine. When he's got a grand total, he slides the magazines into a paper bag emblazoned with an illustration of a tropical Santa steering a sleigh full of books over the ocean beneath a full moon. "Here you are, Mayor."

"Thanks, Vance." Holly takes the bag and drops her change into her purse. "I appreciate you ordering these for me."

Before he can ask what she wants with a bag of wedding magazines, Holly steps out of the shop and walks back to the B&B's lot to get her golf cart. She's put in enough work for the day, and besides, Fiona will be at her house for dinner in an hour. She's stopped in at Tinsel & Tidings to grab a few last minute groceries from the triplets, and with any luck, she'll have everything prepped and on the lanai by the time Fiona gets there.

The air has changed with November fast approaching, and when Holly gets home, she throws the windows wide, letting in the early evening breeze. Pucci is on the top step of the porch, his head hanging over one paw as he pretends to doze. Holly steps over him and gathers the food and magazines from her cart, glancing at Buckhunter's dark bungalow as she heads back into the house.

"You coming in, boy?" she asks Pucci. He gives her the dog equivalent of a raised eyebrow, which she knows is a question. "Is that supposed to mean that we haven't gone on enough walks lately? Huh?" Holly drops everything on the kitchen counter and opens the cupboard where she keeps all of Pucci's things. She picks out a well-worn red ball and whistles for her dog. "Let's go walk on the beach!"

The door is wide open behind Holly as she races down the steps in her Converse with Pucci following close behind. All it takes is the magic "W" word and the sight of his favorite ball, and he's up and running.

The beach is quiet and the tide is out, so Holly kicks off her shoes near the patch of seagrass by the path where Cinnamon Lane ends and the sand begins. Without hesitation, she runs to the water and chucks the ball as far into the ocean as her arm will allow. Pucci dashes into the surf after it, his ears flying behind him as he surges through the waves and reaches the floating red ball.

Holly breathes in through her nose and then exhales as she surveys the beach. It's wonderful to be there alone and to have a few minutes to herself. There have been so many little things happening (and big things, too—Kitta and Deacon's wedding wasn't inconsequential, she reminds herself) that her time alone is usually spent attending to minor details or thinking through the things that are going on. So to have a few minutes to just breathe is a golden opportunity for her, and she takes it in hungrily, letting the breeze from the ocean play with her freshly cut hair.

Pucci is back with the wet ball in no time, and Holly takes it from his mouth and throws it down the beach this time, watching her dog's hindquarters as he bounds across the sand like a freight train headed towards its destination. She smiles at his enthusiasm while a wave washes up the sand and over her bare feet. The water is lukewarm and leaves behind a residue of tiny shells as it retreats. Out of habit, Holly bends over and starts to examine the shells, pocketing any that she thinks might work on her shell wall.

"Find any good ones?" a voice calls out. Holly turns towards the path from Cinnamon Lane. It's Jake.

"I'm looking," she shouts back. His presence isn't unwelcome, but they haven't spoken much lately and Holly feels an unfamiliar separation between them as Jake approaches.

"I tried your house, but the door was open, the lights were on, and nobody was home. This felt like a good guess," he says, pointing at the empty beach.

Holly drags a toe through the wet sand. "Fee is coming over in a bit, so I thought I'd bring Pucci down here before I settle in for the evening." As if on cue, Pucci trots up and drops the ball at Jake's feet, waiting for him to throw it. Jake obliges, tossing it into the waves again.

"Can we talk?"

Holly's stomach sinks. She's not sure whether she's up for a talk with Jake, because it always seems to center around their relationship somehow. "Yeah," she says. "We can talk."

They start to walk in the direction of the Ho Ho Hideaway, which is off in the distance. Jake looks around as they walk, not saying anything for a minute or two.

"So," he starts. "How are things?"

"Things are fine." Holly isn't really in the mood to re-hash the wedding they've just thrown or her discussions with her mother, so she walks along next to Jake, hoping that he'll get to the point soon.

"That was nice of Kitta and Deacon to let the boys off the hook so easily for selling the photos. Katelynn was really grateful."

Ah, Holly thinks. *Katelynn.*

"She had some long talks with Logan and I know Owen felt really bad about it, too."

"Well, as long as they do what Kitta and Deacon wanted and use the money for college, then I guess it's no harm, no foul, right?" She cuts a look in Jake's direction but doesn't stop walking.

"Right." Jake clears his throat. "And I've been spending a fair amount of time with Katelynn lately."

"Uh huh."

"But it feels weird to be hanging out with her and to not tell you about it."

"Jake." Holly finally stops walking and turns to face him. He walks a few steps and then turns around. "Number one, this is not high school and you're not 'hanging out' with Katelynn. Number two, you don't need to tell me anything. In case you haven't noticed, there are zero secrets on this island."

"When you came back from Europe..." Jake trails off. "It seemed like..."

Holly knows what he's getting at. There was a night—a moment of weakness—when she'd turned up on his doorstep even after they'd agreed not to see one another in that light. She'd written it off as loneliness on both of their parts and told herself that comfort between two friends (who were both single at the time) didn't necessarily add up to a full-blown rekindling of their relationship.

"It seemed like we both needed to work through some things." Holly reaches out and puts a hand on Jake's arm. "And thank you for telling me, but it's really okay. It is." She locks her eyes on his meaningfully. "We've got a long history together, and if we're both going to keep living on this island, then communication is key."

A wide smile of relief crosses Jake's face. "Well, I'm not leaving this island." He takes her hand and loops it through the crook of his arm so that they can walk together like old friends. "Are you?"

Holly stops walking and looks at him in mock horror. "Never again. Not unless I absolutely have to."

Jake laughs. "Europe made you realize that everything you want in life is floating out here in the Gulf of Mexico?"

"Yeah," Holly says with a smile. "Something like that."

19

Halloween is bright and sunny. Holly shields her eyes as she looks down Main Street, holding a can of Diet Coke in one hand. She can't believe it's been a full year since the cast and crew of *Wild Tropics* landed on their shores to film the reality show that shook up the island and turned their little slice of paradise into a household name.

"We got it all set up, sugar!" Bonnie calls out the front door of the B&B. "The rooms are ready and the decorations are out!" She pulls her head back into the lobby and disappears from view.

The boat is still a good hour away, but Holly wants to have a look at the decorations on the shops and make sure everything is just the way she wants it. It had been Bonnie's idea to throw a last-minute Halloween party, and with everything settled down after the wedding, Holly had agreed, so long as Bonnie took the lead on planning.

The dock workers agreed to double-up in rooms for a few nights to save space, and Bonnie quickly filled the other guest rooms with friends and family from all over. One of Millie Bradford's daughters and her kids will be arriving on the boat at noon, as will two of Bonnie's sons and their families, a small group of the triplets' friends from Indiana, and a various assortment of other people with ties to the locals.

In order to make the whole thing appropriately festive, Bonnie has insisted that every shop change their Christmas decor to Halloween fare, and she's ordered tons of sparkly orange and black garland, flickering flameless lamps to hang all over Main Street, and yards and yards of fake spiderweb to wind through everything and drape across doorways. The work of transforming the dining room is also Bonnie's job, and she's covered the tables in black linens, switched out lamp bulbs for orange and black lights, and organized a menu of gourmet mini pizzas, cold pasta dishes, and an assortment of salads. Buckhunter will man the bar in the corner of the room, as he does for most events, and then everyone will make their way to the Ho Ho for live music and dancing near the ocean. Holly has to hand it to her friend: it's shaping up to be a great party.

"As if you had nothing else to work on around here!" Fiona shouts from across the street. She's wearing her white lab coat over a pair of cut-off denim shorts and a turquoise tank top, and her hair is twisted into a wavy bun on the top of her head. "You just had to throw another party, didn't you?"

Holly takes a swig of her soda. "This is all Bonnie's doing. I would have been happy to live in isolation for the next six months and just sit around and talk wedding stuff with you like we did the other night at my place, but apparently we needed more action."

Fiona puts one finger to her lips and looks up and down the street like the FBI might be listening. "Shhh!" she says, hurrying across the street in her brown leather sandals, lab coat open and flapping as she makes her way to Holly. "No one knows anything about that."

"Including Buckhunter?" Holly throws a glance over her shoulder and they both look at Buckhunter, who is busy firing up his grill for lunch and overturning the chairs that had been up on the tables all night.

"He agreed to let me run with this," Fiona says, grabbing Holly's shoulders and leaning in close. "Once I realized that he wasn't avoiding the wedding, he just cared more about being married than about a ceremony, I decided to surprise him. I know what he likes, and I don't want him to know *anything* in advance. Got it?"

"You got it, boss." Holly takes another drink from the can and winks at Fiona. After all the drama surrounding their upcoming nuptials, Holly is more than happy to acquiesce to anything Fiona wants as long as it makes her happy. And as maid of honor, it's her duty to be Fiona's right-hand woman and co-conspirator.

"Okay." Fiona heaves a sigh of relief. "Now I need to go and lance a boil on someone's bum. Pray for me."

Holly knows better than to ask whose tail end is in question (doctor-patient privilege and all), but she laughs inwardly as Fiona crosses the street and meets Jimmy Cafferkey at the door of Poinsettia Plaza, holding it open for him as he enters. She casts a look in Holly's direction that's half "This is *top* secret" and half "Oh my lord, please save me from piercing a middle-aged man's hairy bottom with a sterile needle." This time Holly laughs out loud as the door to the building closes behind her best friend.

Main Street does look festive, and the extra pumpkins Bonnie ordered with their last grocery delivery have been carved and set out on the sidewalk. Before the sun sets, Holly will place votives in each one and light them so that everyone will walk out of the B&B and feel like they're at a real Halloween party.

"What are you dressing up as, Mayor?" Buckhunter is standing in the open doorway to Jack Frosty's, watching his niece as she looks around.

"I'm going as Sandy from *Grease*," she says, turning to face him. "Are you dressing up?"

"I doubt Fiona would let me get away with not putting on a costume of some sort."

"So what does she have you going as?" Holly walks up to the restaurant and stands at the bottom of the steps, looking up at him.

"Last I heard we were supposed to be Princess Leia and Darth Vader."

"No way." A grin spreads across Holly's face. "Seriously?"

"That's the rumor."

"This is going to be awesome." Holly is impressed. As always, when they decide to do something, the people of Christmas Key go all out. Seeing everyone in costume is going to be fun.

"I'm not sure if awesome is the right word, but it'll be something." Buckhunter chuckles and turns back to the bar. "I've got dishes to put away here, kid. You wanna help, or you got mayoral duties to attend to?"

"I've got party duties to attend to," Holly says, flipping the watch on her wrist over so that she can check the time. "Bonnie's the boss of this event, and she has me running around."

"Being the boss seems like it'd suit her just fine."

"Oh, it does," Holly agrees. "She's taken to giving me orders like a fish to water."

"Then you better hop to, huh?" Buckhunter waves her off and heads back to the kitchen that's nestled behind his bar. Before she walks away, Holly can hear the clank of clean dishes being unloaded from his dishwasher.

"Bon?" Holly steps into the B&B and tosses her empty Diet Coke can into a recycling bin behind the front desk. She can hear Bonnie talking on the phone in their office down the hall, so she walks into the dining room to make sure things are moving along.

"We need more lanterns over there," Maggie Sutter says, pointing at one corner of the room. Katelynn and Jake are standing on chairs, each of them holding one end of a strand of orange lanterns with little bulbs inside of them.

"Wow, this looks amazing," Holly says. She puts her hands on the back of a chair and watches as Katelynn ties one end of the strand to a hook in the ceiling. From the look of the room, Bonnie's probably ordered every Halloween decoration available from the party store in Key West and had it shipped to the island, but the overall effect is worth it.

"The food goes over there," Maggie says, showing Holly how things will be set up, "and Buckhunter's bar is by the window."

Holly nods. "Looks good to me. Anything I can do to help in here?"

"I think we've got it handled," Maggie says, consulting a clipboard in her hands. "Bonnie said the rooms are all set up, and the boat's scheduled to arrive soon, isn't it?"

Holly looks at her watch again. "Less than an hour."

"Maybe check with Bonnie then?" Maggie suggests. She turns back to Jake and Katelynn. "No, no, no—I think *that* should go over *there*," she instructs them. Holly backs out of the dining room and goes to check in with Bonnie.

"What else do we need to get done before tonight, Bon?" Holly pauses in the doorway of their office and leans against the doorframe.

With a sigh, Bonnie stands and stretches. "Oh, sugar. I think we're close to being ready. Thankfully this is just family and friends and not a bunch of strangers we need to impress."

"But this *would* impress a group of strangers," Holly says, nodding at the window that looks out at Main Street. "Seriously. Look at this place. I think we should consider doing this next year and advertising it. Kind of like we did with the pirate weekend."

Bonnie's face scrunches up at the reminder of the pirate weekend, but she says nothing about it.

"Let's just see how it goes, doll. If it goes well, then maybe we could turn it into some sort of murder mystery weekend over Halloween. A whole themed event."

"Oooooh, I like that." Holly walks across the office and picks up a dry erase marker. "And I *just* talked to Vance recently about trying to put together some sort of murder mystery weekend that involves bringing authors to the island, so it's something I really want to look into."

She pulls the cap off the marker and scrawls *Murder mystery weekend???* on the corner of the board where she and Bonnie keep their running list of possible tourism ideas. So far they've got a few ideas that they've been kicking around, but Holly likes the sound of the murder mystery event—even if it doesn't take place over Halloween.

"Glad you like it." Bonnie smiles at herself, pleased that she's come up with something that Holly's excited about. "But as for today, we could probably use more lanterns hung up around the island. You want to take charge of that?"

"Sure." Holly shrugs. "Are they in the storage room?"

Bonnie nods and sits back down at her computer. "You just go ahead and put them out wherever you think they'll look good. They're solar-powered, so the sooner you get them out there, the more likely those flameless candle thingies will start glowing as soon as the sun goes down."

Holly leaves Bonnie to answer the emails that have stolen her attention, and she loads the boxes of lanterns into the back of her cart in the B&B's parking lot. She spends the next forty-five minutes driving all over Christmas Key and hanging the black lanterns from trees, from fences, and next to the doors of houses and businesses. By the time the sun sets, the island will be glowing.

"Hey!" Logan flags Holly down as she passes by him on his street. "Holly!"

She pulls the cart to the side of the unpaved road and waits as he jogs over. "Whatcha doin'?" Logan asks, peering into the boxes in the back of her cart.

"Just hanging up a few more decorations for the party tonight. You going?"

Logan nods. "Yeah, I am. My mom said that Joe would even let me come to the Ho Ho tonight, as long as I promised not to try and sneak anyone's drinks." He rolls his eyes at the notion of a teenage boy trying to steal a beer or a sip of rum. This makes Holly smile, because she'd done the very same thing half a lifetime ago, and she was pretty sure that almost any teenager would.

"You want to help me hang the rest of these?" Holly tips her head at the box in the back. "I've got about ten or fifteen more."

"Sure." Logan is in the passenger seat and ready to go before Holly even finishes the question. She pulls back out onto the road and rolls along slowly, looking for places to put up lanterns.

"So, Owen's gone. What have you been doing with yourself?"

"It's been a little boring without him," Logan admits. His friend had only stayed a week and a half, and then gone back home to avoid missing too much school. "I put off my classwork while he was here, so I've been catching up with the online stuff."

Holly had done all of her schooling on the island as well, but her studying days had happened before online classes were a thing. In fact, Logan's late great-grandmother, Sadie Pillory, had been a retired teacher and was the one who'd guided both Holly and Emily Cafferkey through their education all the way to graduation.

"Is it hard?" Holly asks, stopping near a tall palm tree and pointing at a branch. "The online stuff?"

"Nah, not really." Logan jumps out and grabs a lantern without Holly giving any more direction. He reaches high and hooks the lantern over a branch. "It's easy. There are just deadlines to meet and papers to write. I have to have video calls with my teachers every week. Stuff like that." Logan gets back into the cart and they move on, turning the corner from Ivy Lane onto December Drive without stopping.

"Does your mom stay on top of all the deadlines?" Holly asks the question without realizing that it makes Logan sound like he needs his mommy to handle his schedule. She wishes she could take the question back as soon as it's out. "I just meant does she like, bug you about your coursework. You know, typical mom worrying." Holly moves her hand around as she talks, sneaking a look at Logan's face.

"No, not really." He stares out at the stretch of hard-packed sand they're driving on. There's been so much golf cart traffic that it's a clearly delineated road, even without the benefit of having been paved. "I can handle it all myself. I'm very organized."

"Of course. Right." Holly nods and smiles at him. "I'm not surprised."

"So what are you dressing up as tonight?" Logan asks, changing the subject.

"Sandy from *Grease*."

"Oh, I've seen that movie. My mom loves it."

"I know. We used to watch it together when we were teenagers. I had it on VHS and we'd watch it in my bedroom when it was too hot to be outside. Amongst other things. We also loved *Pretty in Pink* and *Sixteen Candles*."

"All classic movies of the 80s," Logan says. There's a moment of silence between them as Holly remembers hanging out with Kate-lynn all summer during their teenage years. "I haven't decided on my costume yet," Logan finally says, wiping his palms on the front of his shorts. "But I don't have a ton of choices—it's not like there's a store here on the island where I can just drop in and buy one."

"This is true," Holly says. She stops again and points at a series of wooden posts that run alongside December Drive near the beach. "Hey, how about we hang one lantern on each of those posts?"

Without saying anything, Logan grabs several lanterns and hooks each one onto a post. Holly waits for him.

They turn down Pine Cone Blvd and head towards Main Street when the lantern box is empty, and Holly offers to buy Logan a cold drink at the coffee shop in exchange for his help.

"No, seriously. That's not necessary." Logan slides off the seat in front of A Sleigh Full of Books. "I wasn't doing anything anyway. Happy to help."

"Well, I appreciate it," Holly says, looking up at him from under the roof of her cart. "You're a champ, Logan."

"I'll see you tonight." Logan gives Holly a thumbs-up before she pulls away.

There's still time for a little more work in the B&B's office, and it'll be even more productive for Holly if Bonnie is out doing Halloween stuff. She slows at the curb and peeks in the window of her office: no Bonnie. Perfect. Holly grabs her purse and leaves the cart parked right where it is. She's intrigued by the murder mystery idea, but before she jumps in headfirst, she wants to do a little more research on it while she's got the office to herself.

20

THE DINING ROOM AT THE B&B IS PACKED WITH REVELERS IN COSTUME when Holly turns up later that evening. She'd spent the afternoon digging through various websites boasting murder mystery weekends and come up with tons of valuable information, then gone home and gotten herself dressed for the evening.

"Sandy from *Grease*?" Iris Cafferkey asks in her Irish accent as she takes in Holly's tight black pants, strappy red heels, and black motorcycle jacket over a black tank top. She's curled her hair and made it poofy and then added silver hoop earrings to complete the costume. "You look lovely, lass."

"Thanks, Iris." Holly reaches for a cocktail weiner wrapped in a crescent roll from the tray on the table nearest her. The little paper holder has been squirted with a dollop of mustard to dip the hotdog in, and she pops the whole thing into her mouth and chews. "I like your costume, too."

"Emily and I are doing *Wizard of Oz* this year," she says unnecessarily. Her face is painted green, and she's wrapped in a black cape and wearing a pointy black hat. "She's around here somewhere..." Iris scans the crowd for her daughter, pointing at Emily when she spots her. Emily walks over to them.

"Ahhh!" Holly says, clapping excitedly when she sees her friend. Emily is wearing a tall crown and a floor-length pale pink gown that Holly recognizes from past Halloweens. "Glinda the Good Witch!" She wraps her arms around Emily and pulls her close.

"You look pretty, Holly." Emily steps back and looks Holly up and down. "You look like your boyfriend rides a motorcycle." Emily giggles as she runs a hand over Holly's leather jacket. "You look like Logan is your boyfriend."

Holly frowns for a second as she tries to figure out what Emily is getting at, but as soon as she spots Logan, she knows: he's dressed like Danny Zuko in a black leather jacket that looks remarkably like Holly's own, and tight black pants with a white t-shirt. She watches him as he saunters over.

"Hey," Logan says, giving Holly a look that makes it seem like they've planned their coordinating costumes. "You look really good."

Iris's eyebrows skyrocket up into her hairline and she smothers a laugh. "It's a little late in the year for summer lovin'," she teases, referring to the song from *Grease*.

Holly makes a face at Iris to let her know that she isn't helping the situation. "So my costume inspired you?" she asks Logan.

"I thought it would be cool," he says, turning up the collar of his black jacket like a real Greaser from the 1950s, "to be Danny if you were going as Sandy. You know, since Joe is letting me come to the Ho Ho tonight."

Iris laughs out loud and puts a hand on Holly's shoulder. "You two kids have fun," she says. "Emily and I are going to grab another slice of pizza."

Holly gives Iris and Emily a weak smile as they disappear, leaving her standing in the middle of the B&B's dining room with a sixteen-year-old who seems to think that they're on a date.

Logan's face changes and he suddenly looks uncertain. "This is okay, isn't it?" He looks at his own costume. "I wasn't trying to be a creeper, I just thought it would be funny."

Holly loosens up a bit. This isn't a big deal—it's Logan, and he's a good kid. His crush on her isn't a huge secret from anyone on the island, and it's not like he follows her around like a puppy dog or anything; Logan mostly plays it cool.

"No, Logan," she says, reaching out to straighten his collar. "It is cool. And you look great." The smile returns to his face and he visibly relaxes.

"Sugar!" Bonnie slides over to them and wisely avoids commenting on the matching costumes as she appraises Holly and Logan. "This party is already a knockout!"

Holly can't disagree as she looks around the room and waves at Fiona and Buckhunter in their Princess Leia and Darth Vader costumes. Everyone has done their best to round up creative costumes, and there are clowns, mimes, two witches, and a Frankenstein in attendance. The construction crew has turned up as well, but without access to costumes, they've opted for the freshly showered and shaved look, claiming that clean shorts and t-shirts *do* feel like being dressed up in costumes.

Holly turns back to Bonnie. "It turned out great. And I see everyone's guests are here."

"They are. And I wanted you to say hi to my boys and their families. You haven't seen the kids since they were babies!" Bonnie takes Holly's hand in hers and starts to drag her away. "Oh," she turns to Logan. "I'll bring your date back here in two shakes of a lamb's tail, alright, hon?"

"Bonnie," Holly hisses, following closely behind her friend. "Don't encourage him."

"Oh, come on. It's cute." Bonnie leads Holly over to the table where her boys and their families are sitting and eating pizza. "Sixteen is plenty old for a boy to fall in love for the first time."

"Did Iris pay you to come and give me a hard time?" Holly fluffs her hair with one hand, still holding onto Bonnie's hand with the other. "She got a huge kick out of this, too."

"Honey, we're *all* getting a huge kick out of this." Holly stifles a sarcastic comeback as Bonnie stops in front of her family's table and makes quick re-introductions between her sons, their wives, their children, and Holly. It's been several years since they've all made the trip to Christmas Key, and Holly can see that Bonnie is beyond thrilled to have two of her three sons there for the weekend.

"Will we see you at the Ho Ho?" Bonnie asks her, pulling her out of her thoughts.

"Oh, yeah. Of course. I'm just going to get something to eat and then I'll head that direction," Holly says. "It was really good to see you all." She smiles at Bonnie's family and reaches out a finger to let Bonnie's youngest granddaughter—a teething six-month-old named Charlie—grab onto it.

The food has turned out great. Holly piles a plate high with pizza and snacks and winds her way through the crowd, stopping to admire Maria Agnelli's gypsy costume, the triplets' matching grass skirts and seashell necklaces, and Cap's recycled costume from their pirate weekend.

"Hey, Sandy," Buckhunter calls out, shaking a martini behind the bar in the corner of the dining room. "I think your date stepped outside."

"Funny." Holly shoots her uncle a warning look. She takes a big bite of her pizza and plops down at a table with Jake and Katelynn without asking whether it's okay for her to do so.

"Whoa," Jake says with a surprised laugh. "I had no idea..." He's dressed up like a devil in a bold red button-up shirt and a pair of sequined horns on a headband, and it's obvious that his dark, arched eyebrows are courtesy of Katelynn, who has turned herself into Kim Kardashian with a full face of make-up, flat-ironed hair, and a nude colored dress that she's stuffed pillows under to create the exaggerated posterior that Kim K. is known for.

Holly shoves another mini-hot dog into her mouth and starts chewing so she can't talk.

"Did he con you into that?" Katelynn asks, nodding at Logan as he walks through the door and back into the dining room.

Holly shakes her head and reaches for the bottle of beer next to Katelynn's plate to wash it down. It's a bold move, but she's feeling like Katelynn owes her a swig or two at this point. "Nope," Holly says, setting the bottle back on the table. "I told him I was coming as Sandy, and he showed up like that."

"Hey," Logan says, pulling out a chair. When he joins them at the table, it has the effect of making their foursome look like a double date. Holly picks up the bottle of beer again and drains it.

"Good music," Jake says, filling the gap in conversation. Bonnie's set up a sound system and is playing songs like "Dead Man's Curve" and "Monster Mash."

"Bonnie did a great job," Katelynn adds. She flips her long hair over one shoulder and bites into a slice of pepperoni pizza.

Holly nods and looks around the room again. She isn't sure why, but something is feeling a little off for her. "I'm going to head over to the Ho Ho and see if Joe needs help with anything," she says. She stands and picks up her plate. "I'll see you guys over there."

"You need a lift?" Logan offers. "I have the keys to our cart in case anyone needs a designated driver tonight."

Holly holds up a hand to pause him. "I'm good. But thanks, Logan. I'll see you over there later."

She exits the dining room as "Spooky" by Dusty Springfield comes on.

Outside the sky is dark and the stars are like a patchwork quilt of diamonds. The music follows Holly onto Main Street as her red heels click against the sidewalk. Her annoyance at Logan is minor; that isn't what's putting her off. And seeing Jake and Katelynn together isn't bothering her as much as it had at first, so it can't be them sitting together that's getting under her skin. So what's eating her? She can't put a finger on it, and as she slides behind the wheel of her golf cart and flips on the headlamps, she shakes off the sensation and lets the autumn night breeze blow through her hair.

At the Ho Ho, Joe is setting clean glasses on the bar and humming along to a Bob Marley song that's playing through the bar's speakers.

"Happy Halloween, Mayor," he says, whistling along to the music as Holly's heels click up the steps and into the open bar. He's wearing his usual loose Hawaiian shirt, unbuttoned about one or two buttons further down than would be acceptable anywhere other than a tropical island. "You in costume?"

"No. I'm just thinking of bringing spandex and Aqua Net back into fashion," she says, pausing at the bar and leaning against the counter. "How about you? Dressed like a beach bum for the occasion?"

"Dressed like a beach bum for life." Joe winks at her and bends forward to pull something from the mini fridge under his bar. His snowy white curls and piercing blue eyes have always made him one of the most handsome older men on the island.

"I came by early to see if you needed any help," Holly offers. She glances around the bar and sees that he's switched out the lightbulbs in all the lamps with orange ones, and the tables are covered in black tablecloths just like the ones at the B&B. Other than that, Joe's made little concessions to the holiday, instead letting his homemade rum and the music he'll undoubtedly play on his guitar later on be the backdrop for a great evening.

Joe uncorks a bottle and pours two fingers of dark liquid into a short glass. He slides it across the bar to Holly.

"Nope," he says. "No help needed here. But you look like you could use some."

Holly takes the drink gratefully and sips it. "I'm not sure what I need, to be perfectly honest."

"A man?"

Holly snorts. "Like I need a hole in the head."

"Hmm." Joe sounds neutral, but Holly catches a glimpse of something undefinable on his face.

"What is that supposed to mean?" Holly takes another drink.

Joe shrugs and a wave crashes loudly on the shore just beyond the steps leading down to the beach. "It just means that you've been through the ringer with Jake, and things didn't work out with your baseball player, so maybe it's time to cut your losses and start fresh."

Holly sets the glass down on the bar. "I had no idea you were paying so much attention to my love life, Sacamano."

"What else is there to do here besides make rum and count

waves?" Joe gives her a lopsided grin. "But truthfully, we all care about you, Holly. You know that. And the Jake situation can't be good for you."

"What Jake situation?" Holly's brow furrows as she tries to see how her relationship with Jake must look to everyone else.

"Well," Joe pauses, "for starters, you shot down his proposal."

"True." She nods, remembering how she'd decided that marrying Jake should feel like the best and most exciting decision of her life, and not just something inevitable.

"Then there was the whole thing with that Hollywood gal," Joe says, averting his gaze. He doesn't need to totally repaint the picture for Holly to remember how Jake had fallen for Bridget when the reality show had come to the island the year before, resulting in the ill-fated pregnancy and a messy break-up. The whole thing had further complicated the way Holly already felt about Jake.

"Also true," Holly says, biting her lower lip as she swirls what's left of the amber liquid around in her glass on the bar.

"And now he and Katelynn are running around together quite a bit, but everyone knows that anytime you're both single, one of you ends up knocking on the other's door late at night."

"Joe!" Holly sucks in a breath. This is as close as anyone has come to alluding to her undefined romantic relationship with Jake, and she's shocked that the person calling her out on it is Joe Sacamano rather than, say, Bonnie.

"Hey, I've been around the block a time or two, kiddo," Joe says, holding both hands up in front of him. "I judge nothing." He shakes his head. "I'm just saying that it must be hard to never know quite where you stand with someone." The song on the speaker switches and UB40's version of "Can't Help Falling in Love" starts to play.

"But I had River," she says defensively, as if this justifies everything.

"And is that over?" Joe looks at her with a firm gaze. "Really over?"

Holly thinks about this for a second before nodding. "It's over. Really over."

"Well, then you're basically at the mercy of Jake's relationship status at this point."

"I am not!" Holly slides the glass back towards Joe and he uncorks the bottle again and pours half as much alcohol into it. "I'm happy for Jake if he wants to date Katelynn—he and I have no hold on one another."

"Hey, you two are adults," Joe says. He turns his back to Holly and starts to rearrange the bottles behind the bar. "No one on this island is in a position to decide how you should do things. All I'm saying—as a wise old man and as a friend—is that you might be better off if you truly let one another go. Get over each other once and for all, and start looking for that person who makes you happy all the time, not just sometimes."

Holly nods as she turns Joe's advice over in her mind. He's certainly been married and divorced enough times to have an opinion and to offer advice on love, but she isn't totally sure that anyone else is qualified to parse out the details of her relationship with Jake. Still, she appreciates his candor. And, oddly, something in her has lifted since she left the B&B; that sensation of being bugged by something undefinable has diminished.

"Thanks, Joe," she finally says. "I appreciate the talk."

As Holly drains her glass, the crunch of tires on rocks and shells and sand pulls her attention away from the bar. The first guests from the B&B have started to migrate over to the Ho Ho, and she stands up straighter and smiles.

"Come in, come in!" Holly smiles brightly, waving the triplets and their husbands and guests up into the Ho Ho. Before long, the tables along the edges of the bar start to fill, and the sound of laughter competes with the music on the speakers for airtime. Holly drifts around the room, chatting with everyone and cracking jokes as Joe's rum concoctions start to loosen up the crowd. Maria Agnelli is holding a glass of his coconut lime rum, and as Holly walks by, Mrs. Agnelli reaches out and pinches her bottom through the tight black pants.

"You're looking pretty sassy tonight, Holly Baxter," Mrs. Agnelli says with a warning look. "That outfit is enough to give any man a heart attack."

Both women stop in their tracks as Millie Bradford sidles up to them just in time to catch the end of Mrs. Agnelli's comment. Holly's face falls.

"I'm sorry, Millie," Maria Agnelli says. She puts a gnarled hand on Millie's arm and gives her a watery smile. "I didn't mean to say that."

Millie has clearly been thrown by the heart attack comment, but it's been a few months since Ray's untimely passing, and Millie is a tough broad. More importantly, she isn't the type to expect others to stand on ceremony and watch every word they say. She gives a small shake of her head. "Nonsense, Maria. You don't need to apologize." Millie leans in and puts a kiss on the older woman's cheek. "Now what are you drinking? I think I want one of those."

Holly watches as Millie leads Mrs. Agnelli to the bar. After more than an hour of laughing and talking her way through the crowd, she's suddenly alone in the center of the dance floor, wedged between Cap and Heddie as they sway to a steel drum version of "Brown Eyed Girl," and Fiona and Emily, who are waving their hands around in some made up dance that looks more joyful than rhythmic. Emily is holding a sparkly wand with a star at one end, her crown dipping precariously to one side.

"You look...tall," a voice says from over Holly's shoulder. She turns to see Miguel standing there with a beer bottle in one hand. He's wearing a loose rayon shirt that's unbuttoned to reveal a white shirt beneath. His thick black hair has been washed and combed to one side, and his eyes dance playfully as he takes in her costume. "Those shoes are intimidating."

Holly looks down at her feet and then back up at Miguel. He's right—the shoes add a couple of inches to her height and she now towers over him. "Maybe you're just short," she teases him, putting a palm flat on the top of his head.

He ducks away with a mischievous grin. "Hey, maybe good things just come in small packages."

Holly's attention is drawn to the doorway when Buckhunter and Fiona show up, still in costume.

"You gonna be able to have a beer with that Darth Vader mask on?" she yells out to her uncle, cupping both hands around her mouth so that she can be heard over the music. In response, Buckhunter gives her a thumbs up and lets Fiona take his elbow and lead him to the bar.

"I had no idea you all would be so festive," Miguel says, putting his own bottle of beer to his mouth as he looks around at the costumes and at the dancing locals. "I'm not trying to be rude or anything, but the population here isn't exactly..."

"Young?" Holly finishes for him. "I know. But everyone is incredibly young at heart. You won't find a better group of people anywhere."

He turns back to Holly and looks up at her like the inches between them don't bother him. His gaze is confident. Strong.

Holly smiles as Jimmy Cafferkey passes her and gives her shoulder a squeeze. "I feel really lucky to have been raised here," she says.

"So you really lived here when there were no phone lines and while they ran electricity and water out here?"

"I don't remember it like that, but yeah, we did. My grandpa had a vision, and my grandma was along for the ride. They loved this place." Holly looks out at what's visible of the beach in the darkness. "I went to college in Miami and then came right back here to take over running the island as my grandpa got sicker. Being here on Christmas Key and making his dreams a reality has been the greatest joy in my life."

"You must have sacrificed a lot." Miguel is watching her face intently. Joe Sacamano brushes by them with a tray of drinks in hand; he winks at Holly as he shoulders past.

"Well, I'm thirty-one, unmarried, and have no kids, if that's what you mean by sacrifice," she says. "But I'm happy. One hundred percent."

"You're pretty accomplished for thirty-one," Miguel says admiringly. "I would have thought you were much older."

Holly laughs. "Miguel, never tell a woman you thought she was *older* than she actually is!"

"No, no—that's not what I meant." He waves a hand to clear up the misunderstanding. "I just meant I would have thought that someone much older was in charge of running this place. But you don't *look* older. I actually thought you were younger. Maybe twenty-five."

"Oh, come on." Holly narrows her eyes like she knows he's blowing hot air up her skirt. "You did not."

Miguel shrugs. "My oldest sister is your age, and I wouldn't ever catch her driving a golf cart around all day in a bikini and a skirt with flip-flops."

"Your oldest sister?" Holly's interest is piqued. "How old are you, Miguel?"

"Twenty-three." He takes another sip of his beer. "Last month."

"And how did you end up on my island? Have you been doing construction work for long?"

"Since I was seventeen. My dad had to leave the country, and my mom was raising six kids on her own, so I found work and as soon as I graduated from high school, I got into it full time. It's not exciting, but it pays a lot of bills and it helps my mom."

"What else would you do if you could? What would be more exciting?"

Miguel glances around the bar and his eyes focus on the stairs that lead down onto the beach. "Live somewhere like this. Be an island cop like Jake or work in a shop. Do maintenance for the B&B or just general fixing and building. I don't know. But this life seems like a good one."

Holly thinks for a moment. "It is. This life is a *great* one."

They smile at each other as everyone around them drinks, laughs, and dances to the sounds of the tropical music Joe's still playing over his sound system. Before long, he'll have everyone served and he'll bring out his guitar and start playing requests and favorites.

"You done with that beer?" Holly nods at Miguel's bottle. In response, he tips it back and empties it.

"Yep," he says, setting it on Joe's tray as he winds his way back to the bar. Joe nods at him.

"Wanna dance?" Holly asks boldly.

"Sure." Miguel's smile spreads across his face as he offers Holly a hand. "Why not?"

Why not, indeed.

And so just like that, Holly kicks off her heels and spends the rest of Halloween dancing in the salty ocean air with a man nearly a decade younger than her, laughing as the music floats around her and the wind ruffles her hair.

21

"SO YOU HAD A GOOD HALLOWEEN, HUH?" BONNIE IS WAITING IN THE office for Holly after the island's guests have all cleared out. Her own sons and their families have just boarded the morning boat bound for Key West, and her tears have barely dried from their good-byes, but she's picked up her iced latte at the coffee shop and is ready to roll up her sleeves and get back to work with Holly.

"I did," Holly says casually, shuffling through the papers and envelopes in the wire inbox on her desk. "It was a great party, Bon. You did good work!"

"Hey, I was born to plan parties," Bonnie says. "Throwing a solid shindig is right up the alley of any good Southern girl."

"Well, you did this one up right. It was a good idea, and I think everyone had a fabulous time." Holly sits down at her desk and pulls the sunglasses off the top of her head. She sets them on the desk and opens her laptop.

"Maybe not as good a time as you, sugar," Bonnie says with a nearly imperceptible eyebrow wiggle. "You got your groove on at the Ho Ho, girlfriend."

The right side of Holly's mouth hitches up just slightly as she fights a full-fledged smile. "Oh, get out of town, Bon. I was just dancing like everybody else."

"And with a younger man, no less." Bonnie gives a nod that is clearly approving. "Wait, just how much younger are we talking here?"

"Not much," Holly says, keeping her eyes focused on the screen as she taps her password into the laptop. "He's twenty-three."

Bonnie gives a low whistle. "My aunt Mildred was a certified cradle-robber," Bonnie says knowingly. "She always said that younger men treat you better. Her last husband before she died was only forty-six."

"And how old was Aunt Mildred?" Holly decides to play along, and she leans back in her chair, preparing for one of Bonnie's long and sordid stories that always seem to center on sex or life in the Deep South.

"Seventy-eight." Bonnie lets this sink in. "That's a thirty-two year age gap."

It's Holly's turn to whistle appreciatively. "How'd she manage that? Was she rich?"

Bonnie puts the straw between her red lips and takes a long sip of her iced coffee while she makes Holly wait for more details. "Nope," she finally says, setting the plastic cup back on the coaster next to her computer. "Not at all. But she was a stunner. One of the last great beauties of her generation. A thick head of honey-colored hair right up to the end. Cheekbones you could cut glass on. A figure that held up even as gravity tried to drag it down. And what a personality! Aunt Mildred could swear like a sailor and she loved to laugh."

"So she kept a man more than three decades her junior with just her personality and a booty that fought gravity?"

Bonnie frowns at her. "Well, yes, sugar. That's how love works. It's mysterious and strange, but somehow it works. And when it does, none of the outside stuff matters. Age, money, social status—it all goes out the window. Just like it did for Aunt Mildred and Uncle Jack."

"Uncle Jack?"

"Yeah, he was around for most of my childhood. After Mildred passed, he stuck around for a bit and then left Savannah broken-hearted. Last I heard, he was living on an island off the coast of the Carolinas. He'd become a writer and written a novel about his life with Aunt Mildred. I never read it."

Holly's mouth is slightly agape. "Wait, you never read it? This guy wrote a story about his love affair with your own aunt and you weren't curious?"

"I was busy," Bonnie says defensively. "My boys were young, and then I was widowed. Years went by. I don't know."

"Man, I kind of want to read it."

Bonnie's eyes twinkle and she picks up her cold coffee again. "Looking for some tips on keeping a younger man happy?" She winks playfully.

"Bon, you're gonna kill me." Holly reaches for a pad and a pencil and tries to change their focus from her evening of dancing with Miguel to the work at hand. "So let's talk murder mystery weekends."

She's about to start jotting down ideas and notes when the bell on the back door of the B&B jingles and Fiona comes rushing in. Her strawberry-blonde curls are coming loose from a haphazard topknot, and her lab coat is open over a pair of olive green shorts and a pastel pink tank top. "Hey, ladies," Fiona says breathlessly as she comes to a stop in the doorway. She leans against the frame and tries to catch her breath. "I have news."

"So does Holly," Bonnie says with a cheeky smile. "She's been banned from hanging around high schools and skate parks."

Holly tears off the top sheet of her notepad and balls it up, tossing it at Bonnie with pursed lips and a half-serious glare. "He's twenty-three, and it was one night of dancing," she counters. "Now," Holly turns back to Fiona. "What's the news?"

"Wait, he's only twenty-three?" Fiona seems to have forgotten what she's come to tell them in the first place. "Nice work, Hol."

Holly stands up, shoving her chair back forcefully in the process. "You two better knock it off, or I'm going to come up with every reason I can think of to make fun of the both of you. Every single detail I know about either of you is going to become fodder for jokes."

"Okay, okay," Fiona says, coming over to Holly and putting an arm around her. "We won't tease." She pauses for a beat. "But we will be here to pick up the pieces with you when his mom shows up on the island demanding to know what your intentions are with her baby."

"That's it!" Holly shrugs Fiona's arm off her shoulders. "I'm leaving." She's halfway to the door when Fiona reaches out and grabs her elbow.

"Wait, wait—I came here with serious news." Fiona hangs onto Holly. "I wanted you both to know that I'm getting married."

"This is not front page news, Fee," Holly says. "We're already in the middle of planning your wedding."

"No, I mean, I'm getting married *now*."

"Now?" Holly's stance relaxes. "You mean you guys picked a date?"

Even though she's caught her breath from her mad dash over to the B&B, Fiona's face flushes and her eyes shine like she's winded again. "Yeah, we did," she says. Her smile is so wide that Holly is sure the next step is going to be a cascade of joyful tears. "We're getting married tonight."

"Tonight?" Holly's jaw drops.

"Yes," Fiona says. "Tonight."

WITHIN AN HOUR, THE ISLAND IS A FLURRY OF ACTIVITY. WORD SPREADS like a collection plate in church, with each person adding something before passing the news along. Before Holly has even finished writing her list of things to do that day, Maria Agnelli is standing outside the window of the B&B's office, rapping on it with her knuckles and motioning for Holly to come outside. Holly waves at her to come in. Mrs. Agnelli waves again for her to come out. This goes on for a minute before Holly finally sighs in exasperation and stands up. She walks out into the bright morning sun and puts a hand over her eyes to shield them.

"What's up, Mrs. Agnelli?"

"I heard Fiona and your uncle were going to get married underwater by some scuba diving minister."

Holly doesn't even have a response to this.

"And I just need to say that I don't approve of a girl getting married in a bikini, even if it is a white one." Mrs. Agnelli pulls the arm that's holding her purse in closer to her body and lifts her chin defiantly. "When a woman waits until she's forty to get married, she should do it the right way."

"Mrs. Agnelli," Holly says.

"No," Mrs. Agnelli says, shaking her head. "I won't have my mind changed. And I'm not attending any underwater wedding. So you can just take the pictures with your fancy underwater cameras or what have you—I don't even want to see them." And with that, she turns and totters back down the sidewalk towards Mistletoe Morning Brew.

"Holly!" Heddie is standing on the sidewalk across the street outside of Cap's cigar shop. As usual, she has her white-blonde hair swept into a neat bun at the nape of her neck, and her clothes are crisp and smooth, despite the humidity. It never ceases to amaze Holly how Heddie always looks like a prima ballerina about to take the stage, even on an island and even at her age, which—although she doesn't look it—Holly knows is nearing seventy.

"Hi, Heddie!" she calls out. "You were on my list of people to talk to this morning."

Heddie looks both ways before stepping onto the paved street and crossing over to the B&B. "And you were on mine," she says in her still-thick German accent. "Can we go inside to chat?"

Holly leads the way up into the lobby of the B&B, where they sit in overstuffed chairs and chat for fifteen minutes about the things they need to do that day in order to pull off an evening wedding. The list is long, but the women take comfort in the fact that Fiona will be an easy-to-please bride; her only wish and desire is that, as the sun sets, she can officially say that she and Leo Buckhunter have tied the knot. Without a doubt, they can pull *that* off, but Holly has so many other things she wants to do for Fiona—so many ways she wants to show her best friend how much it means to her that she's trusted her with the details of her wedding.

"So I'll call you as soon as I have these first things done," Holly says, tapping her finger on the notepad that's resting on her knee as she sits in the armchair. "And if you can get ahold of that place we talked about before eleven and get anything sent out here on an afternoon boat, then text me or call me, okay?"

"Of course," Heddie says. Her remarkably unlined face is calm and serene. She reaches over and puts a hand on Holly's knee. "This will be a lovely wedding, Holly. Don't worry about a thing."

"I'm just excited," she admits. "I was worried about Fiona when she didn't even want to talk about the wedding, and the way she acted at the village council meeting when we brought up Kitta and Deacon's wedding—"

"I know," Heddie says. "But they just needed to get on the same page and come to an agreement about what would make them both happy. Have you seen Buckhunter today?"

"No," Holly says. "I haven't seen him yet. I should probably go over to Jack Frosty's and check in with him."

"He's grinning from ear to ear," Heddie says, giving Holly's knee one more pat before pulling her hand away. "Like a little boy who just got exactly what he wants for Christmas. Trust me, everything will be wonderful."

Holly thanks Heddie for stepping up and being as much help as she already has, and as she watches her friend cross the street again, shoulders pulled back, spine straight as a board, she pulls her own back into alignment. She'd like to be as cool and collected as Heddie is at all times, and every time she talks to the older woman, it reminds her to slow down and take a deep breath. And to stand up straighter—always to stand up straighter.

"Hey," Holly says as she walks up the steps to Jack Frosty's. Buckhunter is behind the bar with a stack of receipts. There are no customers because everyone on the island has been assigned a task of some sort that's related to the wedding. "How's the groom feeling?"

Buckhunter taps something into the calculator at his elbow and writes a note on a piece of paper. "Feeling as good as I ever have," he says, setting an empty glass on top of the stack of receipts like a paperweight.

Holly sidles up to the jukebox and fishes around in the pocket of her white overall shorts for a coin. She drops a quarter into the slot and picks Bruce Springsteen's "Born to Run." In response, Buckhunter holds a finger up in the air and bobs his head to the beat as the song starts. They enjoy The Boss in silence for a minute, smiling at each other from across the bar.

"Nothing is going to change, you know," Buckhunter says as he watches his niece lean against the jukebox. "I know we've only officially been family for a year, but it's still you and me, kid."

Holly shrugs and eyes the list of songs under the glass. Fiona is her best friend, and she's over the moon with happiness for her uncle to have found love with someone she herself adores. But there's a weird, lonely feeling niggling at the back of her heart, and somehow Buckhunter has picked up on this.

"I know," she says softly, punching a button repeatedly. "I'm really excited for both of you."

Buckhunter watches her quietly.

"It's just—" Holly runs a finger over the song selection buttons as she fights to find the right words.

"It's just nothing," Buckhunter says firmly. Without Holly even noticing, he's come out from behind the bar and walked over to her. "Come here, girl." Buckhunter pulls her into a tight embrace as they stand in front of the jukebox—this is something he's never done, and it brings prickly tears to the back of Holly's eyes. "Family is whoever you choose, you know? Especially on this island. And I choose you and Fiona."

Holly swallows hard. "I choose you guys, too."

"Then let's have a wedding, huh?" Buckhunter breaks off their hug with a hearty pat on the back. "I need all the help I can get on that one, because I've never done this before."

"I should probably remind you here that I've never done it either," Holly says, laughing as she wipes away a tear that's escaped from one eye.

"Then Fiona had better really love me," Buckhunter says, "because at the end of this, all she's really going to have is me as her husband."

Holly smiles at her uncle. "Lucky for you, I think that's all she really wants."

22

THE EVENING BREEZE COMES OFF THE WATER AT THE DOCK, BLOWING skirts and dresses and ruffling the black and orange tinsel that's still wrapped around the light posts from Halloween. An eighty-foot yacht is moored just off-shore, with Cap's smaller boat tied up at the dock to run passengers to and from the bigger vessel.

Heddie Lang-Mueller holds a clipboard in one hand as she checks items off the list. "Iris," she says. "You have the flowers?"

Iris points at a wagon filled with all the wildflowers that she and Emily could gather that afternoon. They'd spent hours tying them off in bunches, mixing moonflowers with swamp sunflowers and wild pennyroyals. There are also passion flowers and orchids, larkspurs and wild blue phlox, and the bouquets look wild and carefree.

"We got as many flowers as we could find," Iris confirms. "I'm going to take the whole lot of them over to the yacht as soon as Cap is able to run me over, and I'll get everything decorated and set up before we do anything else."

"Excellent." Heddie makes a big check mark next to something on her list. "And has Joe arrived yet?"

"Over here." Joe Sacamano has his hand on an upright dolly that's stacked with bottles of beer and champagne. "I've got all the glasses over there," he says, pointing at another unmanned dolly that's piled high with cardboard boxes. "That'll be another trip for Cap to make when he takes all of this over to the yacht."

"He'll be here very soon," Heddie promises. She checks another item off her list. Holly has entrusted her with the overall event coordination, and with her efficient manner, Heddie has managed to corral everyone and everything needed to pull off this impromptu wedding. She's even managed—with Bonnie's help—to find a yacht to rent on short notice, and since Cap's main job will be to officiate the wedding, they've hired a boat captain to ferry them around the Gulf for the evening.

After working her tail off all morning and afternoon, Holly has disappeared over to Fiona's bungalow, where they're working on getting Fiona prepared.

"You look gorgeous, Fee," she says in a hushed voice as she stands behind her best friend and gazes at the bride's reflection in the full-length mirror before them. Even though the wedding is as spontaneous as it could possibly be, Fiona has long since had the dress of her dreams hanging from a peg inside her closet door. When she'd opened the closet and showed it to Holly for the first time, they'd both inhaled sharply, staring with reverence at the embroidered ivory lace and the deep V-neck that would reveal plenty of freckled décolletage.

"I don't even look like me," Fiona says in awed response. "I look like...a bride."

Holly giggles. "Yeah," she says, sliding her arms around Fiona and hugging her from behind. "You do."

They unzip the dress and hang it back on the closet hook while Fiona sits on a chair in her push-up bra and satin underwear, staring at herself in a small vanity mirror.

"Are you sure you want me to do this?" Holly asks as she picks up an eyeshadow palette. "I'm not really the kind of girl who has a bag full of make-up tricks," she says dubiously. "Not that you need any tricks—trust me, you look beautiful enough already—but I just don't want to let you down."

Fiona smiles at Holly and pushes a cup full of make-up brushes in her direction. "I trust you. Just make me look like myself, only with a tiny bit more mascara and lipgloss."

Holly stares at the jumble of blush palettes and lipstick tubes on the surface of Fiona's vanity table. "Okay," she says. "I can do that." With a deep breath, she picks up a bottle of foundation and starts to read the directions on the back.

"Don't read the directions, you silly girl!" Fiona laughs. "Just put a tiny bit on your fingers and smooth it over my face. Here, like this." She takes the bottle and puts two pumps of the liquid on the tips of her fingers.

By the time Millie arrives with an assortment of brushes and hair tools, Holly has already realized that it's not so much that she's an expert with camera-ready make-up, but more that Fiona wants to spend quality time with her before the ceremony. She's relaxed and done her best work combing Fiona's eyebrows into place with clear gel, and she's applied a light dusting of mauve shadow to her smooth eyelids, finishing the look with several coats of mascara and a soft pink gloss on her lips.

"Doll, you look stunning," Millie says, plugging in a flat-iron and setting the tool on Fiona's vanity while it heats up. She stops to assess Holly's handiwork. "Very natural and like a glowing bride."

"Thank you," Fiona says. She turns to look at her reflection in the mirror again, clearly pleased with the outcome. "I think I'm ready to get hitched."

"Well, you will be after I give you an updo here," Millie says, winking at Holly over Fiona's head. "I want it to be regal—something to match that dress," she says, pointing at the gown that's hanging from the door. "I was thinking of straightening it all and then pulling it into a low bun at the nape of your neck—something really thick and sleek—and then pinning an orchid at the center of it with this." From her pocket, Millie pulls a straight hairpin with a sparkling rhinestone at the center.

"Oooh," Holly says, leaning in to admire the pin. "That's beautiful."

"It was my mother's," Millie says wistfully, turning the pin in her fingers so that the light from the bedroom window catches it and casts rainbow prisms on the wall. "I wore it at my wedding to Ray forty-five years ago."

The women sit in silence for a moment. Millie stares at the hairpin in her hand, Fiona is still perched on her chair in just her bridal undergarments, and Holly sits near the edge of the bed, looking on. The idea that this pin will be the "something borrowed" that tradition calls for overwhelms them all.

"Thank you, Millie," Fiona says softly. "I should be so lucky as to find the happiness that you and Ray had."

Millie smiles at her and her eyes are watery. "I shouldn't say this, but honey, I *hope* you're as lucky as I was. I had an incredibly wonderful and supportive man and a fulfilling marriage. I want that for you."

For a second, Holly feels like an outsider to the warmth of this tableau. Both of the other women have experienced a particular kind of love and joy that she herself has yet to feel, and having never stood on the precipice of matrimony, Holly understands that she really doesn't know what it feels like to fully give yourself to another. She clears her throat as gently as she can and looks at her watch.

"We need to get down to the dock in about forty minutes, Fee," she says in a near whisper. "We're set to sail around six."

"I'll get her ready in a jiffy," Millie says, setting the hairpin down. "Let me get this hair pulled back, and then we'll zip her into her dress and head over there. Do we have arrangements to get her onto the boat without Buckhunter seeing her?"

"Oh," Fiona scoffs. "That's not necessary. We aren't superstitious about stuff like that."

"Nonsense, honey." Millie twists the top half of Fiona's curly hair and clips it on top of her head. "Holly? Can you make sure that's arranged?" she asks, pulling her black flat-iron through the first section of Fiona's hair. "Get ahold of Heddie and have the bride and groom take separate trips over to the yacht."

"Got it." Holly gives a small salute and steps out of the bedroom.

She's grateful to have a task to complete. Something to focus her attention away from the intense joy and unexpected wistfulness that have permeated her day so far. She steps into Fiona's kitchen and pulls her phone from her back pocket, clicking on Heddie's contact.

"Holly?" Heddie says. In the background are voices and the sounds of people moving around and calling out to one another.

"We're getting ready to drive over there, but can you do me a favor and make sure that Buckhunter is already somewhere below deck on the yacht when we bring Fiona on board?"

"Ah, right. The groom must not see the bride." Heddie gets it right away, despite the fact that she, much like Holly, has never wed. "I'll make sure of it."

"Thanks, Heddie. I'll text you when we're on our way." Holly clicks off and stands in Fiona's kitchen, looking around at the neat bungalow. On the fridge are photos of Fiona's family back home in Chicago, held in place with magnets. Holly leans in close and inspects the faces of Fiona and two of her best friends from high school. It's an old picture, and in it, the three young women all have bangs that are teased and sprayed into curly nests. They're wearing pastel skirts and shirts in various shades, and on all of their feet are clean, white Keds.

Holly wanders into the front room and picks the dress she's wearing up off the back of the couch, where she's left it draped. When Fiona asked her to be her maid of honor, Holly had known immediately that the dress she'd choose would be the one she's now holding over one arm. It's a soft pink, and the front of the dress comes up to her collarbone while the back of it reveals most of her back, stopping its plunge just above the waistline. She'd planned to pull her own hair back into a low knot as well, and Fiona has requested that they both carry whatever wildflowers Iris and Emily have gathered.

In the guest room, she quickly zips herself into the dress and pulls a hairbrush and some pins from her purse. It takes her no time at all to smooth her hair into a bun, and as she leans into the mirror and dabs a layer of pressed powder to her forehead and nose, Holly sees the cardboard boxes that fill the guest room closet. The top one is overflowing with clothes, and the one beneath it has "kitchen stuff" scrawled on the side in black marker. She hasn't even asked whether the wedding means that Fiona will be moving in with Buckhunter, but these boxes are confirmation of the fact that she'll soon be next door neighbors with her best friend. The thought thrills her as she imagines evenings spent having happy hour on her lanai, and the possibility that Fiona and Buckhunter might give her a little cousin to look after as he or she toddles around their family property on that side of the island.

Holly surprises herself by even thinking about a baby. At their ages, it's entirely possible that Fiona and Buckhunter won't bother to entertain the notion of parenthood for even a second, but something in Holly secretly hopes that they will.

"Holly!" Millie calls out. "We're ready for you."

In under ten minutes, they have Fiona back in her dress, everything smoothed and tucked, and Holly's laid a clean beach towel across the bench seat of her golf cart for the bride to sit on. She's texted Heddie to let her know that they're on their way, and together, the three women are cruising over the sandy roads of the island, bound for the dock.

As they pull up and park at the end of Main Street, Holly is pleased to see that the yacht has been appropriately tricked out for a wedding. The triplets have strung clear lights all along the boat, and the majority of the guests are standing on the deck, waving at the bride as she climbs out of the golf cart with Millie's assistance.

"Your groom is already below deck," Cap bellows, standing in his small boat and waving Fiona over to him. "Lets get you over there and get out on the water, huh?"

He's dressed in linen pants and a loose linen button-up shirt, his shoulder-length hair corralled in a neat ponytail at his neck. It's a far cry from the theatrical ensemble he'd worn to Kitta and Deacon's wedding, but he looks way more like himself for this ceremony.

"No Marco for this journey?" Fiona asks, letting everyone take her elbows and hands as they help her onto Cap's boat for the short trip from shore to yacht.

"If the bride wants a persnickety bird on my shoulder while I do the honors of marrying her and her beloved, then I can certainly arrange for Marco to attend the nuptials."

"How much desire do you have to be upstaged by a parrot on your wedding day?" Holly teases. "Because if Marco comes along, we might end up back on shore with him married to Buckhunter and you swimming alongside the yacht."

They all laugh because they know it's true: Marco has run the island for as long as he's lived there, deciding who he goes to (more often than not, that's Cap) and when he shows up (mostly for attention or treats).

"I guess I'll take advantage of being the center of attention for one day," Fiona says. She smiles at Holly as they approach the yacht and Holly reaches over to squeeze her hand. "Thank you to all of you for helping me make this day happen."

Cap looks at the water as he eases his boat up to the yacht, but Holly is watching her best friend intently. "Anything for you, Fee. We're family—you know that."

Fiona leans over and puts her cheek to Holly's, careful not to leave her lipgloss on Holly's face. "Love you," she says.

"Love you too."

As soon as everyone is on board, the guests (which include a majority of the islanders, save for Gwen's husband, who has the flu, and minus Maggie Sutter, who isn't a fan of boats and has agreed to stay back and care for Hal Pillory so that Katelynn and Logan can attend) give a whoop of joy and a round of applause. They've done it. In less than a day, they've put it together, and in less than an hour, two of their own will be happily married and on their way to a life together as husband and wife.

The captain steers them out onto open water as Joe Sacamano strums his guitar on the deck. Everyone chats and laughs under a sky that's going lavender and pink with the setting sun, and Iris and Jimmy make the rounds with bottles of champagne, topping off everyone's flutes in preparation to toast Fiona and Buckhunter as they say their vows.

"Could I have your attention, please," Cap says into his microphone. He looks around at everyone, smiling at each of them as they quiet down to hear the ceremony. "We're here this evening to celebrate two of our closest friends, without whom we'd be lost. Without Buckhunter, we'd be short one bar on the island. And if we didn't have Dr. Potts, it would be much harder to get our nitroglycerin pills and hearing aids." Everyone laughs. "But on a more serious note, we're about to witness the union of two people we all love and care about. It's my honor to officiate the wedding of Leo Buckhunter and Fiona Potts. If everyone is ready, I'd like to get things started."

The captain has cut the engine and the yacht is drifting lazily on the calm waves. A gentle November breeze comes off the water as the sun dips her lower half below the horizon to the west. With Cap's signal, Joe Sacamano begins to strum "Can't Help Falling In Love" on his guitar. Eyes all around the deck instantly mist over with tears.

From below, Holly leads the way up the narrow staircase and Fiona follows, holding onto the railing as she comes. Buckhunter is standing at the bow of the ship with his hands clasped behind his back. His graying blonde hair is combed to one side and he's wearing a loose white shirt that's buttoned up to his collarbone and a pair of ironed khaki pants. Holly has never seen him dressed up like this and it's touching to imagine her uncle getting ready for his own wedding day. This thought, coupled with the romantic sounds of the song that Joe's playing, brings tears to her own eyes. She clutches her wildflowers in front of her as she walks towards Cap and Buckhunter, stepping to the side so that Fiona can walk directly to her groom.

Buckhunter meets Fiona's gaze and his eyes soften. He reaches out a hand for her as she draws near, and she gives him the one that's not holding her own colorful bouquet. As everyone watches, Fiona stops next to Buckhunter and they look into one another's eyes for the duration of the song.

As soon as Joe stops playing, a hush falls over the boat. There is nothing but the sound of water lapping against the hull until Cap clears his throat and begins to speak. The ceremony is lovely and short, and once the couple has exchanged vows, Cap pronounces them husband and wife and implores them to "hurry up and kiss already so that everyone can drink champagne."

As Buckhunter wraps his arms around his new wife, glasses are lifted high into the air, and the sparkling champagne catches the last rays of the setting sun. It's a beautiful scene, and Logan Pillory has been quietly capturing the whole thing with his camera, trying to be as low-key as possible as he slides between guests and snaps shots of everyone—especially of the bride and groom. Holly smiles at him and winks appreciatively. He's agreed without any arm-twisting to be the event photographer, and it seems like a fair trade-off for how easily he got off the hook with Deacon and Kitta's wedding. Logan moves his camera away from his face and winks back at Holly with a smile.

For the next two hours, guests drink and mingle just like they would on dry land at the Ho Ho, and Holly walks through the crowd with her bouquet of wildflowers in one hand and her champagne flute in the other. Fiona is holding court at the stern of the ship on a white leather bench seat with her shoes kicked off, and Buckhunter has already untucked his shirt from his pants so that he looks more like himself.

The stars twinkle and mix with the clear lights strung from the sides of the yacht. Bonnie comes up next to Holly and clinks the rims of their glasses together. "Cheers," she says. "We got the doc and your uncle hitched."

"That we did," Holly agrees, putting the flute to her lips and knocking back another sip. The champagne is starting to go to her head and she looks around for a place to sit down.

"I heard so many crazy rumors today," Bonnie laughs. "Before Maria started telling everyone that Fiona and Buckhunter were getting married underwater in their bathing suits, I overheard her at the coffee shop telling Wyatt that we were all taking a speedboat to Orlando tonight so that they could get married at the Magic Kingdom."

"Which would have been fun," Holly says. "I love Disney World." She tries to imagine Buckhunter in a pair of mouse ears and Fiona as the type of bride to sit in Cinderella's sparkling, pumpkin-shaped coach. The image simply won't gel in her mind. "But this suits them way better."

"Damn straight it does. Look at Buckhunter over there, he's grinnin' like a possum eatin' a sweet tater." Bonnie nods her red head in Buckhunter's direction and Holly has to agree: he looks more happy and relaxed than she's ever seen him.

"Sometimes I feel like we're the luckiest people on earth," Holly says. The combination of stars and sparkling wine have her feeling a little giddy.

"That's because we are, sugar," Bonnie says, putting an arm around her friend. "Thanks to your grandparents and their dream— and now thanks to you for keeping it alive—we have everything we could ever want."

"Do we?" Holly's mood suddenly turns pensive. "Don't you sometimes feel like we're missing something, Bon?"

Bonnie's face changes as she thinks about the question and adjusts to Holly's shift in mood. "Well, I don't feel like I am, hon." She runs her hand up and down Holly's arm with concern. "Do you?"

Holly looks into her glass as if she might find the answer floating at the bottom. She shrugs. "I'm usually too busy to feel like I'm missing much. But when the only guy who wants to be my date to a Halloween party is a sixteen-year-old, it does leave me wondering."

In spite of the fact that she knows she shouldn't, Bonnie laughs. "Oh, sugar. You should be flattered that a young man with his whole life ahead of him thinks you're worth pursuing. That doesn't mean you should take him up on it," she clarifies, "but come on. When someone feels good things for you, you should appreciate that."

Holly swipes at the unexpected tear that's rolling down her cheek. "You're right. I need to look at things differently. Have more gratitude."

"Sometimes that's all it is, really." Bonnie gently takes Holly's nearly empty glass from her hands and sets both of their flutes on

Jimmy Cafferkey's tray as he passes. "Just a shift in how you're looking at things. Yeah, you're over thirty and single," Bonnie allows. "But you're never alone on this island—never. And the work you do is amazing and fills all our lives with joy. So it's not thankless work."

Holly nods and tries to discreetly use the back of her hand to wipe away the tears that are now flowing freely.

"But as for finding a man here...the good Lord only knows how and when that'll happen, but I believe it will. I do." Bonnie opens her arms and Holly leans in close for a hug. "When the time is right and your heart is open, it'll all come together, sugar. Trust me on that."

Holly hugs Bonnie tighter. "I trust you."

"Good," Bonnie says, giving Holly a firm pat before pulling back and looking her in the eye. "I would never steer you wrong, doll. You know that."

Holly knows Bonnie is right and for the rest of the evening she's fine. She normally stays so busy and feels so positive about things that doubts never have the chance to creep into her consciousness. It's almost unthinkable for Holly to find herself questioning her life choices or where things are going.

"Mayor," Cap says, walking over to her with a glass of sparkling water in one hand. "Could I request the pleasure of this dance?"

Most of Holly's neighbors are standing along the sides of the boat, talking quietly in pairs or small groups, and a handful of people are dancing to Joe's rendition of "At Last."

"I'd be honored," Holly says, taking Cap's hand as he sets his water down. Watching everyone enjoy the wedding and the night on the water has been a remarkable experience, and as she glances at Fiona and Buckhunter slowly swaying to the song near Joe's perch on a stool at the boat's bow, Holly knows in her heart that things always work out the way they're supposed to.

"It'll be your turn soon," Cap says calmly, holding Holly's left hand in his right one as he dances with her much the way a father might. "Don't you spend a minute worrying that your chance will never come, girl."

Holly's chest tightens in response to Cap's sweet words and she can't speak.

"Look!" Cap says, pulling back from Holly and pointing at the sky with the hand that's still holding hers. "A shooting star! You better make a wish."

Holly leans her head back and lets the dizzying mixture of champagne, floating on open water, and looking at the night sky wash over her. She laughs as Cap grips her more securely, keeping her on her feet as she wobbles slightly.

"I'm wishing, Cap," she says, closing her eyes for a moment. "I'm really, really wishing."

23

"It's something electrical," Iris says to Holly, standing on the front steps of the B&B several days later. "I'm sure of it."

"I bet it's the gas line!" Cap shouts out as his golf cart rolls to a stop at the curb near where the women are standing. "I'd put money on it."

Idora Blaine-Guy is crossing the street, holding each of her identical grandsons by the hand. "Heard things weren't working at the Jingle Bell Bistro," she says, catching her breath as she steps onto the curb. "I wanted to take the boys there for lunch, but I guess I'll have to take them to Jack Frosty's—"

"Still closed," Holly says, shaking her head and glancing at the shuttered bar next to her B&B.

"Oh, right." Idora frowns. "Honeymoon. When do those two get back, anyway? I need to make an appointment with the doctor."

"They'll be back in five days." Holly was adamant that Fiona and Buckhunter get away for a real honeymoon and they'd eagerly taken her up on it. Fiona had managed to book a last minute cruise into the Caribbean and she'd even scored a bargain price because someone else had cancelled. "Fiona has her doctor friend from Key West coming here tomorrow for the day, so if you need to see someone, he'll be here by ten o'clock. I think he's taking walk-ins."

Idora huffs. "Not likely I'd trust my well-being to a total stranger."

"Well, Fiona will be back before you know it, Idora," Holly says patiently. She and Iris exchange a look.

"And that problem you're having at the bistro," Idora says with a grimace. "It's your juju."

"My juju?" Iris's eyes go wide.

"That's right." Idora pulls Mexi and Mori closer to her sides. "You need to burn some sage in there. Maybe find the right crystals and put them around the restaurant to clear the energy and change the vibration."

"Change the vibration?" Iris parrots.

Holly smothers a laugh.

"Hmmm," Idora says, obviously sensing the women's disbelief. "Do what you want then, and none of us will be eating clam chowder and biscuits in the near future." With a little push to the shoulder of each of the boys, Idora propels them all down the sidewalk towards Mistletoe Morning Brew.

"Where can I find sage on the island?" Iris asks, watching Idora's back as she walks down Main Street, head held high.

"I'll have to look into that..." Holly chuckles to herself. The combination of personalities and life experiences on the island never fails to entertain her.

"Hey!" Calista Vance pops her head out of the salon across the street. She watches her mother-in-law retreating with her sons and cups her hands around her mouth. "She talk about some mumbo-jumbo witchcraft?"

Holly tips her head back and forth to let Calista know that she's in the general ballpark with that guess.

"She's mad as a box of frogs. I told you so, ladies." With a raised eyebrow and pursed lips, Calista pulls her head back into the salon.

Iris and Holly look at one another for a moment, bracing themselves for further interruption. When nothing happens, Holly speaks.

"We could get someone out here by tomorrow, hopefully. I need to think about a budget for repairs...this wasn't part of my current plan, but I know we can fix it."

"Hey!" Miguel walks up to the B&B in a sweaty t-shirt. He takes his scuffed yellow hardhat off of his head, revealing damp hair and a line of dirt around his forehead.

"Hi, Miguel," Holly says, although not impatiently. She's pretty good at juggling multiple issues and conversations, though she'd really like to finish this particular chat with Iris so that they can make plans to get someone out to see what's wrong at the bistro.

"Everything okay?" Miguel looks at the two women's faces.

"We can't cook at the Jingle Bell. Something is wrong in the kitchen," Iris says, tipping her head in the direction of the restaurant, though it's not visible from Main Street.

"Gas or electric?" Miguel shifts his hardhat from one hand to the other and squints at the women in the midday sun.

"Gas stove is out. Electricity to the whole place is down."

"Major systems failure," Miguel says knowingly, flashing a big, white smile at Iris. "Mind if I have a look?"

Iris glances at Holly. "A jack of all trades, are you, lad?" she asks him.

Miguel gives them a modest shrug. "Kind of. I know my way around almost anything construction and building-related. Or maybe I should say I know just enough about everything to get myself into trouble."

"Well, I wouldn't mind a bit if you had a look," Iris says with pleasant surprise. "Might help us to get an opinion before we send out for someone to come all the way out here."

"Okay." Miguel spins his hat in his hands. "Well, I just came back here to grab something for one of the guys, but we should be done at the new dock today by about four. Can I come by then?"

"I'll be there," Iris says. "And thank you." She turns to Holly. "So let's put the repairman on hold for the moment and I'll get back to you later on after Miguel has a look at the place, alright?"

"Works for me," Holly says. Iris gives them both a wave and heads back to the bistro.

"You don't mind looking at the kitchen?" Holly asks Miguel as they stand there alone on the steps to the B&B.

"Not at all." He smiles at her. "Happy to help."

"Great. I'll meet you over there around four so we can all see what's up. Since I technically own all the buildings on the island, I have a vested interest in making sure everything is in working order, plus I'm the one who'll have to pay for it, so..."

"So let's figure out a way to fix it without breaking the bank then, okay?" Miguel puts the hardhat back on his head and walks through the front door of the B&B. "See you at four."

Miguel's quick assessment of the Jingle Bell Bistro is accurate. He makes an order from a hardware store in Key West, and the restaurant is up and running again by the time Fiona and Buckhunter get back from their honeymoon.

"So we're back to the regular decorations, huh?" Fiona steps off the boat with a rolling suitcase in one hand. Buckhunter is close behind her. They're both even more tan than they'd been when they left the island. So far, married life seems to suit them completely.

"Of course!" Holly is standing on a ladder on one side of Main Street, unwinding the black and orange tinsel from the lamppost. It's late afternoon, and the sun has dipped low enough that Main Street has a cool, shady feel to it. "It's taken me far too long to get things back to normal here."

"You've been busy," Buckhunter says, smiling up at his niece. "You're forgiven."

"Everybody missed being able to go to Jack Frosty's," Miguel says from the top step of his own ladder just up the street from Holly's. He's already taken down the tinsel on several posts and is wrapping them with the thick ropes of red and white lights that get turned on at dusk every night from November first through New Year's. "We lost power at the Jingle Bell and the triplets made a killing on people actually wanting to buy groceries."

Buckhunter gives Holly an amused grin. "Sounds like we have a new island resident on our hands here." He hooks a thumb at Miguel and they all watch as he focuses on securing the lights to the post. "Is the Jingle Bell up and running again?"

"Yeah, it was a pretty easy fix," Miguel says. "I put in about six hours there one night and by the next morning Iris and Jimmy were serving pancakes and eggs again."

"How'd you trick Miguel into helping you decorate Main Street?" Fiona shoots Holly an impressed look.

Holly tosses a string of shiny black tinsel and it floats to the ground, landing on the pile she's already unraveled. "He saw me out here and offered."

Buckhunter starts to roll his suitcase behind him. "Well, you might want to rent him one of the empty bungalows so you have him on hand for any future emergencies."

"I wish." Miguel holds onto the sides of the ladder as he descends. He stands on the sidewalk. "I love it here. We'll be done with the dock by the end of this week, and I don't want to leave."

The corners of Fiona's mouth are twitching with a suppressed laugh. The look in Holly's eyes is a warning because she knows her best friend wants to tease her about having a younger man in her life. *Another* younger man who appears to be smitten with her.

Buckhunter looks at Holly. "Let me get settled in and get Jack Frosty's opened again, and maybe Holly and I can talk about what the future of having a general repairman on the island would look like."

Hopefulness floods Miguel's face. "Really?"

"No promises, but we're a growing island. It's something we should think about."

"He's not wrong," Holly agrees, coming down from her ladder. "We have big plans and ideas, and we need to keep up with our growth by expanding wisely. And having someone on hand to fix things and keep things running is just smart business."

Miguel looks like he has a million questions, but Holly holds up a hand to slow him down. "We've got a village council meeting coming up soon, and it would be worth pitching the idea to everyone and getting a pros and cons list. Ultimately it will be up to me and Buckhunter to decide, but it never hurts to get an idea of how everyone feels about something. It's how our little community functions."

"Understandable." Miguel gathers the Halloween tinsel they've both discarded and puts it into the box that Holly's brought out from storage. "I'll head home to Miami when we're done with the dock and wait to hear if it's a possibility. But just for the record, I'd be thrilled to call this place home."

"We'll keep you posted," Buckhunter says as he reaches for Fiona's suitcase handle and drags them both behind him. "Now you two better get the rest of this street ready for Christmas. It's a shame to come back and see Halloween decorations still hanging around on Veterans Day. A real disgrace. Somebody should complain to the mayor around here..." He shakes his head playfully and Fiona follows him down Main Street with her hand on his lower back. She looks more content than Holly's ever seen her.

"Welcome back, you two!" Holly says, balling up a length of tinsel and tossing it after them. It catches on the breeze and drifts to the ground like a feather. She and Miguel look at one another and laugh.

24

THE MEETING MINUTES FOR NOVEMBER FOURTEENTH ARE TYPED UP AND sitting in Holly's inbox when she shows up in her office the next morning. She's got an iced latte in hand, and she's dressed in a black tank top and a hot pink skirt. As Pucci walks slowly across the office and settles himself onto the dog bed in the corner, she lifts up the stapled minutes and flips through the pages, skimming all of the topics and decisions.

*Murder mystery weekend: fully supported. Everyone excited to hear more and to participate. **APPROVED**.*

*Dock completion: the old dock will continue to be used for smaller vessels. New dock is complete and ready to begin transport for larger vessels and to commence day trips to Christmas Key via Island Paradise Excursions. All shopkeepers prepared for influx of tourists and day-trippers. **APPROVED**.*

*Full-time island handyman/repairman: all in favor of hiring someone to live locally and be on call for general repairs and maintenance. Mayor Baxter proposes consideration of Miguel Cruz, who has submitted application indicating formal interest. **APPROVED**.*

"Hey, Holly." Logan Pillory is standing in the doorway to the office. "I got all of Fiona and Buckhunter's wedding pictures edited and I'm about to show them. Wanna come?" He holds up the silver laptop that's tucked under one arm.

Holly tosses the meeting minutes back into the inbox tray on her desk. "Yeah! I want to see them."

"We're meeting at Jack Frosty's," he says. "See you over there?"

Holly nods at him and takes another sip of her iced coffee. As soon as he's gone, she jots a few notes onto the pad next to her phone and whistles for Pucci to follow her. She can't wait to see the pictures from that beautiful night on the yacht.

Pucci is already leading the way down the hall when Holly stops. "Oh!" She backtracks to her office. "Hold on one sec, Pooch." She picks up the pencil next to her laptop and adds one final note to her to-do list:

Call Miguel and tell him he's got the job.

"Okay, now I'm ready."

YOU JUST FINISHED BOOK FIVE OF THE CHRISTMAS KEY SERIES! DOWNLOAD BOOK SIX, *BABY, IT'S WARM OUTSIDE*, TO FIND OUT WHAT HAPPENS NEXT!

READY FOR THE NEXT BOOK IN THE CHRISTMAS KEY SERIES?

Tinsel and lights and cocoa and...*murder*?!

The islanders put on their first murder mystery weekend with Santa, Mrs. Claus, and an elf with legs like a Rockette.

Will the magic of the season be lost as the mystery builds? Or will the locals make it a Christmas to remember?

ABOUT THE AUTHOR

Stephanie Taylor is a high-school teacher who loves sushi, "The Golden Girls," Depeche Mode, orchids, and coffee. Together with her teenage daughter she writes the *American Dream* series—books for young girls about other young girls who move to America. On her own, Stephanie is the author of the *Christmas Key* books, a romantic comedy series about a fictional island off the coast of Florida.

https://redbirdsandrabbits.com
redbirdsandrabbits@gmail.com

ALSO BY STEPHANIE TAYLOR

To see a complete list of the Christmas Key series along with all of Stephanie's other books, please visit:

Stephanie Taylor's Books

To hear about any new releases, sign up here and you'll be the first to know!

Made in the USA
Columbia, SC
19 October 2023

24674335R00140